"YOU'VE GOT TO STOP RUNNING AWAY. . . ."

Her mutinous gaze speared him. "Just go back to California, Travis, and leave me alone. It was a mistake to let you stay here." Hurriedly, she turned away, afraid of getting caught up in a situation she couldn't handle.

But Travis grabbed her arm and spun her back, pinning her against the door.

"All of this has nothing to do with what's happening now," he rumbled. "It's because of what happened that New Year's Eve, but you refuse to admit it."

Her face froze. She managed to push Travis away, but before she could take more than a couple of steps, he grabbed her braid and wrapped it around his hand, slowly pulling her toward him. With each step his head lowered until his lips hovered just above hers in a light touch that sent lightning bolts through both their bodies. Kali's eyes opened wide and his own dark ones stared down into hers just as he took her into his arms and brought her flush against his body.

"Let's make sure it wasn't all champagne and holiday spirit the last time," he muttered roughly, just as his mouth covered hers.

QUANTITY SALES

Most Dell books are available at special quantity discounts when purchased in bulk by corporations, organizations, and special-interest groups. Custom imprinting or excerpting can also be done to fit special needs. For details write: Dell Publishing, 666 Fifth Avenue, New York, NY 10103. Attn.: Special Sales Department.

INDIVIDUAL SALES

Are there any Dell books you want but cannot find in your local stores? If so, you can order them directly from us. You can get any Dell book in print. Simply include the book's title, author, and ISBN number if you have it, along with a check or money order (no cash can be accepted) for the full retail price plus $1.50 to cover shipping and handling. Mail to: Dell Readers Service, P.O. Box 5057, Des Plaines, IL 60017.

Only Love

Linda Randall Wisdom

A DELL BOOK

Published by
Dell Publishing
a division of
The Bantam Doubleday Dell Publishing Group, Inc.
666 Fifth Avenue
New York, New York 10103

ISBN: 0-440-20131-4

Printed in the United States of America

Published simultaneously in Canada

September 1988

10 9 8 7 6 5 4 3 2 1

KRI

Only Love

Chapter
1

❧ "Travis? Travis Yates, don't you dare hide from me again, you overgrown cowboy!" A woman's irritated voice rang out through the large photography studio. She hurried across the room, her high heels clicking on the hard linoleum floor, black waist-length hair swaying against trim leather pants with each movement. "Whether you like it or not, I have to talk to you!"

"Give me a break, hoss." Travis groaned, halting at the door to the darkroom. A couple inches over six feet tall, the dark-haired man was an imposingly masculine figure, with black eyes that shone with amusement, and a full mustache dusted with the same silver that tipped his thick, dark hair. His well-worn jeans and chambray work shirt, the sleeves rolled back from his forearms, certainly were not the uniform of a successful businessman, but they suited his rangy looks to a tee. "Can't you see I have important work to do?"

Jenny Chen glared at hearing the nickname she had been trying to break her boss of since the first day she'd come to work for him. She brushed her hair away from her face, now shadowed with displeasure.

"You want to talk about work, fine, we'll talk about work," she insisted, waving a sheaf of pink paper slips in front of his face. "Do you see these?"

"Yep."

"Then you know what they mean?"

"Yep."

Jenny inhaled deeply and counted to ten under her breath. "You have a total of twenty-seven—count them, *twenty-seven*—messages on your desk, and you took care of only one." Her dark eyes narrowed. "Tracy has more to do with her time than field calls from your women. Monica Lambert almost had her in tears!"

Travis sighed, knowing full well that the young receptionist wasn't strong enough to battle some of the women determined to speak to Travis during his workday. "Jenny, I swear to you, I tell everyone not to call me at the studio."

She smiled sweetly. "And where else would they call you? You're never home, and when you are, you refuse to answer your phone!"

He stared at his assistant, a lovely Eurasian woman in her mid-thirties who looked as if she belonged in front of the camera instead of working so hard behind it. He really didn't understand why all those women pestered him. He wasn't vain about his sex appeal; it completely baffled him. When he looked at himself in the mirror, he saw a man whose face was all rough angles and planes, balanced by a heavy mustache and brows and dark eyes that could turn ice-cold with anger or warm with amusement, depending on his mood. He wasn't even conventionally handsome; the photographer in him saw that, yet there was something about him that attracted the women. Funny thing was, he wasn't the playboy many people thought him to be. He was much too busy with his work to party every night and indulge in meaningless affairs. At the ripe old age of forty-one, Travis was looking for more than a roll in the sack, anyway. The trouble was, he hadn't met that special woman yet, and sometimes he wondered if she was even out there. Correction; once he believed he had met her, but the lady had already been taken.

He held his hands up in surrender. "Okay, I'll see what I can do, I promise."

"Deke called. He said you told him you'd take his new publicity photos. He's going to stop by this morning and talk to you about when you'll be able to shoot them."

Travis frowned. "I told him I'd take his photos?" He shook his head, not remembering such a promise.

"It appears this vow was made at that beer bash you went to three weeks ago," she reminded him with a smug smile. "The one that lasted four days?"

He winced at the reminder of one very nasty hangover. He'd given up the heavy beer-drinking parties years ago, and after this last bash he remembered why. The aching head and cottony mouth the morning after weren't worth the alcoholic euphoria he

3

enjoyed in the beginning. Yeah, he was definitely getting too old for that kind of "fun."

"If he comes in here drunk, he's getting thrown out immediately," Jenny said, a warning note in her voice.

Travis sighed wearily. He knew exactly who would be chosen for that task too.

He took Jenny's arm and guided her back to the office area. Then he sauntered back to his own office, stopping long enough to pour himself a large mug of strong coffee.

He glanced at the oak desk, covered with glossy black-and-white contact sheets waiting for his approval, more pink message slips, and stacks of paper filled with his scribbling. The large studio, expensive furnishings, and blown-up photographs of motorcycles hung on the walls were minor trappings of his success. Little had he known fifteen years ago, when he barely made a living photographing motorcycles and their riders, that he would achieve such popularity with the coffee-table photograph books that came out every two years around the holiday season, and trade-size photo books that came out once a year.

The man whose photographs brought lesser-known motorcycle gangs to attention and showed they were more than unkempt men and women who boozed it up and carried knives and guns in anticipation of a brawl, brought that same special touch to his present-day photographs.

In the beginning Travis had saved every penny he could in order to buy better camera equipment. His first book, portraits of hands, was self-published with the assistance of a popular photographer who was also a motorcycle enthusiast. The book turned out to be an instant success. Who would have imagined that pictures of hands—some working at various crafts and skilled labor, others knobby with arthritis and old age, and even those of small children playing— would become so popular. He immediately sank his profits into his next book on endangered species, and from there he never looked back. He started out using the bathroom in his apartment for a darkroom. When the time came, he took the plunge and leased the building he now used for his studio and darkroom. Even though many of Travis's pictures were taken in the field, he still used his studio for special shots.

He settled behind his desk in a deep leather chair and propped his booted feet on top of the desk, scanning the message slips Jenny had handed him.

"Don't you think it's time you shaved again?" she asked, resting her hip on the edge of the desk as she caught the message slips he crumpled up and threw her way. "You look as if you'd recently escaped from the city zoo."

"I shaved Saturday night—and I won't ask what section of the zoo you're referring to."

"Today is Tuesday."

Travis ran his hand over his stubbly chin. "You're a regular nag, hoss. Sometimes I wonder why I put up with you."

"You put up with me because no one else would put up with your insane way of working," she retorted.

"If I talk nice to you, would you take pity on a starving man and go out and get me some breakfast?" he asked with the broad grin that made most women go weak at the knees. Jenny had been immune to his charm from day one, which was another reason why he'd hired her. He could work without the worry of his assistant hoping for more than just a fairly normal working day. Going through the record number of six assistants in the same number of weeks had almost convinced him that he was better off with a male assistant when Jenny walked in the door. Within two days she had Travis in hand, and the office running more smoothly than it had in years. He freely admitted he'd be lost without her, and she always agreed with him wholeheartedly.

While Jenny was gone, Travis attempted to clear some of the clutter from the top of his desk. For the past few weeks he had been mulling over an idea for his next book, but nothing came to mind. At least nothing he would care to put his name to.

Deciding another cup of coffee might help stimulate his brain cells, Travis wandered into the outer office to the coffee maker. As he passed Jenny's desk he noticed a stack of typed sheets of paper set to one side and halted to read the title page. His curiosity aroused by the title, he picked up the pile of paper and carried it into his office. By the time he'd finished the second page, he was totally involved in the story. He quickly glanced through the pages but couldn't find the author's name written anywhere.

When Jenny returned later with his breakfast, he put the stack of paper to one side, deciding not to ask her about the story until he'd finished reading it. Smiling his thanks at her, he asked not to be disturbed until Deke arrived. Jenny nodded and closed the door on her way out.

Absently forking scrambled eggs and honey-topped biscuits into his mouth, he continued reading.

Each page of the manuscript sent his thought processes clicking madly.

Written in first person, it was the story of a woman battling a hostile and obviously insecure husband, fighting to keep her individuality and, ultimately, her sanity. It wasn't a particularly new idea, but the way it was told caught him square in the gut. It spoke of a woman who acknowledged her weak points but still fought to overcome them, no matter how much her husband berated her. The story described the woman vividly, depicting an inner strength that finally surfaced when she needed it most in her struggle for self-esteem. The more Travis thought about it, the more he knew what his next book project would be. He wanted to photograph women with unusual strength and determination. And his first model had to be the author of this story. There was no doubt in his mind that the author was a woman, and he didn't care what she looked like. All he knew was that he had to photograph her. The more he thought about the idea, the more excited he got.

When Jenny announced Deke's arrival, it took every ounce of self-control for him to contain his impatience at the interruption. He decided he would talk to her after his meeting and ask her the identity of the author.

"Hey, man." Deke, a massive, bald-headed man with a large tattoo of a grinning skull on his bare chest, entered the office and settled into the chair across from Travis. Dressed in a black leather vest, frayed jeans, and worn boots, he looked every inch the ex–Hells Angel he was. Now he preferred making films, thanks to Travis's help, and was enjoying his new status as a cult hero of motorcycle movies. "We gonna talk pictures or broads?"

"Pictures," Travis said firmly. "You can concentrate on the other when I've finished the former. I suppose you want these taken in the desert like last time?"

"Damn right I do," Deke said emphatically. "Hell, Travis, I'm not going to sit around in some sissy studio with makeup all over my puss while you pose me one way and another. These ain't for *Vogue* magazine, you know."

Travis shook his head. "Believe me, I'm not going to make you sit around in some *sissy* studio because I'd have to beat the hell out of you if you tried to fool around with any of my models again." He sighed, remembering the stiff muscles and bruises he'd suffered from a previous battle with Deke. The motorcyclist had come into the studio and promptly hit on one of Travis's models. The woman became hysterical, and Travis felt obligated to show Deke just who was boss in his studio. Now, however, he felt a little too old to be trading punches with this behemoth just to prove who was the better man. No wonder he preferred his present work; it was much calmer.

After talking about the old days when they'd ridden together, they settled on a date for the photo session. After Deke left the office, Travis settled back to finish reading the manuscript, "Human Frailties." He was more determined than ever to photograph the author. It was fast becoming an obsession with him.

"Travis—" Jenny walked into the office and stopped short, blanching when she saw the typed pages in front of him.

"Jenny, I've finally come up with an idea for my next book." He leaned forward in excitement. "You have to tell me who wrote this because I want to photograph the author."

"No," she replied in a low voice, reaching out to gather up the pages. His hand grasped her wrist to stop her.

He misunderstood her meaning. "Jenny, I don't care what she looks like. She must have incredible inner strength to write something this forceful, and I want to capture it."

"Forget about the author, Travis," she advised firmly.

Travis was intrigued. Jenny wasn't so much angry as she was upset over his wanting to know the identity of the author. She normally wouldn't have acted so disturbed over a minor matter; he knew her too well.

"There's a good reason for secrecy," Jenny went on. "She doesn't care to have this published."

"You're making a federal case out of my learning a simple name."

"Maybe so, but I have good reason where she's concerned. I'm sorry, Travis. I have nothing more to say about this. If you don't need me for anything else, I'll be going."

He nodded, allowing her to pick up the pages from his desk. He wasn't going to give up his quest this easily, but he'd let it rest for another day. "See you in the morning."

Jenny nodded, her face still taut with tension, and quickly left the office. Travis heard the sound of desk drawers opening and closing, then silence, indicating that he was alone. After checking his calendar for the following day, he left the office as well.

After picking up dinner at a local fast-food restaurant, Travis headed for home.

Having grown up in farm country, Travis had built a ranch-style house in Rolling Hills. The property boasted a small barn where he kept three horses, and a garage that housed his four-wheel-drive truck, a classic fire-engine-red Corvette, and a motorcycle for the rebel in him.

The first thing Travis did when he walked inside the house was to check the answering machine in his office. Replaying the messages, he listened to the women who had called, but was scarcely interested. He didn't care to be disturbed by anyone that evening. After grabbing a can of beer from the refrigerator, he carried his dinner into the den, plopped himself down on the couch by the fireplace, and stretched his long legs out in front of him. He ate absentmindedly as he thought about the story. Pretty soon he was hunting for a pad of paper and making notes on his ideas for some photographs. As he worked, he lost all track of time, something that wasn't unusual for him, since his work was his life. It wasn't until his sore eyes reminded him that it was early morning that he thought about getting some rest.

What kind of person could write something so powerful? he asked himself as he headed for the bedroom. It was purely conjecture on his part, but he'd bet his last dollar that this story was written as some kind of catharsis for the author. He couldn't imagine anyone just sitting down and writing such a moving, emotional story unless a painful episode in the past had prompted it. Sure, it was considered fiction, but there still had to be some kind of background story to it.

He knew he'd have to get some sleep if he intended to persuade Jenny to part with the author's name. He wasn't too worried about her giving him any real trouble, though; his old-fashioned Southern charm hadn't let him down yet.

"Travis, you're beginning to give me a headache. I've told you no a million times before, and I won't discuss this again," Jenny said wearily, two days later. Since Travis hadn't said anything so far that day, she'd assumed the subject was forgotten. How wrong she was.

"Is it so awful to want to talk to this person?" he demanded, stalking her. "You know I can keep a secret as well as anyone else. In fact, you can be the one to contact the author and let her decide what to do. Doesn't that sound fair?"

Jenny sighed. She knew very well that the author would turn Travis down. She just wished she could convince him of that. "Oh, Travis, you don't understand." She fervently wished she'd never left the story out where he could find it.

"Then make me understand. Give me one good reason why I shouldn't meet with this person."

Jenny closed her eyes in exasperation. Travis waited patiently as she silently debated with herself on what to tell him and what not to.

"This is very difficult to explain. It was written by a friend of mine," she began haltingly. "In fact, it was written at my suggestion. She went through a bad marriage—one that almost broke her physically and

11

mentally—and I thought writing about it might drive the poison from her system. It took her a little over a year and a half to write it, and this was the final product. She sent it to me to read and asked that I not show it to anyone else."

"She honestly didn't want this published?" Travis was surprised by the admission. "Doesn't she realize this kind of story might help women in the same situation?"

Jenny's eyes pleaded with him to understand. "It was written to help her keep her sanity, not to head the best-seller lists."

"Fine, I don't intend to use anything from her book. All it did was give me the idea of photographing women who've displayed great inner strength through the years. What would be so wrong in her being one of my subjects?"

"She would never agree."

"You don't know that for sure."

"Oh, but I do."

Travis's eyes narrowed to black slits. "You wouldn't know unless you're trying to say the author is you."

Jenny smiled and shook her head. "No, I'm not the author. And I'm certainly not a good enough liar to make you believe I *did* write it if I thought it would get you off the scent once and for all."

"Look, Jenny, I appreciate and admire your loyalty to your friend, but please look at my side. All I ask is a chance," he requested humbly.

She took a deep breath as she looked into his face and saw the silent pleading in the rugged features, an expression not known to such an inherently proud man. Maybe she should tell him. She knew he wouldn't get any farther in his quest, and he finally just might give up the idea of using the author in his new book if he realized there wasn't a chance of seeking the woman out. "Perhaps in the long run it would be better if you tried to contact her yourself, although it would be next to impossible for you to find her, since she doesn't live in this state."

Travis nodded impatiently, realizing he was finally getting what he wanted.

"Actually I wouldn't be surprised if you've met her in the past," Jenny went on a bit too casually.

He frowned. "I've met a lot of writers in my time, and not one has made a good enough impression to remain in my memory more than ten minutes. I would have remembered meeting the kind of person who'd have written something like this."

"I'm not talking about someone who's made their living at writing."

Travis's eyes narrowed. He could feel the anticipation; deep down in his bones he knew he was going to hear something he hadn't anticipated.

Jenny looked straight into his eyes. "The author is Kali Hughes."

Travis's softly spoken profanity sounded more like a prayer. He'd expected to hear just about any other name but that one. He stood up and walked over to the oak credenza gracing one wall. It took some searching among magazines and bound photo albums, but he soon found what he was looking for. He opened the folder in front of him and scanned the contents. The folder was a few years old.

"Kali Hughes—five foot eight, tawny-colored hair, brown eyes, no distinguishing marks, thirty-one. Married to Blayne Savage; one daughter named Cheryl, aged two. She made the cover of eight magazines, *Vogue* three of those times," he read out loud, then looked up. "They certainly didn't like to give out too much personal information about her, did they? Must've been afraid they'd give away some deep, dark secret. She'd be what, thirty-three or thirty-four by now? Let's see, she divorced her husband almost three years ago, and it ended up pretty messily, even by Hollywood standards. Then there was a child-custody battle that was just as nasty. If I remember correctly, he accused her of taking drugs, which is nothing new in this town; having countless lovers; and engaging in perverted acts. Remembering *his* less than immaculate reputation, I wonder what he considered perverted. And wasn't there an accusation that she deliberately aborted his baby because she didn't want to take the time out from her career to have another child?" He shook his head. Every supermarket tabloid had had a field day, courtesy of Kali Hughes and her handsome actor-husband. At the time all he had thought about was the embittered woman he'd met on New Year's Eve. The vulnerable Kali Hughes he had known was nothing like the cold-blooded woman Blayne Savage talked about during the divorce hearing. "Then she and the girl disappeared, and no one could find out where they went," he recalled, then frowned. "No, something else happened."

"Kali left town alone," Jenny said, correcting him. "Blayne stopped by the preschool Cheryl went to, used his charm on the school director, and walked off with Cheryl. Last anyone heard is that he's somewhere in Europe making 'art' films. If he tries to return to the States, he'll be arrested for kidnapping. Kali was so distraught, she was on the verge of a mental breakdown. Her doctor kept her under heavy sedation for several days because he was afraid she might kill herself. She loved her daughter more than life itself, Travis; loved her so much that losing her almost killed her. To save herself, she finally left town to take stock and make a new life. If she has her way, she'll never return to New York or L.A."

Travis stared off into space. "You two were more than employer and employee, so she sent you the story," he mused. "What's she doing now?"

"Getting her life back together."

Travis looked down at the publicity photograph before him. It may have been black-and-white, but it didn't hide the sheer vitality of the real woman. The loose topknot with wispy tendrils at her ears gave a man the impression that he could undo some invisible hairpin and send the tresses falling down to frame her lovely face. With her slight smile and mysterious eyes, there was a truly elusive quality about the woman. She wasn't beautiful in the traditional sense, but she had that special something the camera loved. All she had to do was smile, and the sun came out in all its brilliant glory. Once Travis had briefly known this remarkable woman, and he would give everything to know her again.

Funny, she'd always told the press she couldn't imagine such happiness as she'd had with her husband and child, coupled with her career. But her husband hadn't found the same kind of fame she had. He'd starred in three television series, but none ever lasted past mid-season. He just didn't have that special spark that made an actor a star.

Travis doubted that anyone would ever know the truth behind the divorce. Kali left the house with her daughter and filed for divorce, but she refused to give any specifics, leaving it up to the press to speculate. It took all of her strength to battle her angry and spiteful husband in court.

But Blayne had enacted his own vengeance by suing for custody of their child. This started another dirty court battle where he brought in his own sleazy type of ammunition. Barely a week after Kali won the case, Blayne kidnapped Cheryl and left the country.

After the tragedy the bereaved woman went into seclusion, refusing to see anyone. Soon afterward, she sold the elaborate family home in the Hollywood hills and the luxurious penthouse apartment in New York, then dropped out of sight. Speculation continued for a time—that she had finally snapped and would be spending the rest of her days in a sanitarium, or that she now lived with a whiskey bottle for company, or even that the court battles were some kind of perverse publicity and she'd left the country to join her husband. But no one bothered to seek out the truth because it was unlikely to sell as many papers as speculation did.

"Damn," he muttered, closing the folder and setting it back in the credenza. He swung around to face his assistant. "You said you suggested she write to relieve her fears. They were that bad?"

Jenny nodded. "She was alone too much, and I thought if she had something to occupy her time, she might be better off. Kali hired a team of private detectives to track down Cheryl and bring her back, but Blayne always seems to keep one step ahead of them. He moves on to another town or country and changes his name and hair color. How he manages it, no one knows. It's as if it's some kind of sick game to him. Meanwhile it's tearing Kali up inside because she doesn't know if Cheryl is all right. She's offered him a small fortune to send Cheryl back to her, but he ignores her pleas. It's as if he's trying to punish her."

Travis considered her words. It sounded like Kali Hughes's marriage had been more hell than heaven. He had to give her credit for having done such an excellent job of hiding the truth. He was sure there was much more behind her claim of incompatibility than ever reached the court.

Closing his eyes, Travis remembered back to the last time he had seen her. Her mouth was swollen from his kisses, her eyes dark with desire, her voice husky with passion. All of it due to him. Maybe he should have said "No thanks" to her, because it ended up as a bitter joke on both of them. She'd wanted to hurt her husband for hurting her, and Travis ended up as the victim in her quest for revenge. Still, he couldn't deny that it had ended up to be a sensual explosion that shocked them both—all because of a simple kiss that promised to be so much more.

But he shouldn't think about that now. She was gone, and no one knew where to find her. It was as if she had dropped off the face of the earth. Of course, he couldn't blame her for getting out while the getting was good. Kali had gone through hell because of her divorce and her daughter's custody hearing. She had been smart enough to get away from her fast-paced life before it consumed her entirely.

"I still want to talk to her," he said abruptly.

Jenny sighed. She wasn't surprised that he hadn't

changed his mind, but she had hoped he might understand and drop the idea. "Travis, I honestly don't know where Kali is. Her mail is sent to me through her attorney, and mine is sent the same way. Her letters give no indication even what state she's living in. She could live outside the country and I wouldn't know it."

"Then I'll talk to her attorney. I need to speak to her even more now. Please, Jenny."

"She won't talk to you, Travis. I doubt she wants anything to do with anyone from her former life, anyone who could be even the slightest reminder of her time here. Besides, in her letters she sounds happy where she is. She doesn't deserve to be hurt anymore."

That was the last thing he would do to her. "I just want to talk to her," he insisted.

"Her attorney is Malcolm Rhodes, and his reputation as a hard-hearted bastard is well earned. He won't give you the slightest hint as to her whereabouts."

Travis smiled, a smile that told Jenny he had a plan up his sleeve; one that would get him exactly what he wanted.

"We'll see."

Chapter
2

🐌 Kali always enjoyed this time of year. The beginning of spring meant rebirth, which was what she was still undergoing in her own life. It was a time when baby animals started revealing their tiny faces in the woods as they followed their mothers and learned all the rules for survival in the wild. The trees and bushes were regaining their leaves and turning a beautiful green as the winter snows disappeared. Oh, it wasn't so much that she hated the snow. Long days of living snowed in didn't bother her a bit as long as she had plenty of wood for the fireplace and the bookcase was filled with reading material to peruse during the long winter evenings.

She had gotten up this morning feeling more

cheerful than she had in a long time. It took no time at all to make her bed and hop in the shower before heading for the kitchen to fix her morning cup of coffee. She smiled at the birds singing outside her window; it felt so good to smile again. For a long time she hadn't had anything to feel happy about. She carried her coffee mug with her as she returned to the bathroom to brush her hair and pull it back into a neat braid. She stared at her reflection in the mirror and saw a woman dressed in a sweater and jeans, no makeup on her face—a far cry from the successful fashion model of two years ago.

"Good morning, Kali, you're doing just fine," she said out loud. "You're in control, and you have a beautiful day outside to celebrate."

Talking to herself wasn't a sign that she had lived alone too long. It was just her daily greeting to herself as a reminder that as long as she could speak positively to her reflection, she could still consider herself a part of the human race.

Kali thought over what she would do that day. She had driven into town the day before for supplies and her mail, pleased to find two letters from Jenny, forwarded through Malcolm's office. She had hoped to receive another report from one of the private detectives she'd hired to find Cheryl but wasn't lucky in that respect. Oh, well, maybe she was better off not reading any bad news for a while. She'd read Jenny's letters the previous night, pleased to learn how much her friend had enjoyed her story and eager to hear the latest gossip. Kali had been surprised when Jenny took a job working for Travis Yates. It wasn't that she was a snob about L.A.'s caste system, but she couldn't imagine her glamorous ex-assistant working around former Hells Angels and motorcycle jockeys, even though Travis was now better known for his photo books than for his previous work. There were other reasons why Kali didn't like hearing about Travis; he brought back memories of a night she wanted to leave forgotten. Trouble was, as long as Jenny worked for the man, Kali doubted she would be able to forget his name. She was glad she no longer lived in L.A. and wouldn't accidentally run into him when she least expected it. She couldn't afford a repeat of that night three years ago.

In her letter Jenny had hinted that "Human Frailties" was the perfect kind of story to be published, but Kali wasn't interested in seeing her name in print. She was just glad to get so much of her hurt and anger out of her system by writing about her marriage. Lately she had been wondering if she would ever marry again. One thing was sure: If she could ever trust another man, it wouldn't be anyone from L.A. or New York. No, sir—next time she'd choose a down-home country boy. Of course, if she was smart, she just wouldn't remarry, period.

In the end, Kali decided it was the perfect kind of morning to spend baking bread. When she'd first returned to Virginia, she had forgotten so many of the household tasks that had been a habit during her teen years. During her first bread-baking attempts the dough had either refused to rise or tasted as if she used too much salt. Now it tasted just as good as it used to. Funny, she used to work out daily in the large exercise room in the house in order to keep her weight down. Now she ate anything she wanted, yet was probably a good ten pounds thinner due to her walks and horseback rides in the woods.

Late that afternoon, after putting aside a fourth loaf of warm bread, Kali debated whether to go to the trouble of fixing a gourmet meal for dinner, as she did every so often, or just taking the easy way out and cooking an omelet. She planned on spending the evening reading, or watching one of the new video-tapes Malcolm had sent her. Since many of his clients were in the film business, he received a lot of new films, but claiming that he barely had time to watch the news on television, he sent them on to Kali to enjoy. She had just come to the conclusion that she wasn't in the mood to fix an elaborate meal when she heard the roaring sound of a motorcycle climbing the hill that led to her cabin.

Figuring the rider was using the road to make a turn, she thought nothing of it until she heard the loud engine silenced just outside her front door. Not sure if her visitor was friend—few of the locals came to visit, since they knew and respected her wish for solitude—or foe—she lived quite a distance from town, so she was vulnerable in many ways—she checked her shotgun to make sure it was loaded. Standing near the front window, she peered outside at the ominous-looking motorcycle in front of the cabin.

The heavy dust layered over the cycle told her it had undergone a lot of hard driving, and the blue-and-gold California license plate warned her that this visitor must be foe. She cursed under her breath, wondering if a reporter had somehow found out her whereabouts and was coming to look for *the* story. If that was the case, she had a special load of rock salt just for this occasion. She took the few minutes to study her unwanted visitor a bit more closely.

Only Love

The man straddling the bike was tall and lean. The adjective *dangerous* also came to mind before she even saw his face. Her blood suddenly chilled as she realized his identity. He pulled off a black-and-silver helmet and shook his head, the black, wavy strands curling down around the collar of his leather jacket. Rugged angular features, a thick dark mustache dusted with silver, and an unshaven jaw seemed to jump right out at her, along with heavy-browed black eyes that she swore bored right through the thick walls and could see her standing by the window. She knew that face, all right. And he was the last person she wanted to see out here.

Kali turned away, shaken by the unexpected intrusion into her new life. How had he found out where she was? Her first thought was Jenny, but no, she didn't know where Kali lived, and Kali had never given her the slightest hint. Malcolm? No, he understood and respected her need for privacy and wouldn't tell the devil himself where she was. So how had he found out?

Her body burning with anger at this intrusion, she hefted the shotgun in her hands and headed for the door, yanking it open angrily.

I'm not ready for this! her heart cried. *All I ever wanted was to be left alone.*

Travis remained straddling his bike. He watched the slender woman carrying a shotgun in a manner that indicated to the casual observer that she not only knew how to use it but would with the slightest provocation. One brow lifted in acknowledgment of her firepower.

"Hello, Kali." His deep voice carried across the yard.

"You're trespassing on private property," she said roughly, refusing to call him by name. She saw no reason to be polite. He certainly hadn't been invited.

"I drove almost three thousand miles to see you, Kali. Do you think I could at least have a glass of water before you empty that load in me?"

"There's a stream three miles south of here. Try there. The water's not too muddy this time of year."

He couldn't help grinning at her retort. He admired her feisty attitude. And, Lord, she was still beautiful, now even more than before. "What happened to the good old-fashioned Southern hospitality you Virginians are known for?" he said, taunting her.

"It died out a hundred and twenty years ago. But I will give you some advice. The nearest decent hotel is sixty miles away, and in order to reach it, you're going to have to drive a narrow, winding mountain road. I suggest you get started now so you'll arrive there before dark." She tapped the gun barrel against her palm.

Travis looked up at the rapidly darkening sky. Judging by that and the wind gusting around him, he'd hazard a storm was closing in fast.

"I don't appreciate uninvited guests," Kali shouted above the wind, brushing her hair from her eyes. "So do us both a favor and get out of here."

"What will you do if I don't want to leave, call the cops?"

Kali's face tightened. She thought of Red Gorman, the town sheriff. She knew that the overweight man, whose idea of relaxation was going fishing with a keg of beer for company, was no match for the man in front of her.

Travis watched her standing stiffly on the edge of

the porch. There was no denying her anger at his intrusion. After all, it wasn't as if they had been the best of friends—although once they'd been on their way to knowing each other very well. Looking at her set features, he doubted she would care to be reminded of that night. He had a pretty good idea she wouldn't think twice about using that gun on him. He was going to have to indulge in some pretty fast talking if he wanted to stay in one piece. Luckily Mother Nature decided to help his cause. The threatening storm turned into fact, and the rain poured down heavily.

"You'd better get down the hill before the road washes out if you don't want to ruin that fancy bike," Kali yelled, wishing with all her might that she could just shoot him and get it over with.

"Hey, you wouldn't want me to drive in this rain, would you?" he said, protesting with a wide-eyed innocence that didn't suit him one bit.

"Wouldn't bother me at all."

He zipped up his jacket against the cold downpour.

"Kali, have a heart. The roads are probably slippery by now, and I could have an accident," he argued.

"Tough."

"No decent human being would send an animal out in this rain!" he shouted back.

"You're right, I wouldn't send an animal out."

Travis sighed. This was turning out to be more difficult than he'd feared. What had happened to the charming woman he'd known years ago?

Kali tried not to show how cold she was standing out on the porch. Deep in her heart she knew Travis was right. The rain was coming down harder by the minute, and from past experience she knew the hilly road would soon be impossible to traverse. While she didn't care if he broke his neck driving down the hill, she knew any publicity regarding his accident would reveal her whereabouts, and her peace would be gone forever.

"There's a shed around back." She gestured with the gun barrel. "You can leave your bike there." She turned away and went back into the house.

Travis climbed off his motorcycle and pushed it toward the rear of the house. "I've seen more charm in a Gila monster," he muttered, exhaling as he maneuvered the heavy bike through the mud. He assumed he'd find a back door near the shed. If he didn't think she'd shoot him, he'd take a chance and waltz in the front door, muddy boots and all.

Kali put the rifle back in its place by the door and walked into the kitchen, resisting the urge to throw anything breakable.

I don't want him here! she thought frantically.

But it's raining. Her softer side persevered. *He could skid on the road and have an accident. Would you want that on your conscience?*

I don't have a conscience. She poured herself another cup of coffee and leaned against the counter. She wanted to know why he was here, but something prompted her not to ask. She'd let him stay only until the rain let up enough so that he could get back down the hill and on his way. She could hear Travis moving around in the shed, then the sound of the back door opening and closing. She was staring into the dark coffee, as if she would find all the answers there, when Travis entered the kitchen.

"It's really coming down now," he told her, pulling off his jacket and placing it over the back of a chair. He eyed her steaming mug with undisguised envy. The cold rain had left him chilled to the bone.

"There may be a cup left." She waved a careless hand in the direction of the coffeepot. If he could stand a cup from the bottom of a very strong pot of coffee, he was welcome to it.

Undaunted by her rudeness, Travis rummaged through the cupboards. He looked around the kitchen, noting the round butcher-block table set in one corner with four cushioned navy tweed chairs. The appliances were gleaming white, with brightly colored tiles set along the wall for accent. The dish towel and pot holders echoed the same cheerful floral pattern. It was a homey kitchen. He sipped the coffee and uttered a low sigh of appreciation as the hot liquid warmed his throat.

"How did you find out where I was?" Kali demanded, holding on to the coffee mug in hopes that it would warm her cold skin. She slowly raised her eyes to face him squarely. The once smiling and laughing Kali Hughes wasn't evident in her unwelcoming stance and icy gaze. It didn't take much to sense she didn't want Travis there.

"I guess you could say I'm very resourceful," he quipped. Kali didn't crack a smile.

"Malcolm knows better than to reveal my whereabouts to anyone."

"Yeah, and no one keeps secrets better than that old bastard. Don't worry, he never said a word, but that didn't stop me from finding another way."

"You broke in!" she accused shrilly. "You broke into Malcolm's office and went through his files. That's the

27

only other way you could have found out, and a hood like you *would* resort to such a despicable thing."

Travis shrugged, crossing one foot over the other. "I don't recall making any confession."

Kali's cheeks turned bright red with anger. He was playing games with her and she didn't appreciate it one bit.

Travis could see he was pushing her a bit too hard. It was time to back down temporarily.

"Where can I wash up?" he asked amiably.

"There's a well next to the shed."

His lips twitched. "You saying you don't have indoor plumbing?"

Kali resisted the urge to grind her teeth in frustration. Why couldn't he be obnoxious so she could be as rude as she wanted to be? On second thought, she'd be obnoxious no matter how nice he was. Then maybe he'd leave, rain or no rain.

"It isn't that I mind visiting the outhouse during a rainstorm, or even in the middle of the night, but my daddy installed an honest-to-God bathroom when I was eight years old, and I kinda got used to having indoor facilities."

Kali raised her eyes heavenward in a silent plea. Too bad no one was listening to her.

"Down the hall, first door to your right."

Travis nodded. He set the mug down and ambled toward the doorway. He halted and turned. "Thanks for letting me come in out of the rain." Then he had the audacity to wink at her!

Kali clenched her hands so tightly, the nails left imprints in her palms. She wondered if a good healthy scream of outrage would help her keep her sanity. How dare he be so nice to her!

Only Love

While Travis washed up, he thought about the many changes he'd noticed in Kali. If he thought before that she was the perfect model for his book, now he *knew* it. The lighthearted woman he'd known long ago had survived the traumas to emerge a much stronger woman.

He'd also noticed that the designer label on her jeans read Levi Strauss, and her watermelon crewneck wool sweater was inexpensive. Her tan Western boots were scuffed, the heels slightly worn down. His dark eyes had studied her over the rim of his mug. Her hair was longer, and he'd bet a good many of those lighter strands were gray instead of tawny blond. With all she had endured, she'd certainly earned them. There were tiny lines fanning out from her eyes, and an expression in the nutmeg depths that could only be described as haunted. He'd also seen the faint lines around her mouth and eyes, scored there by emotional pain and stress. Yet they didn't detract from her beauty but rather enhanced it.

He'd also noticed she had quite a temper. He knew it was pure luck that he wasn't presently nursing a bullet wound or suffering from a dose of rock salt in his ass at the very least. He wouldn't put it past her to use it to keep away any intruders. Since she lived so far off the beaten path, she had to be strong enough to fight her own battles. He knew his time was limited and he would have to use every second he had to plead his cause.

Kali knew it was close to dinnertime—her stomach had already informed her. And now it appeared she had a guest, whether she wanted one or not. Trouble was, if she had to have a guest, why couldn't it have been someone she would appreciate seeing?

When Travis returned to the kitchen ten minutes later, she was stirring eggs in a bowl.

"Dinner will be ready soon," she said crisply, not bothering to look up from her task.

His eyes brightened. "Sounds great. I haven't eaten since breakfast, and I have to admit I'm starved."

Kali smiled briefly as she poured part of the egg mixture into an omelet pan.

Travis looked on in dismay as Kali deftly prepared two cheese-and-mushroom omelets. To a man of his size and metabolism, it was nothing more than an appetizer.

"Looks good," he said weakly, eyeing the medium-size omelets. "Ah, are we going to have any hash browns or toast with this?"

"I'm on a diet." She set the coffeepot in the middle of the table after topping off her mug.

Travis consumed his omelet in tiny bites, hoping his stomach would think he'd eaten a large meal. Too bad his stomach wasn't gullible.

"You have a very nice place here," he commented, wanting to break the thick tension surrounding them. "It appears well built; real cozy. Did you have to do any remodeling?"

Silence.

"It looks pretty old."

More silence.

Travis exhaled. "Would it kill you to say one lousy word to me?"

She raised her eyes. "I came here for the solitude. If I had wanted to talk to someone, I would've bought a dog, since they don't talk back." She returned to her meal.

He rolled his eyes. The lady was a great deal more stubborn than he'd expected. Oh, he didn't think she would greet him with open arms, but he didn't expect the silent treatment, either. He couldn't blame her entirely; he had intruded on her when all she wanted was peace and quiet. He knew that if it hadn't been for the rain washing out the road, he would have been out there cursing the hard-hearted woman who refused to give him shelter.

He wanted to talk to her immediately about his new book, how her story had given him the idea, but he knew if he discussed it with her now, he would be effectively ignored and quite probably turned out, rain or no rain.

"You know, strange as it sounds, Jenny didn't talk about you a lot," he commented, pouring himself another cup of coffee. Kali didn't appear at all interested. "I guess you could say she respected your privacy."

"Too bad you didn't feel the same way."

By now she was trying very hard not to look curious, but it was difficult with this man sitting across from her. Kali blamed her unease on the fact that she'd seen so few people in the past couple of years and that Travis represented a time she'd prefer to forget. She knew she'd have to keep her wits about her as long as he was in her house.

She would need her wits to find out the real reason for Travis's visit. Her little hideaway wasn't exactly easy to get to or to find. Located in an out-of-the-way part of Virginia, Newton's Gap boasted a general store, combined with a post office, a gas station complete with mechanic, a tavern, and a small building that passed as a police station and town hall. If a resident needed medical attention, Newton's Gap had a county nurse, but anything major required a twenty-mile drive to a medical center in Bixby. Bixby was another small town but much more cosmopolitan than Newton's Gap. If someone wanted to see a movie or find other entertainment, they drove to Bixby, where they could find a pool hall, a movie theater, and a tavern complete with live music and pinball machines.

"Nice country around here," Travis remarked. "Any good hunting?"

"Enough so that no one goes out alone or wanders in the forest too much during hunting season," Kali said curtly. "Outsiders don't have a chance if they hunt out of season. Red Gorman, our sheriff, thinks he's a regular Kojak."

Travis chuckled. "Sounds like where I came from. Our sheriff used to visit the high school and remind us that if we didn't watch our p's and q's, we'd end up in his jail."

"And did you ever end up in his jail?"

"Most of us did, one time or another."

"Where was that?"

"Texarkana," he replied, glad that she was finally talking to him. "You wouldn't find it on any map."

"And the country boy ended up in wild and woolly L.A.," she mused dryly.

"Just like the country girl."

Her eyes narrowed. "I never said I was from around here."

"You didn't have to, and I'm not as stupid as I sometimes look. When I first saw you, you had all the trappings of a high-fashion model, but now you look like the small-town girl you really are," he told her. "Sorry, lady, you can't hide your beginnings."

Her eyes turned cold as ice. "Don't try to tell me who you think I am, because you have no idea who the real me is." *Because I don't even know who I really am anymore.*

Travis looked at her curiously. Something about her past bothered Kali a great deal. He wasn't the type to pry, because there were a few gray areas in his own past he preferred to keep quiet. Still, he couldn't help wondering why she'd returned to her hometown when there didn't appear to be good memories for her. She could have gone anywhere in the world to live; why move back to a small town that had little going for it and live like a virtual hermit?

"So, what do you do around here for fun?" Travis quipped, hoping she would warm up to him if he could prove to her he wasn't a threat. He should have known better.

"Keep to ourselves."

Travis dropped his gaze to the coffee mug he held between his palms, wishing it was Kali's slender neck he had his hands wrapped around.

The moment Kali finished her meal, she picked up her plate and coffee cup and carried them to the sink. In a matter of moments they were washed, rinsed, and set on the drainboard. Without a word she left the kitchen.

Travis watched in stunned disbelief as she walked out. He doubted he had ever met such a hardheaded woman and would give anything to teach her some manners. He gathered up his own dishes and washed them up. Needing a few minutes to himself, he walked out the back door to check on the rain.

Meanwhile Kali paced the living room in short, agitated steps. *How dare he come here! He has no right to barge into my home. I came here to get away from people like him.*

She felt her head pounding, her breathing growing heavy.

It isn't fair! she swore. If anyone had to show up here, why did it have to be him?

Kali wished she could forget all about the New Year's Eve three years ago, but she never could, not as long as Travis was in her house. All the details were still too clear in her mind.

It had begun at a New Year's Eve party when she'd found Blayne in bed with a blond starlet. Her pain was coupled with intense anger, and she was suddenly determined to seek revenge. A few drinks had served to give her the courage to choose a victim. Why she had picked Travis, she couldn't explain— except that he was a stranger and she preferred her victim not to be someone she knew. The electricity that sizzled from their first kiss to that last caress was a shock to her senses. She left the party disgusted with herself, ashamed that she would have been willing to go to bed with a man she didn't even know. Thank goodness she'd come to her senses in time. Ironically Travis hadn't condemned her for pulling back but seemed to understand her self-recrimination. He showed her a great deal of understanding that night, but she couldn't help but hate him, anyway. She wanted no sympathy or pity from anyone, especially from him. She thanked her lucky stars she wouldn't have to see him again and firmly pushed the episode out of her mind. Now he was here for some unknown reason, and she resented his bringing back painful memories—

"How about an after-dinner drink?" Travis said, his voice breaking into her thoughts.

She spun around, unaware of how vulnerable she appeared to him with her wide eyes and pained features.

Travis gestured with the bottle of brandy he held in one hand.

"I brought this along with me for nights after a long day on the road." He set two glasses on a nearby table and poured the amber liquor in them.

Kali accepted one of the glasses and sipped cautiously.

"All that anger bottled up inside isn't good for you," he said casually, settling in an aqua tweed easy chair.

"I didn't realize you had a medical degree."

Her sarcasm wasn't lost on him, but he preferred to ignore it.

"Stress isn't selective." He sipped his brandy with an appreciative air. The air outside had been freezing cold, and the drink was doing its part to warm him up . . . although he wouldn't mind if the lady across from him assisted in the warming-up process. "And you've certainly had enough problems piled on your plate to warrant feeling so angry at the world. All I ask is that you don't take it out on me."

"I have no feelings toward you one way or the other." She perched herself stiffly on the edge of the couch, looking ready to bolt at the slightest provocation.

Just as Kali's thoughts had careened back to New

Year's Eve, so had Travis's. He would have brought
up some light quip about that night but wisely decided against it. She sat too close to that shotgun of
hers, and he wouldn't put it past her to use it. But
that didn't stop him from noticing how her worn
jeans clung to her trim hips and thighs, the way her
sweater curved delicately over her high bosom. His
palms itched with the memory of caressing those
luscious breasts. How satiny smooth her skin was, and
how tantalizing was the memory of her passionate
moans when he'd kissed her. He shifted in his seat,
feeling his body reacting to his heated memories.

As if sensing the direction of Travis's thoughts, Kali
swallowed the fiery liquid and jumped up.

"You can sleep in the loft," she said icily. "Don't
worry, you'll find a perfectly adequate bed up there."
With that, she strode down the hall to the last room
and slammed the door behind her.

Travis remained sitting in the chair, wishing he
had brought up "Human Frailties," even if it had
meant being kicked out. On second thought, since he
would be tossed out in the morning, anyway, he
might as well talk to her then. He figured he'd be
able to get out at least two sentences before she
grabbed the rifle.

He took the two glasses into the kitchen and
checked the doors before climbing up to the loft
bedroom. The room turned out to be decidedly chilly
—just like his hostess.

Chapter
3

🦤 Kali didn't feel very secure behind the closed bedroom door, even though she doubted Travis would enter the room without an invitation. Still, she suspected she wasn't going to have an easy night. His arrival had stirred up painful memories, and she feared a recurrence of the fitful nights she'd experienced the first year after the kidnapping. Then she had been plagued by nightmares of Cheryl coming to some harm. It had taken her a long time to come to terms with what had happened—that her daughter was gone, stolen from her. All the while she worked hard to contain the pain inside her, pushing it far from the surface. She didn't cry as often anymore; she could finally eat a meal without becoming violently ill; and, most of all, she discovered she could go on living and praying for the day her daughter would be returned to her. She never gave up looking for Cheryl because she always felt in her heart she would get her back. And if Blayne ever showed his face again, Kali would take the rock salt out of her gun and replace it with the real thing!

She undressed and curled up in bed even though her usual bedtime hour was a few hours off. Better to be alone in her bedroom than listening to Travis's all too sexy voice. It disturbed her to find him so appealing when all she truly wanted to do was order him from her house and return to her self-imposed solitude.

Funny, for the first seventeen years of her life Kali had thought of nothing but escaping Newton's Gap. Her mother ran away when Kali was five, and she honestly couldn't blame her. Kali's father felt the best way to prove who was in charge was to physically beat his opponent. Kali was free from him only when she was in school or clerking at the general store.

It was while leafing through fashion magazines during the slow hours at work that she thought about working as a model. When she once mentioned her dream to her father, he slapped her across the face and informed her that only sluts worked as models, and she'd be better off getting married and doing something proper with her life. Kali never mentioned her dreams again, but she knew she couldn't go along with her father's plans for her. Three weeks after her high-school graduation, and four days after her seventeenth birthday, she ran away with her boyfriend, Harold Gresham, who aspired to be an actor, and the pair hitchhiked their way to L.A.

She found a lot of openings for waitresses and sales-clerks in the glitzy town, but very few for models unless she cared to pose in the nude. She was flatly informed that a model's career usually began in New York, and besides, she'd never make it as one. She just wasn't what they were looking for. But that didn't stop Kali from seeing one agent after another, until one woman saw something special in her and took her under her wing. The first change made was Kali's name; Calliope Sue Howard became Kali Hughes. Harold had already known his name wouldn't look impressive in print, and changed it to Blayne Savage because he thought it sounded sexy. At the same time he decided his career just might be better off if he didn't have any ties, meaning Kali would have to go. But around that time Kali was chosen for a swim-suit ad, and the manufacturer began to ask for her on a steady basis. With her growing popularity, Blayne just as quickly changed his mind and told her he thought they should get married as soon possible. Within a few weeks they were the picture of the perfect couple.

From the beginning Kali learned that fashion mod-eling was a lot of hard work, but that didn't deter her. She was used to hard work, and what made it worth-while was that this time she was doing something for herself. At first she went along with Blayne's sugges-tion that they not have children right away, even though she wanted it all: a house, a career, children. She held off, knowing they had to settle in as a mar-ried couple before starting a family. Cheryl turned out to be a happy accident as far as Kali was concerned. While Blayne would have preferred Kali to have had an abortion, she insisted on going through with the pregnancy. Loud and vicious arguments echoed through their house for months afterward. Still, she remained stubborn about having the baby and, after a remarkably short and uneventful delivery, was blessed with a healthy baby girl who was the apple of her mother's eye.

Kali's eyes filled with tears. She loved Cheryl so much. The little girl had always been her weak point, and when Blayne decided to exact vengeance, he knew exactly where to hit her—where it would hurt the most. She rolled over and punched the pillow, wishing it were Blayne's pretty-boy face. At the same time she cursed Travis Yates for barging in and bringing the past back to torture her.

Curled up on her side, she could see the shadowy figures of two stuffed animals sitting on the edge of the dresser: one a sleepy-faced lavender dragon with outstretched wings and a lopsided pink tongue; the other a brown teddy bear with one of the saddest faces she had ever seen. A sad face that many days matched her own. They'd been Cheryl's favorite toys, and she'd always refused to go to sleep without them beside her. Unfortunately Blayne hadn't taken them along when he snatched Cheryl, and Kali wondered how the little girl got to sleep without her beloved toys. When Kali escaped from L.A., she had left everything pertaining to her life there except for those two animals. To her they were a reminder that the day would come when their owner would return to claim them.

During the day they sat in the middle of Kali's bed, and at night they graced her dresser where she could see them if she woke up in the middle of the night. They always brought such a clear picture of the little girl to her mind. How Kali loved her! And she'd felt that she was a good mother, always making sure she took time to listen to Cheryl's tales from preschool, trying to be with her and comfort her when she was sick in bed. Many times her schedule had been hectic, but when possible, Kali took Cheryl with her. With Jenny there to help look after the small girl, Kali never worried. Blayne never bothered spending any of his free time with Cheryl, his excuse being that he was better around the older girls.

Yet he had kidnapped Cheryl and kept her with him all these years without a word to Kali. She would have paid any amount of money to get her daughter back. But Blayne allowed her to beg, and he kept on the run to continue punishing her for divorcing him. He hadn't been a faithful husband, but he enjoyed the idea of keeping his other women at bay with the mention of his wife.

She was so afraid that Cheryl wouldn't remember her after all this time. She had been so little when she was taken. Tears pricked Kali's eyelids. She didn't want to relive her pain right now, and it wasn't fair that she had to. She rolled over onto her other side so she couldn't see those lonely stuffed animals. Toys that were as neglected as she was.

The rain slowed to a steady drizzle, and the clock read just past three o'clock when Kali finally fell into an uneasy sleep.

It took a bit of searching, but Travis finally found bed linens stored in a cedar chest in a corner of the loft. He made up the bed, and after grabbing a book

41

out of his duffel bag and shucking his clothing, he climbed under the covers.

Trouble was, he didn't have reading on his mind. Not when he wanted to think about Kali Hughes. There were times when he was sorely tempted to shake some sense into her, but that feeling was quickly squelched when he saw the pain in her eyes. It had been more than two years, and she was still hurting from the hell her ex-husband had put her through. How many women could have endured what Kali went through and still retained some remnants of sanity?

He knew she didn't want him there, but that wasn't going to stop him from imposing on her. He climbed out of bed and walked over to the window overlooking the front of the cabin. There was only a little moonlight, and from what he could see, the hilly road leading to the main road was washed out.

A slow smile lit up his harsh features. It appeared the lady wasn't going to get rid of him as easily as she hoped to. With that cheerful thought he returned to bed and his book.

Travis couldn't imagine a better way to wake up than to the homey aroma of bacon cooking, and coffee brewing. He pulled on his jeans and made his way down to the bathroom for a quick shower and change of clothing before heading for the kitchen. He walked in with a huge grin on his face, his mouth watering at the thought of a huge breakfast.

"Good morning," he said, greeting Kali cheerfully.

She looked up from the magazine in front of her, barely nodded her head, and returned to her reading.

Only Love

Travis took in the spring-patterned stoneware plate filled with two eggs, sunny-side up, two crisp slices of bacon, one English muffin liberally covered with butter, a glass of juice, and a cup of coffee. Two frying pans, recently rinsed, were stacked in the sink.

He wanted to laugh out loud. The little witch had fixed just enough breakfast for one person! Even the coffee maker was empty, showing that she'd gone to the trouble of preparing only the one cup.

"I see you're already eating," Travis ventured, hoping she would take pity on him. "Sorry I overslept. It was probably all that fresh mountain air."

Kali's gaze was cool. "If you want breakfast cooked for you, I suggest you visit your mother. This isn't a bed-and-breakfast inn."

Travis chuckled. "If you had ever tasted my mom's cooking, you wouldn't say that. All of us were grateful my dad was a good cook. Mom is the only woman I know who can't even boil water."

Kali lifted an arched eyebrow, silently indicating that she could care less about his mother's culinary habits.

Travis sighed and headed for the coffee maker. Like his mother, he couldn't cook worth a damn, but he had learned to make a decent cup of coffee out of sheer necessity.

Kali finished her breakfast, picked up her dishes, and carried them over to the sink to wash and put them away. Travis looked her over, noticing she wore red socks with white hearts on them, and no shoes.

Someone who wore such whimsical socks couldn't be all bad, he decided while rummaging through the refrigerator.

"Don't forget to clean up when you're finished," Kali tossed over her shoulder as she headed for the laundry room. There, she pulled on a pair of mud-encrusted boots and a faded denim jacket.

Travis guessed she was going to check on her horses, although she didn't bother to volunteer any information. From the look of it, she probably hadn't slept well the night before. He could see the signs of tension in her demeanor. Her knuckles had been white as they clutched the coffee cup, her mouth taut, her eyes shadowed with strain. He had a pretty good idea his presence was getting to her.

Outside, Kali first walked around to the front of the cabin to check the road. Road, that was a joke; right now it was more like a sea of mud.

Damn! Wouldn't she ever get rid of him? If she weren't so angry, she'd sit down and have a good long cry.

Kali didn't want Travis there. Travis in his skintight jeans, boots, and shoulder-hugging shirt. Why did he have to be so damn sexy? She fumed, walking around back to the barn. Why does he have to smell so fresh, like the earth after a spring rain? Why does he have to look like the devil himself but be so gentle that a woman couldn't help falling under his spell? After all, she should know.

She pushed open the barn door and stepped inside, halting to press her hands against her mouth to stifle the sobs welling up in her throat.

For the past two years she had taught herself not to feel. She had refused to allow any emotion to enter her life, whether it was joy or pain. That was the way she lived her life, and if it hadn't been for Travis Yates barging so unceremoniously into her life, she could

44

have continued living that way as long as possible. In the space of one night he had begun altering her life, and she hated him for that. She had been a bitch toward him and she wouldn't deny it. But it was so much easier to hate him than fall for his good-old-boy charm. To fall the way she had years ago.

She took deep breaths to calm her nerves, inhaling the warm, familiar scent of horseflesh and hay. Stiffening her backbone, she repeated the same words she had recited every morning for the past two years: *You're going to be fine, Kali Hughes.* No matter what, she intended to keep control of her emotions. Then she began the dirty task of mucking out the stalls and feeding the two horses, intending to stay out of the house for as long as possible.

Why had Travis come all this way to see her? It was strange, but she dreaded asking him, fearing she wouldn't like his answer. It would be so much easier if she could throw him and his motorcycle down the hill and be done with him. Naturally it wasn't that simple. The weather had to go against her and create a sea of mud in her front yard.

When Kali entered the house two hours later, she felt tired but much calmer. She found Travis sprawled in the easy chair watching television.

"Hi." He looked up when she walked into the room. "I didn't know this movie was out on tape. I saw it when it first came out and thought it was great."

"It isn't out yet," Kali replied. "Some of Malcolm's clients are film producers, and they give him tapes of their latest work. He claims he doesn't have time to watch the news on TV, much less these, so he sends them to me."

Travis studied Kali's features. He had hoped she might have worked out most of her hostility toward him in the barn, and it appeared she had. Today she wore a delft-blue V-necked pullover sweater with a blue-and-rose plaid shirt underneath. He could have believed she was softening toward him if it hadn't been for her next remark.

"I suppose you'll want to be on your way now that the rain has let up."

His eyes widened. "With all that mud out there? You've got to be kidding. I'll skid before I get two feet."

"So slide down the hill," she suggested softly.

Travis's good nature finally evaporated. "Lady, you're really something, you know that?" He threw himself out of his chair and paced the floor. "I swear, a vulture has more compassion than you do."

"You weren't invited here!" she retorted. "If it weren't for all that damn rain yesterday, you'd already be gone. I'd have made sure."

He stopped and fixed her with a quelling gaze. "You sure can play the coldhearted bitch, can't you?"

Kali was stunned. As long as she'd been able to keep herself on the offense she felt confident, but Travis had very neatly, and cruelly, turned the tables on her.

"Why are you here?" she demanded. "And please don't insult me by saying you just happened to be in the neighborhood, because that story won't wash."

Travis uttered a sound of exasperation. "Now she asks me," he muttered to the ceiling, standing in the middle of the room, his hands folded across his broad chest. He spun around to face Kali.

She shifted uneasily under his scrutiny, not liking

the way his sharp eyes swept over her from the top of her head to her toes, lingering on the rapid rise and fall of her breasts.

"The reason you're upset isn't because you've ended up with an uninvited guest but because your precious privacy has been invaded," he mused. "And I'm the invader."

"I don't know what you mean." She denied his allegation too hastily and refused to look at him.

"I think you have just as long a memory as I do," he continued in a deadly soft voice. "What's upsetting you is the fact that I'm a reminder of that New Year's Eve when little Miss Perfect Wife fell off her pedestal. You don't like to recall that night when you happened to be the seducer instead of the seduced."

Kali jumped up and swung her arm around to hit him as hard as she could, but his reflexes were too quick and he grabbed her wrist before her hand slapped his cheek.

"Don't try that again," he warned in a steely voice, tightening his grip just enough to get his message across. "Or I just might forget I was raised to be a gentleman."

That didn't stop her from glaring at him, her eyes glittering with anger and unshed tears.

"And I thought *Blayne* was a bastard," she whispered, finally pulling her wrist free.

Travis cursed himself for hurting her but knew the truth had to be aired now.

"Kali, I'm sorry," he said with a sigh. "It's just that I came up here to see you, and I was greeted with a shotgun between my eyes and treated like a muddy hound dog coming in through the front door after the floors were just washed and waxed. Honey, if I

47

have to fight back every time you get nasty, I'll use whatever ammunition I can. Besides"—his voice softened—"wouldn't it be better to bring it out in the open now than to allow it to build between us?"

"There won't be time for anything to build between us," she argued, wishing he wouldn't stand so close to her, especially since he looked as if he could cheerfully strangle her. "Because you're going to be out of here in five minutes."

Travis's slow smile signified pure danger. "Think so?" he inquired lazily, stepping even closer until they stood practically nose to nose. Kali tried to retreat, but Travis's grip on her arm prevented any escape. "Then maybe we should just get everything out in the open before I leave."

His casual suggestion left her suspicious, especially if he was thinking about the same thing she was.

"You're blaming me for something that wasn't my fault, Kali," he reminded her in a harsh voice. "I wasn't the one who approached you that night; you came on to me. In a pretty explicit way too. But you don't want to remember it happening that way, do you? You want to keep yourself lily-pure and remain the innocent victim when you weren't. You were hurt and you wanted to hurt him back, although that bastard probably could have cared less what you did as long as it didn't interfere with his own fun and games."

He was right. Even if she didn't want to remember what had occurred that night, it still had to be aired between them. She just didn't feel now was the right time—but that didn't stop Travis from continuing.

"The way I heard it, Blayne celebrated most of that New Year's Eve with a little blond starlet in one of the guest rooms," he went on ruthlessly. "Rumor has it that you walked in on them."

Kali turned away, feeling her face burn with humiliation. How carefully she had worked to keep up the facade that their marriage was the kind dreams were made of, even after her shattering realization that not all was as it should be. She had been so naïve back then! How many nights had she convinced herself that Blayne was working late when he actually had been shacked up with some young actress?

New Year's Eve three years ago had opened her eyes. It was late, and Kali was ready to leave. The party turned out to be much wilder than she had anticipated, and she was eager to return home to their daughter. While looking for her husband she hadn't expected to find a very naked Blayne in one of the guest-room beds with a well-endowed blonde. Afraid that this wasn't the first time it had happened, she fled downstairs and searched for the bar. She needed something to ease the pain of her husband's infidelity. She also wanted revenge.

Kali consumed several double Scotches, a great departure from her usual glass of wine, and looked around for her victim. Then she spied the tall, mustached man standing near the patio door. She knew him as Travis Yates, a popular photographer, although they had never worked together, since he didn't shoot fashion layouts. He was known as a rebel and somewhat of a ladies' man, so she deemed him perfect for the game she was determined to play. Forcing her most seductive smile, she sauntered over to him. From there, it was almost too easy. Little did she know that the man's unconscious and very potent charm would hit her right between the eyes.

49

They headed outside and ended up in a deserted cabana not far from the pool area. Kisses and intimate caresses were shared, words of desire whispered, and clothes were beginning to be shed when a woman's voice sounded nearby.

"Did you see little Miss Modest Kali Hughes with Travis Yates?" she said in a slurred voice. "And here I thought she didn't look at other men, even though her husband's slept with every woman at this party!"

"Honey, if anyone should know about that stud, I do. I've had firsthand experience!" the other woman commented with a drunken giggle. "Wouldn't it be funny if Kali and Travis were off screwing around like Blayne and Gloria are upstairs?"

The crude words had been more effective than a cold shower for Kali. She pulled away, apologized tearfully to Travis, and stumbled out of the cabana, anxious to get as far away as possible. What she hadn't expected was that he would follow her in his car to insure that she reached home safely. During her long drive she imagined him watching her with those haunting dark eyes. He walked her to her door, flashed a brief smile, and left her with a softly spoken apology. She sensed it was meant as a sympathetic gesture after overhearing the woman's comments about her husband and had nothing to do with their aborted lovemaking. Kali was mortified that she'd allowed her guard to lower so abruptly, and vowed she would make sure not to see Travis Yates again. When Blayne arrived home hours later, she never mentioned seeing him with the blonde. It wasn't that much later when she began divorce proceedings, and any lingering thoughts of Travis Yates were pushed to the back of her mind. Until now.

"You thought going to bed with me would make everything right." Travis's blunt words intruded on her painful thoughts.

"Except that I didn't go to bed with you," she said, correcting him in a harsh voice.

"No, but if we hadn't heard those women, we would have made love."

"We would have had sex."

He shook his head. "Oh, Kali, it still upsets you, doesn't it?" he asked gently, his eyes warm with an unspoken emotion. "It still bothers you that when I touched you, you responded to me, asking me to—"

"No," she cried, shaking her head and holding her hands over her ears to keep out the insistent sound of his voice. She turned away, but he refused to let her escape him. He pulled her hands away, spinning her around to face him.

"Listen to me, Kali. You've twisted this all around in your mind. I didn't unzip your dress that night, *you* did. You were the one who kept asking me to make love to you, telling me how much you wanted me. You were the one who came on to me so strongly."

"Stop it!" Kali screamed. "Just stop it! I don't want to hear this."

"At first you did it out of revenge because your husband was cheating on you. Then you changed after I first touched you. You felt the electricity flowing between us, so don't deny it. I've read your story, Kali, so I know what you were feeling."

Kali's eyes flew open, the expression a combination of shock and horror.

"How do you know about that? Jenny, she told you! She promised she wouldn't show it to anyone!" Her voice rose hysterically. "How could she have done this to me?"

"She didn't show it to me, Kali." He lowered his voice, hoping to calm her. "Jenny kept her promise. I found it by accident and read it."

Kali breathed deeply to regain her composure. "My name wasn't anywhere on the story, so how did you find out I wrote it?"

"I bullied the author's name out of her. Believe me, she didn't have a chance."

She smiled wanly. "No one can bully Jenny, and we both know it." She freed herself and walked to the other side of the room, her head bent in despair.

Travis told her, "I read it and it gave me the idea for my next book."

"You're a photographer, not a publisher."

"True," he conceded. "Just remember that when I first read it, I had no idea who the author was, but it did tell me that it was written by someone familiar with pain, and strength was born from that pain. That's when I thought about a book dealing with women of strength. And the person I most wanted to photograph was the author of 'Human Frailties.'"

"No!" Kali shouted, spinning around. "When I left L.A., I vowed I wouldn't go before the camera again, and I mean to keep that vow. I didn't write it just to begin a new career and return to the public eye."

His patience was being sorely tested. "Kali, I don't give a damn what you do with that story. Burn it, throw it away, publish it, I just don't care. When I thought of the author of 'Human Frailties' posing for my book, I didn't care if she was tall, short, thin, fat, or had a wart on the end of her nose. All I knew was that if she had the character to write such stirring words, she had that same character in her face, and I wanted to capture it on film."

Kali pressed her fingertips against her temples in a feeble attempt to ease the pain raging through her head. Writing about her marriage had helped banish some of the demons haunting her since the divorce. She'd let Jenny read it only because it had been due to her urging that Kali had undertaken the task. The words were private, full of a woman's intimate thoughts. She hadn't expected anyone else to read it —especially someone like Travis, who would see far more in the words than she cared him to.

"This could be just what you need," he said quietly, walking over to stand behind her. "You can go back to L.A. in a blaze of glory and show everyone you don't give a damn what they think of you."

"I don't give a damn now."

He placed his hands on her shoulders. "Oh, but you do. If you didn't care, you'd still be living there holding your head high and smiling that icy, 'damn-the-world' smile you're so fond of bestowing on people. Instead, you're hiding out here where your friends can't find you."

Kali turned around and stepped back out of his reach. "It didn't take very long to learn exactly who my friends were, and I can count them on one hand. I wanted to be where life was uncomplicated, where no one cared what kind of car you drove or what hairdresser you went to. Where all that mattered was that you did your work. No one around here cares what designer label you wear on your clothes, or what exclusive resort you're going to on your vacation. These people keep to themselves, and outsiders are not tolerated. But if you're in trouble, they'll be the first to help without it seeming like charity, because they're proud as hell. I didn't run away; I left a town with no heart for one with more soul than anywhere else in the world. I only wish I had realized that when I was younger. And when my daughter is returned to me, we'll continue living here. I want her to grow up among people with the right kind of values."

"Did you ever stop to think that you might have a better chance of finding Cheryl if you were back in L.A. where you can make the proper contacts?" Travis wandered around the room, picking up a color photograph of a smiling toddler, obviously Cheryl, with her mother's hair color and eyes.

"I have an excellent attorney in charge of the case, so there is no need for me to live where I don't care to. And this is as good a place as any to close the subject. I suggest you pack your things and get on the road before dark. After all, you wouldn't want to meet up with an unfortunate accident on an unfamiliar road, would you?" Her insincere smile told him she hoped he would do just that.

Travis's mustache twitched with amusement. "Lady, you've been so hot under the collar, you haven't noticed that the rain's started up again. It appears you have me as a guest for a while longer, like it or not."

Kali's face reddened as she seriously thought about screaming the rafters down. This time maybe she'd just toss him out, rain or no rain. Why was this happening to her just when she felt more like her old self again? Was someone playing some macabre joke on her? She could tell by the smug expression on Travis's face that he figured on talking her into posing for him. Well, she hoped he didn't mind a long wait, because it would be a cold day in hell before she returned to L.A. and posed in front of a camera again.

Chapter
4

Travis didn't like having a roommate, especially a woman. After all, they left their cosmetics scattered all over the bathroom counter; likewise their clothing in the bedroom. And they always seemed to be on the latest fad diet, whether that meant high-protein, high-carbohydrate, all fruits and vegetables, or no food at all. Oh, how they could talk about dieting!

Kali wasn't that way at all. For one thing, she didn't use any cosmetics other than cleanser and a moisturizer he found in the bathroom cabinet. And his few glances inside her bedroom told him that she was scrupulously neat. Judging by the way she ate, she didn't seem to know about that nasty four-letter word—*diet*. And as for talking his ear off, well, he certainly didn't have to worry about that. She ignored him more often than not, which alternately amused and irritated him.

This new Kali Hughes was a revelation. Once known as a gracious and warm hostess, she made life for Travis just barely tolerable. She talked to him only when necessary; the only meal she cooked for two was dinner, and then it was always something more suited to a woman's delicate appetite than a man's hearty one. She read a lot in the evening, while Travis usually watched videotapes. All he knew was that if the intermittent rain continued much longer, he might kill her after all. He was well on his way to getting cabin fever, not to mention having erotic ideas every time he looked at Kali.

As for Kali, she hated to admit that Travis wasn't a bad houseguest; he never left a mess in the bathroom, and didn't try to force his company on her in the evenings. She only wished she could ignore him altogether. Then life would be the way it used to be.

No, she thought, silently correcting herself. She could never feel that inner peace again. Travis had stirred things up so much that she could never go back to her quiet life.

As was her pattern during the past few days, Kali rose earlier than her normal hour, fixed herself breakfast, and went out to the barn to care for her horses. Travis had offered to help, but she refused curtly, wanting that time to herself. She was grateful he didn't offer again.

It was the third evening of their enforced confinement, and Kali was feeling restless. She sat in the easy chair, trying to watch the tape Travis had put in the VCR.

Why did he have to look so damn comfortable? she thought, resenting him for fitting into her home so easily. He lounged on the couch, his sock-covered feet propped on the edge of the coffee table, hands clasped behind his head as he watched the comedy film.

"Say, do you have any popcorn?" he asked suddenly, turning his face in her direction.

"No." Her gaze was as stony as Mount Rushmore.

Travis sighed. "And here my mouth was drooling for a big bowl of popcorn loaded with salt and real butter."

"Try Bixby's movie theater."

During her lifetime Kali had disliked few people. It wasn't in her nature. Even her father she had feared more than hated. It took Blayne's flagrant infidelities for her to begin to see the worst in people and despise herself for being so naïve all those years, but even then she still didn't hate him. Now she sat in the chair wishing she could hate Travis with his torso-fitting shirts, tight jeans, and rugged features that were neither handsome nor ugly. Even unshaven, he looked sexy as hell.

"Don't you ever shave?" she blurted out, making it sound more like an accusation than a question.

Travis's mustache twitched with amusement. "Is it Saturday?"

Her brow wrinkled. "No, but what does that have to do with it?"

"I shave on Saturdays."

"Along with your Saturday-night bath?" She knew she sounded bitchy, but she couldn't help it.

"Truth is, I hate to shave," he confessed.

"Then why don't you just grow a beard?"

"I hate beards just as much as I hate to shave." Travis leaned back and closed his eyes, dreaming of a giant tub of butter-drenched popcorn. "Food has a bad habit of sticking to it, and you have to keep it trimmed for it to look good. Too much trouble."

Kali sat there watching him, alternately wanting him to leave and hoping he would stay. She blamed her erratic emotions on unbalanced hormones. In the past three years she hadn't been around a man under the age of sixty. What could she expect when confronted with a healthy male in the prime of life? If she had any brains at all, she'd kick him out in the morning and try to resume her old way of life.

Kali kept that thought in mind when she woke up the next morning. She showered and dressed quickly, wanting to have her breakfast out of the way before Travis got up. This time she wasn't lucky. She entered the kitchen to find Travis standing over the griddle, turning oddly shaped circles that bore a faint resemblance to pancakes.

"Good morning," he said, greeting her with that endearingly crooked grin. "I thought I'd surprise you."

"I thought you couldn't cook." She eyed him warily.

"I can't, but I watched my dad and sister cook pancakes plenty of times. There's really nothing to it," he replied with faint surprise in his voice. He piled three golden, lopsided pancakes on a plate and set it on the table, gesturing for her to sit. He took six for himself and sat across from her. He pushed the bottle of warmed maple syrup her way. "Dig in."

Kali poured syrup over her pancakes before cutting into them. She smiled slightly as she ate the first piece; just as suddenly the smile froze.

A leathery crust covered a substance she had to admit tasted like the library paste she'd eaten once in kindergarten. Come to think of it, the paste had tasted much better.

"How is it?" Travis asked, looking so hopeful, she couldn't bear to hurt his feelings.

She managed a sickly grin as she swallowed the gooey lump. "Very good. It's difficult to believe you've never really cooked before."

Travis's face lit up, proud that he had been able to do something nice for his hostess. "I can't believe I did it right." He dug into his own breakfast with gusto. Within moments his face contorted. "This tastes like sh—." He stopped, wondering if it would be a proper description.

Kali's lips quivered. "Like library paste."

"You tried that culinary delight too?"

"When I was five."

"I was much more precocious. I was three when I tried it." Travis stood up and grabbed Kali's plate along with his own.

"Just what did you put in them?"

"Flour, sugar, salt." He tossed the pancakes into the trash.

"If you had explored the cabinets a bit more, you would have found a box of biscuit mix that can be used for making pancakes. And they have the recipe for them printed on the back. Let me give you a hint. One major ingredient in pancakes is eggs." She opened the pantry door and found the yellow box of buttermilk biscuit mix and quickly assembled the ingredients in a bowl.

Travis leaned against the counter, drinking his cup of coffee. Their truce was as fragile and delicate as a bone-china tea cup, but it was a beginning.

Kali had indeed relaxed a bit around Travis. It was hard not to when he was such an undemanding guest, though still an unwelcome one. But how could she stay angry with a man who made the absolute worst pancakes she had ever tasted?

After a breakfast of *real* pancakes Travis offered to help Kali in the barn, but she refused, still needing that precious time to herself. He smiled and shrugged his shoulders, saying he'd do the dishes while she was outside.

Ten minutes later, alone in the warm barn, Kali set to work cleaning the stalls and rubbing down each horse with extra care. The ground wasn't as spongy today; in two or three days, if the good weather held, Travis would be able to leave her hill. So why wasn't she eager to see him gone?

More than two hours later, Kali was pleasantly tired from her chores and ready for a hot shower to ease her aching muscles. She found Travis seated at the kitchen table, reading from a stack of papers, a cup of coffee near his left arm.

"The ground is almost dry enough—" she began, only to stop when she realized what he was reading. Suddenly she saw red. *"No!"* she cried, snatching the papers out of his hand and tearing them to pieces. "How can you do this to me?" she accused, her chest heaving.

Travis leaned back in his chair, looking very relaxed and unrepentant. "Why don't you take a few deep breaths to calm yourself down."

She drew in a deep breath. "I just wasn't expecting to see you reading my manuscript."

He leaned forward, looking at her with an intensity that was frightening. "Kali, you should be very proud of yourself. This is a beautiful piece of writing."

"Compliments about my writing are not going to persuade me to pose for you." Her eyes blazed.

He shrugged, looking remarkably relaxed, while she felt ready to explode. She wished she could sit down in a corner and cry. His fingertip brushed his mustache as he sat watching the many emotions crossing her face. She was hurting inside—he'd be a fool if he didn't see that—but his reason for coming here had to come out in the open. While he enjoyed her company—at least some of the time—he had to return to L.A. soon. No matter what, he still wanted her to pose for him.

Kali sank into a chair, looking down at her tightly clasped fingers in her lap.

"I wish I could make you understand. That story was more fact than fiction," she related in a low voice. If she didn't look up at him, she just might be able to tell him why she couldn't have it revealed to the public. "It took me almost a year to write it, and during that time I suffered more anxiety attacks than I thought possible for one person to endure. I cried buckets of tears, I suffered from horrible nausea every time I ate anything, and I went out into the woods and screamed until I was hoarse. Writing it was a living hell, but when I finished, I knew I had purged the poison from my system and I would be able to begin living a pretty normal life."

"A normal life without your daughter?"

Her breathing stopped for a split second. "I've employed so many private detectives . . . but Blayne, dear con man that he is, seems to keep one step ahead of them. I've heard that he's now working in Europe under a variety of aliases, but no one can ever catch up with him. He makes 'art' films." Her wry tone indicated what kind of art was depicted. "I want Cheryl back, and I'll sell my soul to accomplish it."

"What if you run out of money before they find her?" Travis asked gently.

Kali shook her head. "My needs are very minimal, and most of my money is in high-interest-bearing accounts. Besides, I'm sure I'll have her back by the end of the year." She didn't mention she'd felt that way the previous year.

"And if you don't?"

She blinked rapidly against the scalding tears. "Why do you have to be so damn pessimistic?" she demanded. "I sit here every day waiting for word, anything, the slightest hint about my daughter while I hope and I pray I'll have her back with me, and all you can insinuate is that it won't happen. I won't listen to this!"

Travis remained silent during Kali's outburst, letting her vent some of the anger and frustration she was feeling. When she'd finished, he finally spoke.

"You can argue about it all you want, but I'd still like to photograph you," he told her, leaning forward. "Just give me a chance to talk about it before you jump down my throat again."

Kali stiffened suspiciously but didn't say a word.

"You've turned into a very strong woman emotionally, and I'd like to show that," he went on, keeping his voice level and calm in the tension-filled room. Kali's face was so pale and wide-eyed, she resembled a frightened animal ready to bolt. He was determined to keep the atmosphere as calm as possible so she wouldn't be frightened away. At least her anger had finally disappeared.

She laughed, a sound as brittle as glass. "Me, a woman of strength? Give me a break, Travis. A guppy has more strength than I do."

His face creased in a slow smile. "Oh, honey, you're stronger than you realize. If you weren't, you wouldn't have survived the past few years. How many women would have put up with a bastard like Savage with all his affairs? Why you didn't just shoot him where it counts and have done with it is beyond me."

She swallowed the lump in her throat. "I was a naïve idiot," she admitted, refusing to look him in the eye. Why should he believe that someone who had lived in freewheeling Los Angeles could have been so blind? But she had been. She had been so caught up in her career and the mistaken idea that her marriage was storybook perfect, she hadn't bothered to read the signs that her husband was occupying beds all over town. "And after I did find out, I felt I had to protect Cheryl from the malicious gossip as much as I could—" Her voice broke. "Except I didn't do a very good job of it in the end." She was so caught up in her misery, she didn't notice Travis rising to his feet and crossing the room to sit on the arm of her chair. "All through my pregnancy I did everything the doctor told me so the baby wouldn't be harmed. I refused to have a nurse or nanny who didn't understand *I*

65

wanted to take care of her. I refused to be a part-time mother. I sent her to one of the finest preschools in the city. I wanted her to have everything I didn't have while growing up, but I wasn't going to spoil her in the process. She would have as normal a childhood as I could give her." By then the tears couldn't be contained. She wrapped her arms around her body, as if she'd suddenly grown very cold. Her blood felt frozen inside her veins, and her body began to shake from the pain she'd revealed. Her breathing grew shallow as she felt all control leave her body, and she hated herself for revealing her vulnerability.

Travis didn't hesitate in his silent offer of comfort. He wrapped one large, warm palm around the back of her neck and drew her up into his embrace. Kali had no chance to protest even if she wanted to, as he kept his arms around her in a hold that bore no passion, only the need to protect someone from further pain. Even as she cried out for him to let her go, he held her as he waited for her to calm down. It was several minutes before she was able to speak coherently.

"Damn you," she swore in a low voice, wiping her wet eyes with the back of her hand. "I was doing just fine until you showed up."

"Were you?" he retorted mildly. "All you managed to do was delude yourself into thinking everything would be peachy keen as long as you hid out here. It doesn't work that way, Kali. There are times you have to take a chance, and I think your number has just come up."

"I won't pose for you. I've told you that before," she mumbled, finding it nice to have a man's arms around her again. It had been a long time since she had been comforted by a man's touch, and strangely it felt right coming from him. But why did it have to be someone who looked as if he'd just escaped from a chain gang who could make her feel safe?

"A chain gang?" Travis chuckled. "That's a new one for me."

Kali was horrified that she had unwittingly spoken the last words out loud. "You're making me say and do things I don't normally do," she said with a moan, burying her face against the curve of his shoulder. The warm scent of his skin assaulted her nostrils, bringing to mind tumbled bed covers and a naked, hard-muscled body. It gave her ideas she had no business even thinking of.

Hormones, she decided, feeling horrified at the explicit pictures crowding her mind. It was just time for her hormones to go out of whack, and Travis happened to be there when it happened. She wondered if a good dose of cod liver oil would put things to rights. Her arms crept stealthily around his waist and hung on for dear life.

Travis didn't miss her arms slowly slipping around him. He wondered how long it had been since a man had held her, just held her without passion or need, to silently let her know she was safe from any harm.

"How about we make a deal?" he asked, his lips perilously close to her ear.

"What kind of deal?" she mumbled, deciding she liked the way his mustache tickled the top of her ear.

"How about allowing me to stick around here for a while?" He ignored the little voice inside, reminding him of all the work waiting for him in L.A. This was much more important. "No pressure about you posing. Just a chance for you to get to know me and find out I'm not so bad after all. If you say no, I'd understand, although I hope you'll give me a chance. And no one will ever learn your whereabouts from me. But I hope you say yes."

Kali ran her tongue over her lower lip. How was he able to make it sound so innocent when she was sure he had other things in mind than just talking. After all, she hadn't forgotten that one New Year's Eve.

"Dare I ask where you plan to stay, since there's no hotel in town?" she asked coolly, although she had a pretty good idea what his answer would be.

"What's wrong with the room upstairs?" he asked. "I didn't find any bedbugs, and the mattress is good and firm. I'm reasonably housebroken, as I've shown you. I know how to pick up after myself, and I can even help with domestic chores as long as you don't have me cooking." He was pleased to hear her laugh at that. He added for her peace of mind, "I don't go where I'm not invited, Kali."

She understood his meaning right away. He wanted her to know he wouldn't enter her bedroom unless asked.

"You mean it about no pressure regarding my posing? You'll leave it alone?"

Travis nodded. "I give my word. Besides, I haven't had a vacation in six years. Communing with nature just might be what I need."

Kali looked skeptical but found herself hard pressed to come up with a logical argument other than she just plain preferred to be alone. "I would think your idea of communing with nature would be checking out the local bars."

One corner of his mouth lifted. "That sounds like a

good idea too. I bet Saturday night is something else around here."

She stepped away before she softened too much. If she wasn't cautious, all her carefully erected walls would come tumbling down. "To be honest, I don't think it will work, but I always was a gambler. I'll be up front and tell you that if you mention 'Human Frailties' just once, you're out on your ear." She nodded her head toward the door to make her point. "I'll probably regret this in the end."

"I'll make sure there won't be any regrets." He held out his hand to seal the bargain.

Kali accepted it hesitantly, feeling the calluses on his palm graze her hand as she shook it. She didn't want to be aware of him as a man, so why was she allowing him to stay with her for the next week or so? She blamed the hormones again. She remembered once reading that a woman in her thirties was at her sexual peak, so there was good reason for her to feel the way she did, even as she reminded herself that she had cut out all soft feelings from her heart years ago.

Every muscle in Travis's body relaxed. He hadn't expected Kali to go along with his suggestion as amiably as she had. While he still wanted to photograph her, he wasn't about to abuse the privilege by discussing it again until she brought it up.

He looked down at her and said the first thing that came to mind. "You deserve a lot of nice things."

Kali's smile wobbled. "Such as a hot-fudge sundae with extra fudge and nuts and loaded with real whipped cream," she countered. "And cotton candy at the fair, and a day at the beach during the summer."

He shook his head. He knew she was trying hard to evade what he really meant, but he didn't intend for that to happen. She had retreated from the real world for too long a time. He wanted to see her back in the mainstream of life full-force, and he intended to be the man to lead her there.

"How do you feel about moonlight swims?" he suggested in that drawling, tender voice that sent dangerous shivers up and down Kali's spine.

Yes, she could visualize that scene. A quiet, rippling lake with the silvery moonbeams floating across the surface and two figures holding hands as they waded into the warm water. Two figures who were gloriously naked and obsessed only with each other. No, she mustn't think of such a thing. That kind of dream would only make her crazy. What was it about him that prompted such scenes in her mind? Had she been alone too long?

Kali walked away from Travis's presence, desperate to put distance between them. While he had held her, she'd become aware of him as a man and she didn't like that. She didn't want to notice that his jeans fit him like a second skin, or that his faded blue flannel shirt with the sleeves rolled above his forearms revealed a tattoo peeking out from under the cloth. She was curious as to what kind of tattoo he had but feared that if she asked to see it, he just might take off his shirt to show her and that might be a bit too much for her in her vulnerable condition. She was right that first day. This man was dangerous to her peace of mind, and she was taking an enormous chance by having him stay. She would have to watch herself very carefully because the longer she was around him, the more sensitive to his every word and movement she became. If only she hadn't chosen him that New Year's Eve, this never would have happened! She'd lost the war between the sexes once before and had just barely recovered. This time might not be so easy, because the man she would be battling had something Blayne never had had: the intimate knowledge of the pain in her soul.

Chapter
5

For the next few days Kali played the part of the perfect hostess, which was quite a change from her earlier hostility. Travis was relieved and suspicious all at the same time. The first day she'd aimed a shotgun at him; now she was cooking meals for two. She even took him out to the barn to introduce him to her two horses, a bay named Brandy and a dark chestnut called Cognac.

She smiled, even talked to him in the mornings, but still kept her guard firmly in place. Travis knew it was going to be difficult if she remained wary of him all the time he was there.

During those first few days Travis saw a side to Kali Hughes of which the public had no idea. Here, she wasn't one of the most popular models in the country. All she cared about was making sure the barn was clean, food was in the pantry, and the dirty laundry didn't pile up too high. He especially liked the way she wandered around the cabin muttering to herself.

It wasn't as if she floated around the cabin in sheer negligees guaranteed to drive a man crazy. Her jeans were well-worn and faded; her colored T-shirts, coupled with a flannel overshirt or pullover sweater weren't tight; but she still managed to impart a sensuality most women worked hard to achieve and never truly attained. He even liked the crazy-looking socks she wore.

"Where's the sugary, yet sexy, temptress fashion magazines knew?" he once asked during an hour of relaxation before bedtime.

Kali eyed him sardonically over her brandy glass. "She grew up. She finally realized the pot of gold at the end of the rainbow was pure gilt and wasn't worth the pain of pursuing."

Travis stared down into the amber liquid, the glass cradled between his palms. "He did quite a number on you, didn't he?"

There was no need to pretend she didn't know who he was talking about. Kali set her glass to one side and leaned back in the chair, her hands clasped behind her head. "In a way, I had two children because Blayne refused to grow up and accept responsibility for any part of our marriage. As a result, I had to learn to be the stronger one."

"Then why did he take your daughter?"

Kali's eyes narrowed. "My, you enjoy using the sharp edge of the knife, don't you?"

"It's the best way to find out anything I want to

know. Besides, your ambivalent feelings toward your ex at the end of your marriage were pretty well known."

"Ambivalent?" She chuckled. "That's a ten-dollar word if I've ever heard one. Say *hate*, that's more like it." She stared off into space, gathering up the jumble of words and emotions running through her mind. "Blayne hated to lose, he always did. His way of getting back at me was through Cheryl, and what better way to punish me than by taking her from me?"

"It's surprising your P.I.'s haven't picked up any clues about his whereabouts," Travis commented.

Her eyes clouded over, and she silently commanded herself not to cry. "Blayne has been a con artist since birth." She stood up, preferring to end the conversation before she revealed too much. What was it about this man that prompted her to want to talk so freely about the painful past when she hadn't uttered a word even to her closest friends? "It's still very difficult to talk about, so I believe I'll say good night now." She headed for her bedroom.

"Kali." Travis's quiet voice halted her escape. "Let me help."

She shook her head, instinctively knowing what he was talking about. She realized that giving in to him on this would mean giving him everything when she really had nothing to give to anyone. "If a team of highly rated investigators can't do anything, what makes you think you can?"

"High-priced investigators don't necessarily have the right friends in low places."

Tears stung her eyes at his sincere offer, and she wrapped her arms tightly around her body. Deep down she doubted he would have better luck than the men she had hired over the years, but she did appreciate his offer.

"Good night, Travis." She continued toward her bedroom and closed the door behind her.

Kali undressed slowly, willing herself not to cry. And here she had been doing so well too. It was having Travis around that was making her feel uneasy. She decided a trip into town the next day might be an excellent idea. It would also get them away from the confining walls of the cabin.

She heard the sounds of water running in the kitchen, the loud clicks of dead bolts thrown, then the creak of the steps leading to the loft.

Why had she allowed him to stay? If she wanted company, there were a few other friends she could have chosen from. If she was smart, she'd ask him to leave in the morning. No excuses, just that she wanted him gone. If he mentioned "Human Frailties" to her, she'd give him a flat and final no. She knew she couldn't live through that hell again, and her return to L.A. would just dredge up memories better left dead and buried. When all was quiet overhead, she finally drifted off to sleep with dreams that both disturbed and aroused her, although she remembered nothing in the morning.

When Kali awoke the next morning, she could smell brewed coffee. That was one good thing about her unorthodox houseguest—lately he had been getting up early and fixing a pot of coffee, and she appreciated his thoughtfulness. He was a perfect houseguest, always picked up after himself, helped with the dishes, and even chopped wood one afternoon.

Kali showered and brushed out her hair, letting it

dry on its own. She dressed in jeans, a cobalt crew-neck sweater, and purple socks with pink polka dots.

"Good mornin'." Travis greeted her with a slow, sleepy grin. With a sexy voice like his, she was surprised he hadn't tried to break into films. He certainly had the rough-and-ready look for them. He held up a steaming cup, an act of temptation along with the man holding it. "I just made it."

Tempting. What an apt word, because that was exactly what he did to her—tempt her into experiencing emotions she had long kept hidden.

She grasped the cup, making sure not to touch his fingertips, an action he didn't miss.

"Since the ground is probably dry enough, I thought I'd drive into town today and see if there's any mail. Would you care to ride along?" she asked, concentrating on drinking her coffee. "You can meet some of our more colorful citizens."

"Sounds fine to me."

"We'll leave in fifteen minutes, then," she said crisply, looking anywhere but directly at him.

"Don't you want any breakfast first?"

She shook her head, remembering the last time he had tried to fix breakfast. Her stomach couldn't handle that kind of abuse again. "I'm not hungry. I'll check the supplies and see what I need to pick up."

Travis stood up with the lithe grace of a mountain cat. "Sounds fine to me. It'll give me a chance to get a better look at your town."

"Don't expect too much," she advised good-naturedly.

A little over fifteen minutes later Kali ushered Travis into her jeep, drove it down the hill and along the highway like a Parisian taxi driver. One arm was braced on the open windowsill, the other hand loosely guiding the wheel. Only when she needed to change gears as she maneuvered the treacherous curving roads did she use both hands.

"You didn't tell me you once drove in the Indy 500," Travis shouted above the roar of the engine.

She flashed him a broad grin. "And I suppose you don't speed around and do wheelies or whatever motorcycle jocks do!"

"Maybe you should go to one of our rallies," he suggested slyly. "You'd certainly add some class to them."

"I think I can live without the privilege." Kali pulled up in front of the general store, which doubled as the meeting place for the town gossips.

Travis followed Kali into the dim interior, which smelled of freshly ground coffee beans, various spices, and the earthy smell of fish bait.

"Good thing you came in today, Kali. You're savin' me a trip out to your place, and you know how much I hate that damn hill of yours," a man's gravelly voice greeted her from behind the counter.

"Did you think I'd stay away from my favorite man for too long?" Kali teased, walking up to the storekeeper and kissing him soundly on the cheek. Travis saw the first natural smile appear on her face. He wished she would smile that way for him. "You're looking good, J. C. Are you remembering to take your pills like the doctor ordered?"

The older man grimaced.

"I've got a bum ticker," he explained to Travis, who stood behind Kali. "And this one thinks she's my mother and my wife all rolled up into one neat package. The first one passed on thirty-two years ago, and the second kicked the bucket eight years ago. It's been nice having some peace and quiet all these years—until this little twit pushed her way back into my life to turn it upside down." He held out a hand. "J. C. Thomas, owner and postmaster and whatever else sounds good at the moment."

"Travis Yates." He shook the older man's hand, not surprised to find his grip strong and sure.

J. C.'s eyes narrowed. It was apparent that his age hadn't diminished his faculties. He knew Kali hadn't had any visitors in all the time she lived at the cabin, and doubted Travis had been invited, what with her avid distrust of any member of the male sex.

"You visitin' Kali?" he asked.

Travis nodded. "We met a few years ago, and since I was in the neighborhood, I thought I'd stop in."

"You don't look fancy enough to be a model."

Kali turned her head to hide her grin.

"I'm a photographer," Travis explained.

"Oh, so you took pictures of her?" J. C. pulled out a box and several envelopes from a shelf behind him, placing them on the counter near Kali.

Travis shook his head. "My photographs are in specialty books." He watched Kali wander around the store picking up various foodstuffs and setting them on the counter. "Hard to believe she grew up so far back in the hills. When I first heard she was from Virginia, I expected to see a Colonial mansion and servants at her beck and call."

"She does make people see her in a different light without even being aware of it," J. C. replied. "When she first came back here, she found the cabin not fit for a dog to live in—'course, it never was much to begin with—but she didn't waste any time. She

79

called contractors to come in and fix it up and used my guest room as a home base until it was finished."

"Doesn't she have any family?"

J. C. spat into the nearby brass spittoon. "Her pa died, oh, six years ago; good riddance to trash. Let me tell you, he was one of the meanest ole coots around here. There's only two good things he did for this world—make the best white lightnin' in the state and produce Kali. But he wasn't the kind of man a woman could live with for long. Kali's ma ran off when Kali was just a baby, and he held it against the girl, more's the pity."

Travis frowned. This was a surprise to him. Kali had always kept her family background a secret, so he'd naturally assumed someone who had appeared to be all sweetness and light would have had a normal, happy childhood. Instead, she had followed her mother's example and run away from home before she was beaten down by an embittered old man. He waited for the garrulous J. C. to say more, but Kali, with ice glittering in her eyes, approached them.

"That's enough, J. C.," she said politely, but her voice carried a hidden warning.

"He 'pears safe to me," he argued.

"You talk too much," she accused mildly.

J. C. shrugged, not offended by what had to be the truth. He looked over at Travis. "Got a tongue like a viper, that one," he told the younger man.

Travis grinned. "I've been bitten more than once myself."

J. C. chortled, slapping his thigh, while Kali stared at both men as if she wished them a horrible death.

"No wonder I gave up men for Lent—and all the other days of the year." She turned away and marched out of the store, calling over her shoulder. "Put these on my tab. I left a list of what I picked up by the register."

"Nice to have met you, J. C." Travis extended his hand.

"You must be special, son, if she let you stick around for more'n five seconds." His smile disappeared. "She's had a rough time of it. The two men she shoulda been able to trust let her down, and it's left a bitter taste in her mouth and a lot of scars." He cocked his head to one side, listening to a jeep engine revving up outside. "You best be goin' 'fore she takes off without you."

"Yeah, she'd do it too." Travis's forefinger touched his forehead in a salute. "See ya around."

A stony-faced Kali sat in the jeep waiting for her passenger. The minute Travis swung his body into the seat, she took off with a squeal of tires on the paved surface. The drive back to the cabin was conducted in chilly silence. Travis merely settled back and smiled to himself. He liked the lady when she got her hackles up and displayed the temper she tried very hard to keep under wraps. It proved she had substance, after all. From the hints J. C. had dropped, he sensed she'd needed that iron backbone just survive.

Kali brought the jeep to a bone-jarring stop by the cabin's back door and jumped out. Travis beat her to the bag of supplies and mail and followed her stiff figure inside. He put away the groceries and watched her fix a pot of coffee.

"Why are you so afraid of someone finding out about the real you?" He folded the empty bag and placed it on the counter.

She spun around and braced her hands on her hips. "I'd rather just forget about my past, if it's all the same to you," she replied in a clipped voice. "It's easy enough for you to say I shouldn't hide what's gone on in my life. *You've* never gone through a divorce, Travis. And you've never had to sit in a courtroom filled with reporters staring at you like vultures waiting to sense the least bit of malice in your voice so they can print it for their avid readers. I heard stories about myself that should have been upsetting, but I couldn't allow that to happen. I had to keep up a false front to the public so no one knew how badly I was hurting inside. I couldn't put that weapon into anyone's hands—" She halted, surprised that she had spoken so frankly to a man who was still a stranger in many ways.

"Writing 'Human Frailties' let some of the poison out of your heart, but not all of it, Kali," Travis said quietly. "You've remained here erecting these damn walls to hide behind so no one can help. Trouble is, the day may come when you want help and you'll be too far gone to ask."

She shook her head rapidly to discourage his words. "That's why I came here; to get away from meddlers like you."

Travis's fingers itched to take her into his arms and soothe the raw pain he sensed she felt but he knew any overture on his part would be icily rejected. Frankly he was surprised she hadn't ordered him out of the house after what he'd said. What had stopped her?

The same question echoed in Kali's brain. Why didn't she just ask him to leave so she could get on with her life? But then, what kind of life did she really have before he'd showed up? She lived alone because she was afraid to let anyone close after all she had gone through.

Travis leaned past her to retrieve two mugs and fill them with coffee.

"Come on, let's see what your Care package brought you," he suggested, walking into the living room. "If there're any good videotapes in that box, we can watch movies and eat popcorn all night."

The package from Malcolm had five videotapes enclosed and a letter addressed to Travis in Jenny's unmistakable script, along with a letter to Kali.

Travis scanned the letter that outlined what had gone on in the office in his absence, and her sweetly worded assumption that he was either still with Kali or Kali had shot him on sight and buried his body in the woods. If the latter was true, could Jenny please have his James Dean poster collection? Travis laughed out loud, reading the last lines to Kali.

"I'll keep that in mind in case I do decide to shoot you." Kali chose a cassette at random and inserted it in the VCR. Then she stood up and headed for the kitchen.

Several minutes later Kali returned carrying a large tray filled with potato chips, popcorn, a jar of chunky peanut butter, and several cans of diet Coke. She set her booty on the coffee table and curled up on the other end of the couch.

"What's the peanut butter for?" Travis asked curiously.

"For the potato chips." She demonstrated by using the knife to spread a thin coating of the peanut butter over the rippled surface. Two bites and the chip was gone. "Better than onion dip. Try it, you might like it," she invited with an impish grin, her earlier hostility now gone.

Travis was very tempted to try something else he was pretty sure he'd like, but he decided rejection wasn't for him. Instead, he tried the potato chip/peanut butter combination and announced it wasn't so bad.

They spent all afternoon and much of the evening watching three of the videotapes. After their film festival Travis talked about his days on the road, telling her about the time six of his riding buddies had held an impromptu beer party and belching contest. And the time a group tried playing polo using their bikes instead of horses with a crushed beer can as the ball. Not to mention the several rough-looking men comforting a little lost girl at a carnival with cotton candy and hot dogs until her parents could be found.

The more Kali heard, the more she saw a man any woman could respect and like, she admitted grudgingly.

Kali sat on the couch Indian-style, her back braced against the cushioned side, her palm cupping her chin as she listened to his tales. In return she talked about her work more freely than she had in a long time.

Travis recognized that his low-key manner helped weaken her self-resurrected walls faster than any arguments could. He watched her stiff posture loosen, her eyes lose their frosty glaze, and she smiled at him.

Lord, she has a beautiful smile, he thought, enjoying watching her in her old jeans and sweater, not to mention her ridiculous socks. *If I'm not careful, I*

*could fall in love with her—and that would turn out
to be the ultimate torture.*

Funny how a hardened bachelor like him could
find that idea a little sad. The more he listened to her,
watched the way her hands moved as she talked and
saw the many emotions that crossed her face, the
more determined he became to see her before his
camera.

Kali wasn't sure when her body began to shut
down. One minute she was listening to Travis talk
about his photography, the next she opened her eyes
to find the TV off and the lights dimmed. She was
snuggled warmly in Travis's arms with a quilt thrown
over them.

"I'm sorry," she apologized, trying to sit up, but his
hand on her shoulder pulled her back against him.

"Don't worry, my ego isn't so fragile that I ever
thought I was boring you," he said teasingly.

This time Kali did sit up. In keeping her balance,
her hand rested intimately on his muscular thigh.
Both froze, staring into each other's eyes. For long
moments all that could be heard was the sound of
uneven breathing. Kali's cinnamon-brown eyes
never blinked, even as Travis stared back at her with
an almost frightening intensity. The fire in his eyes
was hot enough to erupt a volcano, and potent
enough to snare her gaze and keep it captured for
endless time. Kali felt the flames lick along her body,
sending heated messages to every nerve ending.
With a surge of primitive feeling she wanted to feel
his lips on hers. At that moment she knew she
wanted him. She certainly knew he wanted her, and
reveled in the knowledge. The tip of her tongue

moistened her lower lip with unintentional sensuality.

"Go to bed, Kali," Travis ordered roughly, forbidding himself to touch her when all he wanted to do was haul her into his arms and carry her up to his bed. "Go to your room, shut the door, and if there's a lock on it, use it—because I don't feel very noble tonight."

She managed a wobbly smile. "I know exactly what you mean." She stood up and walked out of the room without a backward glance.

Travis remained on the couch listening to her door closing and the click of the lock turning. He cursed himself for not taking advantage of the moment even though he knew the timing was all wrong. He went up to the loft to spend a the night wondering why he was such a fool for sticking around when Kali was determined to be a recluse.

No, it was no longer just the hope of buying her story or taking her photo that kept him there. He wanted to stay long enough to see her smile and laugh the way he knew she could. And he wanted to be the cause of it.

Travis uttered a curse. He should have known better than to be attracted to a woman who was even more stubborn than he was.

Kali woke up feeling as if a dark cloud had descended upon her. One look at her calendar confirmed the reason for her misery. She showered and dressed before wandering out to the kitchen. Travis was already there, tucking into a plate of black bacon and scorched eggs.

"I'd offer you some, but I wouldn't want you to accuse me of trying to poison you," he said, not missing the lines of strain around her eyes. Evidently she hadn't passed a good night, either.

"I'm not hungry," she muttered, picking up the coffeepot.

Travis arched an eyebrow in surprise. Kali always ate a large breakfast, claiming it was what kept her going through the day. But today something was troubling her a great deal.

"You feeling all right?" he asked, concerned for her.

"Fine." Kali managed to smile, but it didn't reach her eyes. Instead of sitting down at the table, she leaned against the counter while sipping her coffee.

"I'd better muck out the stalls first thing," she murmured, finishing her coffee and rinsing out her mug.

"I'll help." Travis stood up. Her unease bothered him, and something made him feel she shouldn't be left alone.

Kali didn't reply as she hurried outside.

All day Travis watched her work in the barn as if she were meeting some sort of deadline. The stalls were cleaned out in record time. Travis watched her exercise each horse, cool them off, then brush and curry them until their coats shone. She fixed veal parmigiana for dinner but ate no more than three bites. Travis offered to do the dishes, figuring she was so jumpy that she'd probably break them.

"You're treating me like a child," she said crossly.

"If I am, it's because you're acting like one," he informed her as he gently pushed her in the direction of the living room. "Go sit down and twiddle your thumbs or take up knitting."

Kali went into the living room and sat down only because she couldn't think of a sufficient argument.

But she couldn't sit still for more than a minute. She wandered around the room, picking up a vase and putting it down, turning on the radio and turning it off.

Travis finished the dishes in no time, determined to find out what was bothering Kali. Once everything was put away, he walked in to discover her sitting on the edge of a chair and staring off into space.

"What is wrong with you?" he demanded. "You're as nervous as a whore in church."

Kali gave a short laugh. "How my father would have liked you." Travis wasn't sure it was a compliment. "He enjoyed those old sayings."

"Something's eating you up inside, Kali. Is today the anniversary of your divorce?"

Her laugh was bitter. "On the contrary, that's the day I dance with joy and thank God I was sane enough to get out when I did. Tell you what, why don't you draft your ideas for your new book for me? Show me what you want to do, and then we'll talk," she crooned, as if promising something special to a child.

"You're only changing the subject so I won't probe any more."

"Is it working?"

"No. Afraid I'll find out the truth?"

Yes! she wanted to scream. She bent her head, her loose hair draping the thin contours of her face. "I promise I will give your ideas serious consideration," she murmured. "After all, you did come all the way out here to see me about modeling for you. The least I can do is listen to your ideas."

"Are you sure you're telling me the truth, or are you just humoring me?" he said challengingly.

Her head snapped up, her eyes flashing fire. "I may be weakening on part A, but don't push for Part B unless you want to lose it all," she warned in a hard voice. She walked out with her head held high and without saying another word.

Travis remained sprawled on the couch in the living room, watching the flames die down in the fireplace. He couldn't understand the reason for the abrupt change in Kali's personality. None of it made any sense. He couldn't imagine he'd said anything that might have triggered such an emotional turnaround. Would he ever be able to figure her out?

As the room grew cooler he thought over the past few days he'd spent with her. She was feistier now than he remembered her to be, more willing to stand up to people and speak her mind. Of course, there was one thing about her that hadn't changed—she was just as beautiful as ever. He closed his eyes to think of her, but that only gave him ideas about her he knew he shouldn't be thinking. Oh, how he wanted to see her flushed with passion, those wicked eyes slumberous from his lovemaking.

Deciding the direction of his thoughts was leading him into dangerous territory, he pushed himself off the soft cushions and ambled over to the fireplace to bank the coals before heading to his lonely loft and equally lonely bed. If he had any brains at all, he'd pack up tomorrow, head for home, and throw himself into his work. If nothing else, the battles between him and Deke would keep his mind off the bewitching brunette in the next room.

He cursed under his breath as he pulled off his

boots and socks and began peeling off his jeans. Nope, nothing was ever going to make him forget her. And bedding her would only turn the illness from critical to terminal.

Chapter
6

That night Travis lay in bed trying to figure out what had caused Kali's abrupt mood change that day. He remembered the lines of strain around her eyes, the look of desperation on her face as she moved around the house. Something was very wrong, but he couldn't figure out what. He finally dozed off but was unable to sleep more than short periods of time for worrying about her.

It was a few hours after midnight when he awoke to sounds filtering from the living room. Wondering if something was wrong, he climbed out of bed and looked over the railing to find Kali seated on the rug before the fireplace, photo albums scattered around her. She appeared to be crying. He quickly pulled on a pair of jeans and quickly descended the narrow stairs. She didn't even look up when he approached.

Kali sat cross-legged on the rug, a floppy-eared teddy bear clasped in her lap as she stared at the photos before her. She was so lost in her thoughts, she didn't even acknowledge Travis when he squatted down beside her. Even though the room was cold, she wore only a thin nightgown and showed no signs of chill.

"Kali?" He spoke softly, reaching out to touch her shoulder.

She didn't look up. "She was such a beautiful baby, wasn't she?" she murmured, holding up a color photo of a newborn child. "She wasn't red and wrinkled like most babies when they're born. And she always smiled, especially for me."

Travis plucked the photo from her fingers and gazed at the tiny baby. Turning the photo over, he cursed softly as he read the date, written in a neat, feminine hand. Four years ago to the day. No wonder Kali had been so distraught. It was her daughter's birthday and there was no little girl around to spoil shamelessly, no one to throw a birthday party for, no little friends playing in the yard, no happy shouts of excitement—only dreams of what might have been.

"This is Boo Bear." Kali held up the lop-eared bear. "Cheryl never went anywhere without him. How she must miss him." She wiped her tears away with the back of her hand. "I wish I knew where she was so I could send him to her." Not missing a beat, she turned the pages, pointing out pictures that had special meaning to her. "She was beginning to walk here. We'd tease her because she seemed to waddle like a duck. She refused to hold on to anything . . .

this was her first birthday party here. Poor thing, one of the older boys, our agent's five-year-old son, decided to throw his piece of cake at her, then pushed her face in the ice cream. It seemed to take forever to clean her up. . . . Cheryl's first time on a pony, she wasn't frightened at all. She was always so independent. Blayne said she got that from me, although he was certainly never one to back down from a battle." Kali sniffled. "I miss my baby, Travis. God, how I miss her. Why am I being punished? I was never a bad girl. I always did what I was told. Why should my baby be taken away from me? Why can't she be found? I want her back with me so badly."

He pulled her into his arms and held her tightly. "You aren't being punished for anything, Kali. Your ex-husband wanted you to suffer, and he found the perfect way to do it. You'll get her back, I promise you."

Kali sighed, burrowing her face against the cool skin of his bare chest. "Oh, sure, the detective agency says that every time I mail them a check, but I haven't seen any results," she said, scoffing. Warm tears slid down her cheeks and landed on his chest.

Feeling the chill of her skin and fearing she'd get sick, Travis stood up and gently pulled her up with him, steering her toward her room. "Like I said before, you're using the wrong people. But you can't afford to worry about it tonight. You get your rest and we'll see what we can do."

The rigors of the day had already caught up with her, and her eyelids drooped as Travis put her to bed and piled the covers around her. "Last year I tried to get drunk, and I couldn't even do that right." Kali's words were slurred from exhaustion. "Hangovers are very disgusting."

Travis grinned. "No kidding. Get some sleep, and everything will look brighter in the morning." He only wished he could offer her more comfort than that.

Kali reached out and grasped his hand tightly. Her face was pinched from the tension still holding her emotions hostage.

"One more thing." She turned her face away, as if unable to look at him. "I'm sure you know about the story Blayne told about my having the abortion to spite him." Her hand tightened as she worked hard to relate a tale that still carried a great deal of pain in her heart. She swallowed the lump in her throat. "Cheryl came down with a case of German measles, and I later had a bad case of them. Shortly afterward, I was told I was ten weeks' pregnant."

Travis swore softly under his breath. He felt her pain flow through her hand into his body.

"There was no question of my not having the baby," she whispered, still staring off into space. Her free hand hovered over her abdomen, which once had protected a tiny life. "The doctor was adamant and Blayne was relieved. One child was more than enough for him, and I was feeling so bad, I doubted I could have made any other decision."

Travis silently cursed the terrible misfortune that had befallen this woman. Without stopping to think, he sat on the bed and gathered her into his arms.

Kali didn't hesitate. She accepted Travis's comfort and relaxed against his hard frame. For the rest of the night they huddled together as if they were all that was left to ward off the evil in the world. Even after

Kali finally fell asleep, Travis remained awake. Now he knew he could never let her go. It was just a question of convincing her of that.

When Kali woke up late the next morning, she felt a jumble of emotions; embarrassment over spilling her woes to Travis; and relief that he wasn't still lying in bed with her. She wasn't used to betraying her feelings to anyone, and she didn't feel she could face him just yet.

She lay under the warm covers and realized this was the first time she'd woken up the day after Cheryl's birthday not feeling as if her world had ended. By talking about the pain of three years ago, she felt freer and more relaxed than she had in a long time.

A hot shower helped clear away the balance of the cobwebs in her brain, and she dressed in record time. She walked out to the kitchen feeling a bit shy at meeting Travis.

"Mornin'." He greeted her in a casual voice, as if nothing had happened, which Kali appreciated. He smiled at her as he filled a mug with coffee. "Looks like it's going to be a beautiful day," he commented. "What would you say to a hike?"

Kali would have preferred staying around the cabin but knew she would only start moping again. "I guess the exercise wouldn't hurt after so many days of inactivity." She didn't sound convinced.

Travis recalled the feel of a soft, yielding body in his arms and thought of another kind of exercise that was very beneficial but knew better than to suggest it. He hastily pushed the idea aside and handed Kali a plate of warm toast topped with butter.

"At least I didn't burn it," he said with a grin. "Just

don't look in the trash or you'll see what happened with the other thousand attempts."

Kali wanted to protest that she had no appetite, but thought better of it. Instead, she ate all four slices, then shyly suggested that she would fix a picnic lunch for them to take along on their walk. Travis hid his triumphant smile and went to put on his hiking boots. Within twenty minutes they were walking outside in the early spring sunshine.

"Oh, I almost forgot. I still have to feed the horses." Kali sighed, heading toward the barn.

Travis grabbed her arm and pulled her back. "It's already done."

She stumbled, and only his restraining arm kept her from falling. She looked up, seeing the expression she remembered seeing the night before—the very male expression that stated he wanted her. She slowly pulled her arm away and stepped back a few paces.

"Thank you for taking care of them for me," she murmured, afraid to look up at him again.

"You can't run away forever, Kali." His low voice reached her ears, but she refused to acknowledge it. He wanted to bring back the memories she had successfully kept hidden for years, and she wasn't going to allow him to revive them now.

Their hike was a disaster. Kali couldn't seem to relax enough to enjoy their walk into the hills, and Travis continued to watch her with knowing eyes that made her even more uncomfortable. During their stop for lunch Kali sat against a tree trunk and only nibbled at her food. All she could think about was the way she'd confessed her sorrows the night before and practically invited Travis into her bed. What was wrong with her?

"Is something the matter?" she asked waspishly when she noticed him staring at her.

He shook his head. "Just watching the way the sun shines on your hair. It's beautiful, like gold."

Kali sniffed but said nothing. She may not have known what was wrong with her, but Travis did. He wasn't vain about his charm, but he knew there was some kind of attraction between them; there had been since that New Year's Eve. And Kali wasn't sure how to handle it. She had bottled up her feelings for so long, she didn't know what to do with them. He chose not to say anything at the time, preferring to give her space enough to come to terms with her feelings.

Finally unable to take any more of the tension festering between them, Kali suggested after lunch that they return to the cabin. Her unspoken suggestion that Travis return to his own home hovered in the air around them.

Muttering an excuse about checking on the horses, Kali disappeared into the barn. Deciding not to give her time after all, Travis followed her.

"What is this? Are you bucking for the job as my keeper?" she demanded, spinning around to face him when she realized he had entered the barn after her. Why did he have to look as if he understood the pain she was still going through?

"You've got to stop running away and face your past, Kali."

"I don't recall hearing that you've recently obtained a degree in psychology, so I believe I'll pass up the advice." Her mutinous gaze speared him with no lasting effect. "Just go back to California, Travis, and leave me alone. It was a mistake to have you stay when I don't even like you or the so-called books you put out." Not ashamed of her rude outburst, she continued to glare at him, watching his anger build in terrifying degrees. Then something began to change. Feeling something else more elemental begin to pass between them, she hurriedly turned away before she got caught up in something she couldn't handle.

But Travis wasn't about to let her walk away from him again. He grabbed her arm and spun her back around, pinning her against a stall door.

"All of this has nothing to do with what's going on now," he said in a rumbling voice. "It's still because of what happened that New Year's Eve, but you refuse to admit it. That's also the reason you don't want me here, so go ahead and admit that right along with everything else."

Her face froze. If her arms hadn't been pinned to her sides, she probably would have hit him, because the last thing she wanted to remember was that particular night. She managed to free her arms and push Travis away. Before she could take more than three steps, he had caught hold of her braid and was wrapping it around his hand, slowly pulling her toward him. With each step his head lowered until his lips hovered just above hers in a light touch. Kali's eyes opened wide, and his own dark ones stared down into hers just as he took her into his arms and brought her flush against his body.

"Let's make sure it wasn't due to too much champagne and holiday spirit the last time," he muttered roughly as his mouth covered hers. His tongue thrust roughly between her parted lips in an intimate motion that should have been meant for longtime lovers. There was no doubt that their other kiss had not been a fluke. Travis felt the heat steal up from his booted feet, through his thighs, and into the part of him that ached so badly for her. She felt so good against him that he never wanted to let her go. His hands roamed up and down her back, from the base of her spine to the soft area of her nape. He was unable to stop touching her.

Kali found herself falling under the same bewitching spell as before. She caressed his face, neck, and broad shoulders, which were covered by flannel under the heavy jacket. She was eager to touch all of him, the angle of his hips, the hard curve of his buttocks, the rock-hard muscles in his tensed thighs. Her hands, her entire body, ached for the feel of him. There was no blaming her hormones this time; now it was a pure and simple case of wanting a man so badly, she was blind to everything else. She opened her mouth wider, hungry for the taste of him, her tongue darting into his mouth to mimic the same motions. One arm curled around his neck while the other hand crept along his chest and downward, to press boldly against the surging heat of his arousal. Her senses were starved for him. She wanted to press closer to the warmth of his skin, burning through the heavy layers of clothing; she ached at the feel of his hands roaming over her, and the hard, lean body that pressed against hers, not to mention the bulging masculinity nestled in the soft cradle of her thighs. She wanted it all. One of his knees gently nudged her legs apart and moved even more rhythmically against her. The warm, musky scent of his body wove another spell around her.

"Travis!" She gasped, pulling her mouth away from the tempting lips that turned her to fire.

"You know how much I want you, Kali," he breathed in a rough voice that betrayed his arousal. He drew air into tortured lungs, feeling an almost uncontrollable urge to make love to her there and then.

She wanted him just as much but was afraid to accept even the slightest idea of a commitment. She shook her head and whispered, "I can't."

"Because we hardly know each other, or because of the past?"

She raised her hands and pushed him away. "Because of me," she said tautly.

Travis couldn't miss the tears in Kali's eyes, and knew they weren't caused by what had just happened. It wasn't that she was ashamed of her unbridled behavior, it was because of the pain she had known in the past. He could feel it just as surely as if she had told him so.

"I'm not Blayne, Kali. I'm not the kind of man to promise you one thing, then strip you of all you know and love," he said harshly, instinctively knowing that any sign of pity would raise the barriers between them.

She smiled wanly. "I realized that within five minutes of talking to you." She stepped away to escape the spell his nearness had wrought. She had to think clearly to explain her fears. "You have to remember that I've been living alone for a long time and that I've chosen not to have a man in my life. Oh, not because of what Blayne did to me, but because of what I felt I did to myself by allowing him to hurt me so badly during the years we were together. Not that he ever hurt me physically; he had other ways that hurt just as much, if not more, and he left very deep scars. I made a lot of mistakes I can only blame on youth. I ran away from a set of problems instead of trying to work them out, not realizing I was only running into another set of problems that were just as bad.

"By the time the smoke cleared from the divorce and Cheryl's kidnapping, I was in pretty bad emotional shape. So I did what I knew best; I ran away. I came back to the home where I had grown up, and the people who knew the person I used to be. It took a lot of months of self-imposed solitude and a great deal of soul-searching before I felt that I was growing into the person I should have been in the beginning. Maybe if I had known then what I know now, I wouldn't have allowed myself to get in such a complicated mess. The biggest mistake I made was in not protecting myself. The media, with Blayne's help, found all my weak spots, and I could only hide away, licking my wounds instead of fighting back. It taught me never to allow myself to be victimized again."

Her voice suddenly hardened. "The fashion model Kali Hughes isn't the Kali Hughes standing before you, or even the Kali Hughes I hope to be in time. Even the name isn't real; I was christened Calliope Sue Howard a little over thirty-four years ago." She smiled bitterly. "I was a sham out there, Travis, just a figment of my agent's imagination, but I went along with it because I thought that was what I wanted. Then the time came when I couldn't live with that particular Kali Hughes, and it's taken me this long to find the real me. And I've just begun to like what I've learned about myself. I don't intend to lose my self-respect again."

His slow smile was almost her undoing. It was amazing how just a slight twist of facial muscles could turn her knees to jelly. He grasped the back of her neck with his hand and pulled her into the comforting pillow of his chest.

"Oh, Kali, I never looked at the woman in the magazines or the eternal smiler at parties," he explained quietly, moving his lips over the soft cloud of hair. "I looked at the woman behind the glossy pages, and I liked what I saw. The woman I saw that night is the one I wanted."

She was stunned by his revelation that he had wanted her then. "But I was married. I had a child."

"For the first time it didn't matter to me that a woman was married, and believe me, I have my standards. I never have had the slightest leaning toward a married woman until I met you." He smiled faintly. "You, Kali Hughes, were different."

"I never knew," she whispered, at a loss for words.

A shadow crossed over his face. "You weren't supposed to," he muttered, suddenly turning away from her. "Well, now I've poured my guts out to you, so you can have your laugh or put on ladylike airs, 'cause you wouldn't want to be caught with a man like me. A man with a few things in his past that he'd rather forget, and a bunch of friends who have police records as long as your pretty arm. Why did I bother coming to ask you to pose for me when you'd be better off not having me around?"

Kali was startled at his sudden vulnerability. He had always seemed so sure of himself, so determined to get what he wanted. Could it be that he felt a bit uncertain around her and now regretted admitting how he felt?

"Travis," she said softly, laying her hand on his arm, "you're right, I have been hiding my head in the sand. I admit I'm still not sure I want to pose for your book, but I'd be willing to do anything else to help you work on it."

"Posing would help me," he said, countering.

She shook her head. "The hurt is still here. I honestly would prefer staying out of the limelight."

"That's running away again," he said, arguing.

Kali smiled sadly. "No, it's playing it smart. Right now I don't feel confident enough to return to L.A. and the fast lane." Her voice was so soft, he barely heard the words, but he did hear the pain beneath and he understood. Deep down he felt Kali wouldn't be free of the past until she returned to L.A. and confronted her fears. And he hated the thought of her sitting out her days in this lonely cabin when she should be living a much fuller life among other people.

"You can't keep your hideaway a secret forever," he warned, knowing she would expect at least a token argument.

Kali shrugged. "Maybe, maybe not." She walked over to one of the horses and picked up a currycomb. "But I can't worry about it now."

Travis followed her and plucked the comb out of her hand. Keeping hold of her fingers, he led her out of the barn. "Come on, I'm starving—and I'm sure you are, too, since you barely ate anything during lunch."

Kali had to admit she was feeling a bit hungry, and suggested roast beef sandwiches and clam chowder, then couldn't help laughing when Travis agreed it was a good start.

The atmosphere was more relaxed during dinner than it had been at lunch. They washed their food down with beer and tried to top each other with bawdy limericks and stories.

"Where did you learn all those?" Travis found himself laughing so hard, his eyes were tearing.

"J. C. has books of them," she confided before telling another. "Of course, he doesn't realize I know where he hides them." She flashed a gleeful grin.

The more beer they drank, the more uproarious they grew. It was as if the emotional scene in the barn dissipated the tension between them. Before long, both of them were laughing hysterically, until Kali held her hands up in surrender.

"I give up," she said, choking, then wiping the tears from her eyes while the other hand was pressed to her aching side. She glanced up at the wall clock, surprised to find that it was after three o'clock in the morning. She couldn't remember an evening when the time had passed so quickly, and she knew the company had something to do with it. In fact, it had everything to do with it. "I didn't realize it was so late." She stood up.

Travis did the same, then locked the back door while Kali checked the front one.

"When I grew up here, I couldn't remember a time when those doors were locked unless my dad wanted to keep the sheriff out," she said sadly. "But with so many teenagers roaming around with nothing useful to do, it's become the norm."

"And you thought that when you came back here,

things would be the same as when you were a kid, but it didn't happen," Travis commented.

She smiled. "Sure, why not? You could trust people then." She turned to head for her bedroom.

Travis grasped her arm and gently turned her back around. One hand cupped her chin, tilting it upward. "You can trust me, Calliope Sue Howard," he said in a voice rough with desire, and something else more heart-stirring. He lowered his head, brushing her lips lightly. Keeping his eyes on hers, he slowly released her chin and stepped back. "Sleep well, Kali. I'll see you in the morning." He walked toward the steps leading to the loft.

Kali remained frozen to her spot, her fingertips touching her lips. For a moment she though he was going to invite himself into her bed, but she should have known better. Travis wouldn't need to use any coercion. If a woman wanted him, she'd go after him without a moment's hesitation. Kali easily could have become one of those women, but memories of past hurts intruded, and she knew she would have to be free before she could go to him.

Upstairs, Travis listened to the soft sounds of the bedroom door closing, and later bedsprings creaking under a slight weight. He had hoped . . . God, how he had hoped. But this wasn't the time. He knew it wouldn't have taken much to have to persuade her she needed him that night, but he didn't want to persuade her, he wanted her to want him. And when that time came, they were in for a night of loving they both richly deserved.

Chapter
7

Kali woke up the next morning with conflicting feelings after what had happened the night before.

Let him be gone! her brain pleaded.

Give me a break. Do you really want him to be gone? her heart countered scornfully.

Truthfully she should want him gone. During this time he had wheedled his way into her emotions and forced her to reevaluate the reclusive way she had been living. How many times had J. C. suggested she invite a friend out for a visit so she wouldn't be alone all the time, or that she indulge in some traveling? Perhaps she should have listened to him instead of wallowing in her misery for so long. The truth struck her like a hard blow.

Was that what she had been doing for the past three years? Had she been crucifying herself for having a failed marriage and losing her daughter instead of reconstructing her life the way she had been telling herself to do? Had she been lying to herself all this time? The answer was an unqualified yes.

It took her longer than usual to shower and dress. She walked into the kitchen and found only silence.

He was gone, after all. Her shoulders slumped and her steps slowed. Well, her wish had come true, so why wasn't she relieved?

"He could have at least said good-bye," she muttered.

Kali might have thrown herself into a blue funk if she hadn't found the note on the table, anchored by the salt shaker.

Had to make a quick trip into town.
Be back by lunchtime.

Travis

She was grateful he wasn't there to hear her sigh of relief. She noticed the coffeepot sitting smugly on the counter, and was thankful he had left her her much-needed caffeine. Not feeling very hungry, she settled for an apple with her coffee and proceeded to strip the sheets from her bed and throw them into the washer. With Travis gone, she decided it was a perfect time to clean the loft.

Funny, Kali hadn't felt lonely before. In fact, she had welcomed the solitude after years of living in a virtual fish bowl. But Travis—with his slow, sexy

smile; easy drawl; and uncomplicated company—
had changed all that. Now she woke up in the morning looking forward to more than a lonely ride
through the countryside or driving into town where
she sometimes sought out the sound of another human voice. It took Travis to prove to her that not
everyone from L.A. was a shark.

She chuckled to herself. Well, she suspected Travis
could be the biggest and meanest shark in the ocean
when necessary, but he hadn't acted that way around
her. She would miss him when he left. She was so lost
in her thoughts, she didn't hear the roar of the motorcycle outside. It took the sound of the back door
opening and closing to rouse her.

Kali's eyes swept over Travis as he entered the
house. "Have a nice trip?"

"Yeah. I wanted to make a couple of phone calls,
but the phone at the gas station was out of order, so
J. C. let me use his. Didn't you see my note?"

She stiffened. What had the garrulous old man told
him? Wasn't she meant to have any secrets?

Travis watched Kali's face change as he draped his
black leather jacket over the back of a chair. So she
figured J. C. had been saying things he shouldn't, did
she? Okay, maybe he had, a little. After all, a taste of
moonshine in a cup of ink-black coffee at eight
o'clock in the morning would loosen anyone's
tongue. He wasn't about to tell Kali that, though.
He'd prefer to hear it all from her, if she ever trusted
him enough to really talk to him the way she had the
night of Cheryl's birthday.

"It's a real pretty day outside. What say we go for a
ride and you show me some of the countryside?" he
suggested.

Kali didn't respond as readily as he'd hoped. "The ground's still kind of spongy."

"A little mud never hurt anyone. I'll even help fix a picnic lunch."

Maybe his idea wasn't so bad, after all, but Kali groaned at the idea of Travis working with any kind of food. "I'll fix the lunch. That way we won't have to worry about ptomaine poisoning."

"I'll go change." Travis headed for the loft to change into a different pair of jeans and boots. When he entered the small bedroom, he couldn't miss the signs of cleaning and fresh sheets on the bed. Hmm, maybe he was getting to her, after all!

Within twenty minutes the horses were saddled, and Travis took charge of the saddlebags holding their lunch.

"What's in this thing, a seven-course meal?" he said teasingly, hefting the canvas bags in one hand.

"With the way you eat, I'd need to pack *two* seven-course meals just so I'd get some too," she retorted.

Travis dropped an arm around her shoulders and pulled her to him, placing a light kiss on the tip of her nose. "If that's a hint that I eat too much, I would just like to remind you that I'm still a growing boy," he said gravely, a twinkle in his eyes.

"And here I thought it was my cooking that prompted all those second and third helpings," she responded with a playful pout.

Travis enjoyed Kali's lighthearted banter. He liked seeing her smile and hearing her laugh, and he especially enjoyed being the one to cause it. He assisted her in mounting up, unable to keep his eyes from the enticing sight of her shapely bottom as she swung herself into the saddle.

For a split second he pictured her bare skin, pink and flushed from her bath or, more importantly, from his lovemaking. He forced his attention away from the erotic view and headed for his horse, hurriedly mounting and silently cursing the suddenly tight fit of his jeans.

Following Kali, Travis thought about his morning errands. He wanted to tell her about his phone calls, but he didn't want to get her hopes up. He remembered J. C. listening unashamedly to the four calls he made and the way the older man smiled broadly when he hung up.

"Son, I have an idea that if anybody can pull it off, you can," he told him in his deep voice.

"Even after all the time and effort already put in by those other P.I.'s?" Travis said lightly, tucking his telephone credit card back in his wallet.

J. C. slipped his glasses off, wiped them with his handkerchief, and replaced them on his nose. "You achieve your goals because you don't believe in playing by the book. I'd say you're the kind of man to look over a situation with a careful eye and then plow in and accomplish it your own way, come hell or high water."

Travis's eyes had darkened. "How could a man who had supposedly loved her so much hurt her so deeply?"

The older man sighed. "Men have been hurtin' her since day one. Her pa always believed the best way to raise a kid was to apply the rod on a regular basis whether they needed it or not. As for her husband, he wasn't a man, he was still a boy playing grown-up, and not doing too well at it. She made good and he

111

didn't, so he was going to hurt her where it hurt most, and he sure as hell did that."

"Then why did she come back if there were so many bad memories for her here?"

J. C. shrugged. "She needed the land and the mountains to put her back together. You didn't see her when she came back. Damn, she was all uptight and couldn't sleep more than an hour at a time. Food was just somethin' to pick at. Memories didn't even come into it. Her pa's dead and can't hurt her anymore, so there was no reason why she couldn't come back. She means to stay here for the rest of her life unless someone is strong enough to pull her out of her hole. That's why I think if anyone can do it, you can."

Travis didn't feel as positive, but that wasn't going to stop him from trying. Even as he and Kali rode up the path, he thought over what J. C. had said and wondered just how right he was. Didn't she have friends she missed? No, she'd said a majority of her friends dropped her after the divorce. Judging from some of the names she'd mentioned, she was better off without them.

J. C. also had warned him that when it was all over, he would either be lauded as a saint or branded as a devil for interfering in Kali's business.

"Just remember, she's a crack shot with that shotgun of hers," he told Travis before the younger man left the store.

"Then it's a good thing I'm a fast runner." He grinned, undaunted.

"What country did you say we were going to?" Travis asked, returning to the present after they had ridden for almost an hour.

Only Love

Kali laughed, half turning in her saddle. "Come on, cowboy, don't tell me you're feeling a little saddle-sore?"

"No, but I was beginning to wonder if we had any border guards to sneak past. You didn't tell me I would need a passport where we're going."

Kali chuckled. "It's just a little farther up the hill. Don't worry, the ride is more than worth it."

A little farther meant another twenty minutes, but Kali was right, Travis decided as he dismounted. It was more than worth it. The meadow was high up in the mountains, a tiny oasis dotted with heavy green grass and tiny flowers.

Kali guided her horse to a small nearby stream and allowed him to drink before leading him to a clump of trees, unsaddling and tethering him. Travis did likewise.

"When I was little, this place used to be my escape from the world," she explained, taking a blanket from behind her saddle and laying it on the grass. "I'd come up early in the morning after my chores were done, and wouldn't go home until I absolutely had to."

Travis sat in the middle of the blanket and pulled her down next to him. "Tell me," he urged. "Tell me what your father did to make you run away."

Her smile held no joy. While she had hoped never to talk about those days again, she felt the need for him to know. "It was more like what he didn't do. My mother was a tramp, according to him, so I had to be reared to his idea of a lady. He was going to insure that I didn't end up like her. When I was fourteen, he dragged me with him over to a neighbor's farm where he was having one of his cows bred. I wasn't

113

repulsed by the sight—after all, it was a fact of life on a farm. That night he sat me down and coldly informed me, 'Girl, you're comin' of age now where boys are gonna come sniffin' around you like a bull after a cow in heat. If I find out any boy has gotten into your pants, your backside's goin' to be whipped raw.' She had imitated the harsh, impersonal voice that must have been her father's. "I wanted to hate him, but how can you despise someone who tried to raise you the best way he could? I don't even hate my mother for leaving me with him, but I used to wish she had taken me with her."

Travis put his arms around her and pulled her against the comforting warmth of his body. His father had been rough on his sons at times, but only when they needed it, and the Yates boys were well known for doing their fair share of hell-raising. He had a pretty good idea that there was more than the brief synopsis she had just given him, and he wondered when he would hear the rest—or if he ever would. For the first time in his life he wanted to gather a woman in his arms and protect her from all that might hurt her.

His mustache brushed the top of her ear in a silky caress. "You're an incredible woman, Calliope Sue Howard."

She wrinkled her nose as she leaned farther back against his chest. "Call me Kali and you can say all the nice things you want. Try calling me Calliope again, and I just might pour the wine I brought all over your head."

"No wonder those bags were so heavy. What else did you smuggle up here? Tins of pâté? Caviar?" He turned her in his arms and nuzzled her throat.

114

"That tickles!" Kali laughed, trying to turn her head from the sounds he uttered against her skin, but he refused to let her go just yet. "Travis!" She dug her fingers into his waist and discovered the perfect way to get even.

"Okay, that's enough!" Travis choked, trying to evade her teasing fingers. But Kali was having too much fun after learning Travis was ticklish. The two rolled around on the blanket like puppies until Kali ended up on top, perfectly aligned to Travis's body. All of a sudden their play took another turn. Kali's hands braced themselves against his shoulders, his hands on her waist. Their eyes spoke dozens of silent messages. Travis's hand traveled up to wrap around the nape of her neck and pull her face down to his.

"During the night I dreamed of the way you taste," he said huskily, as her mouth hovered a breath away from his.

Kali's smile sent shafts of pure sunshine through his body. "Then let's make sure it wasn't just a dream." She took the final step, her fingertips fluttering over his cheeks as her mouth settled on his with the delicacy of a butterfly.

Sensing her need to take it at her own speed, Travis lay docile under her as Kali rubbed her lips over his, then laved his lower lip with the tip of her tongue.

"You taste like midnight," she murmured.

He smiled. "How does someone taste like midnight?"

"Mm, dark, smoky, forbidden." Her tongue slipped inside his mouth for another one of those forbidden tastes. "Dangerous." Her low voice was pure seduction.

115

Travis put his arms around her and rolled over with her. "I'll show you dangerous," he said roughly, bending his head and plunging his tongue deeply into her mouth as he pushed her hands down farther, to the throbbing evidence of his masculinity.

Kali matched the rough exploration of his tongue thrust for thrust and felt the impatience in the touch of his fingers on the swell of her breasts under her flannel shirt. Her nipples contracted from his heated touch, aching for more, setting off tiny explosions of ecstasy throughout her body. She had never forgotten the way he had made her feel that New Year's Eve, and that was nothing compared to what he was doing to her now.

"Do you feel how much I want you, Kali?" Travis demanded, rolling his hips over hers until he lay nestled intimately in the cradle of her thighs. "And it isn't just sex I want from you. It's more than that, and you know it too."

"Maybe so, but that doesn't mean I'll give in to you so quickly," she admitted, tucking her hands inside the back of his jeans. "Travis, I haven't made love to a man in over three years, and I'm not sure what to do anymore. Sometimes I wonder if I honestly did know what was involved in the act of making love, because I don't see this as sex, either. That frightens me even more. I don't want to disappoint you." She had to tell him, no matter how much she hated to admit her vulnerability. That was why she hadn't wanted him to stay at her place, why she hadn't wanted him even to talk to her, because what had started that New Year's Eve long ago was just the beginning and was destined to culminate now.

He trailed light, teasing kisses over every inch of

her face. "You couldn't disappoint me, Kali, even if you tried your damnedest. You can relax for now because I don't intend to make love to you our first time in some field, no matter how beautiful it is, where a low-flying plane or some backpacker could come upon us. I want us to have absolute privacy."

"Too many mountains around for planes to fly in, but there is Joe."

"Joe."

Kali nodded. "He lives in a run-down old shack somewhere around here. No one has ever been able to find him, and they really don't want to, since he's considered an ornery old cuss. He's known to shoot first and never bother asking any questions. Rumor has it he's run the same still for the past fifty years and makes the best corn liquor in the county."

Travis rolled away and threw an arm over his eyes. "Wonderful. I can just picture it now. A grizzled old man carrying a shotgun and threatening to blow my brains out."

Kali's lips twitched. "Joe does look pretty grizzled, and his shotgun is probably older than he is. He is also very protective of these mountains."

He moved his arm and turned his head to look at her, pleased to see her cheeks flushed, eyes sparkling.

"Well, if we can't fool around, do you want to eat that hundred-pound lunch you had me tote up here?" he asked. "No use in letting it go to waste."

Kali smiled broadly, grateful for his thoughtfulness in lightening the mood. She had to be careful because this man instilled emotions she wasn't sure how to handle. From the day he'd arrived on that huge motorcycle and walked in her door, she knew her life would change. She just hadn't realized how much.

117

The only reason she wasn't burrowing her head in the sand and ordering him out of her life was because he admitted he was just as in awe of this new turn in their lives as she was. She couldn't see him as a permanent fixture in her world because it was too remote from the hustle and bustle of the photography studio where he belonged, but that didn't bother her, either. In fact, Travis Yates was just what the doctor ordered to pull her out of the darkness of the past and into the bright colors that signified her new future. Maybe his photographing her would be her first step toward returning to the real world—if she got the nerve to go through with it. She turned on her side and placed her hand against his cheek, finding it scratchy against her cheek.

"I like your mustache, it makes you look sexy," she crooned, using her fingertip to trace the thick hairs.

Travis reached up and grasped her wrist, keeping her hand against his face. He was convinced she was a witch with healing properties because he had never felt more wonderful than he did just then. "I never thought of myself as sexy, although I've been told that before." He grinned devilishly.

"Oh, who else told you that?" She hated herself for imagining a voluptuous blonde toying with his mustache the same way she was.

"My mother."

"Mothers don't think of their sons as sexy."

"Mine does," he argued amiably, reaching out to touch the petal softness of her cheek. "She once said my brother, Rory, is the brawniest in the family, James is the most intelligent, and I'm the sexy one."

Kali wrinkled her nose. "I'd have to meet your brothers before I would agree with your mother."

"Oh, no, I think I'll just keep you for myself," he said huskily, bringing her face down to his for a lengthy kiss. He released her with a great show of reluctance. "No use in giving old Joe a free show. We'd better eat before I decide to say the hell with caution and take you here."

Kali felt an excited tingle race through her. It wouldn't be long now; she felt it in her bones, and especially in the darkest reaches of her body. The time would soon come when they would be lovers, and from then on her life would never be the same. She was surprised to discover she wasn't frightened any longer.

For the next two hours they munched on sandwiches of smoked turkey, ham, and various cheeses, accompanied by a crisp white wine and chocolate cake for dessert. Kali laughed when Travis broke off a piece of his cake and held it out to her. She, in turn, offered him a bit of her cake.

"In some countries this would make us engaged," he said quietly, spearing her with a hot look of desire.

Her breath caught in her throat. "And here I thought you were only romancing me in hopes that I'd pose for you," she said with a lightness she didn't feel.

Travis's eyes darkened with anger. He stood up and walked over to the horses. "Damn you," he said gruffly, picking up a blanket and saddle and tossing it on his mount's back. "If you honestly believe that, I may as well leave when we get back. Otherwise, you can expect to have that pretty little neck throttled."

Kali scrambled to her feet.

"Why can't you understand?" she murmured, holding her hands out. "All the men in my life seem to do is hurt me. How can I be expected to trust another?"

He tightened the cinch before walking back over to her and grabbing her by the shoulders. "That's the operative word, Kali. *Trust.* Dammit, if you can't trust me—by now you should know I wouldn't hurt a hair on your head—then you'll never be able to trust anyone." Fearing he might do harm to her after all, he pushed her away from him and stalked away.

Kali watched him through a stinging film of tears. No, she couldn't allow him to leave her like this. Not when he was willing to bare his soul to her even though she was afraid to let go of the tiniest part of hers. "Travis," she whispered, holding out her hand. "Teach me how . . . please."

He just managed to hear her soft plea. Spinning around, he covered the distance in long strides, catching her up in his arms. Holding her tightly against him, he buried his face against the curve of her throat. He felt her arms creep up his back to his shoulders. For long moments they stood here, just holding each other while Kali's tears wet the front of his shirt. Without saying a word, they parted. In unspoken agreement, Kali gathered up the rest of the food and packed the saddlebags while Travis saddled Kali's mount. Their long ride back to the cabin was silent, with Travis following Kali the same way he followed her up to the meadow, the way he would always follow her if he had his way.

Now he knew why she always held some kind of magical spell over him. It wasn't just a photographer's appreciation for a beautiful woman. It was a man's much deeper appreciation for a woman, and from that appreciation was coming something much more meaningful. Travis knew he was falling in love with Kali Hughes, but it was going to take more than his saying the words to bring her fully to him; not just her body but her heart. Why should she ever come to trust him? He was going to do everything in his power to show her the pain was over if she would allow herself to open up. He only hoped he had enough time before he had to return to L.A.

When they reached the house, Kali carried the saddlebags inside, and Travis led the horses to the barn. As she put away the remainder of the food, she found her hands shaking. Setting the packages down, she braced her hands on the counter and took a deep breath. The fear wasn't gone. For a few moments in the meadow she had been convinced she was free from the past, but that wasn't possible as long as she feared opening herself to more pain. She was so engrossed in her thoughts that she didn't hear Travis enter the kitchen. Deciding it was time to take the decision out of her hands, he crossed the room and pulled her into his arms, turning her to face him. When his mouth took possession of hers, her very breath was taken from her.

There was no gentleness in him and she wanted none. His hands tangled in her hair, pulling the band from her braid and freeing the heavy strands.

It's been so long, she kept thinking, opening her mouth even wider for his marauding tongue. *So long since a man has wanted me, but it's never been like this. Why hadn't anyone told me a kiss could take me into another world?* She was hungry for his deep passion, desperate for more. She strained against him, returning kiss for kiss, caress for caress.

Travis swept Kali up into his arms and carried her

into her bedroom. In the late-afternoon light he undressed her slowly, savoring each glimpse of her splendid body.

"I'm not sure I can remember what to do." Kali whispered her halting confession. "There's only been the one—" Her words were stopped by the gentle pressure of his mouth on hers.

"Just relax," he said quietly. "This isn't a studio, and there's no camera watching us. And I'm sure not going to direct you every step of the way in this new shoot of ours. We'll just improvise on the script and do fine, you'll see." He pulled the covers away from the bed and eased her down with him. The late-afternoon sunlight shone through the sheer curtains and set dancing lights over Kali's nude body. He doubted he ever could have choreographed such a beautiful picture.

Kali blushed under Travis's thorough regard. Even Blayne, during his most loving moments, had never looked at her the way Travis was now. She traced the colorful leaves of a vine tattooed along his forearm, then cautiously inspected the coiled snake etched around the vine. "Aren't you afraid it might decide to change locations and strike a vital area?" she asked with a teasing lilt.

Travis grinned. "I've had it since I was nineteen. I don't think I have anything to worry about now." He was discovering there were other things he wanted to concentrate on instead of his tattoo.

"Skin of gold," he murmured, burying his face between her breasts and inhaling the warm, womanly fragrance of her skin. The most expensive French perfume couldn't compete with Kali's individual scent. He swept his hand down her side and along the gently rounded hip. "The lady sunbathes in the nude." There was a light teasing note in his voice.

She smiled. "Something tells me you're not complaining."

He lifted his head and looked down into her face. "There's nothing about you I could complain about." He lowered his head and took her nipple into his mouth.

Kali cried out with joy, fire racing through her veins as Travis suckled at her breast, teasing her into an unbearable state of arousal. She lifted her foot and rubbed it along his calf while her fingers clung to his broad chest, feeling a rapid heartbeat that matched her own. Wanting to feel every inch of him, she let her hands wander down to his pulsing erection and stroked it almost shyly.

Travis groaned and captured her hands with his. "Honey, too much of that and this will be over before we've even started." His mouth trailed over the top of her breast. "This is all for you, Kali."

She wasn't sure if one hour passed, or three, as Travis explored every inch of her body. His mouth and hands now knew her better than she knew herself. His whispers of praise to her beauty and body were dark with passion and erotic with intent. Her skin flushed a deep pink, and her breathing grew labored.

"Travis, please," she whimpered, grabbing hold of his shoulders. Her open mouth moved over his throat and up to his mouth.

Their tongues mingled wildly, and soon he pulled her beneath him. One thigh parted her legs, and his fingers slid upward, finding her more than ready for him.

"Now, Travis." Kali's fingers encircled the heavy shaft and guided him to her as she arched up to encompass him completely. "Please."

Even now he wasn't about to hurt her by possessing her too quickly. Watching her with loving eyes, he thrust gently inside her. Kali gasped, not with pain but with pleasure as he filled her with his pulsing warmth. She ran her arms around his shoulders and curled her legs over his calves. When Travis was buried fully within her, he halted for a moment. They stared into each other's eyes, silently saying words their lips were afraid to express out loud. Travis began to move slowly, but the temptation of Kali herself and the response she gave him was enough to throw him over the edge. She lifted her head for his kiss, and their mouths met and held as he pleasured her over and over.

Kali felt the tingling begin in her toes and work its way upward. Her body arched, accepting more of Travis, greedy for all he could give her. Her fingertips dug into his back as she moved with him in the primitive dance. When the time came for her release, her cries mingled with Travis's own.

As they lay together sharing the tiny aftershocks of their loving, they instinctively knew what they had just shared was a blending of two souls into one, and that they would never be the same again.

Chapter
8

They spent the rest of the day in a sensual haze, and thanks to Travis, Kali couldn't stop smiling. They spent several pleasurable hours in bed talking and caressing each other until hungry stomachs forced them from their warm haven. While Travis showered, Kali slipped on a robe and went into the kitchen to fix them a late supper. She was so intent on watching the ham frying in the skillet, she didn't realize Travis had sneaked up behind her until he slid his arms around her waist and pressed his mouth to her ear.

She turned her face sideways in his direction, then shivered as his mouth trailed silkily across her cheek, then to the corner of her lips. Unable to resist his allure, she turned around and linked her arms around his waist. As their mouths met, she could feel his smile.

"Know what? I feel as if I've discovered sex for the very first time," she murmured, then said, scolding, "And don't laugh at me!"

Travis chuckled. "I'm not laughing. In fact, I feel very much the same way."

She arched one eyebrow, unconvinced. "Hmm, why can't I believe that?"

His hand moved over the curve of her buttocks and pinched lightly. "*Now* who's being the tease?" he muttered, eyes darkening as he captured her mouth in a kiss that took her breath away. Only the faint smell of smoke from the skillet broke them apart before they forgot themselves entirely and risked a burned dinner.

"We'd better eat so you can keep up your strength," Travis advised with a straight face as he gathered up plates and silverware.

"*My* strength? If I recall, you have a few years on me, meaning I should worry more about your health than my own," she said, teasing, forking slices of ham on each plate and adding flavored rice and a green salad to their meal.

The expression in Travis's eyes could only be described as hot and hungry—and not for food. "I think I've already proved that a few years difference in our ages didn't hinder me for a moment."

Kali smiled, remembering only too well what Travis had proved. And she knew he would be only too happy to repeat the performance after dinner. She also knew the age difference wasn't all that gave him such expertise. Having made love to only one

man in her life, she'd had no idea that there was
more to lovemaking than a man's possession and a
few cuddles afterward. Travis had taken his time
with her, praising her body and encouraging her to
take the same freedom with his. Just thinking about it
was enough to heat her blood. The feeling was scary,
too, because she was afraid of losing her identity to
this man.

What have I done? she wondered. *After all this
time, why have I given up so much to a man I barely
know?*

Travis caught the look of concern in her eyes and
correctly interpreted it. "You lost nothing, Kali," he
said quietly, leaning forward to cover her suddenly
chilled hand with his warm one. "We gave to each
other a special gift. We shared something few people
know about. Remember that."

She managed a wan smile. "I'm trying to tell myself that, but it's difficult. I'm not the kind of woman
to go to bed with just anyone." The image flashed
before her of their entwined bodies in that cabana
years ago. Her face whitened at the memory. "Or am
I?"

Travis caught the look and suspected what she was
thinking. "You were looking for revenge that night. I
think if it had come down to it, you wouldn't have
gone to bed with a man just for revenge. Even
though alcohol gave you the nerve to start something, I don't think you would have had the courage
to finish it." He raised her hand and brushed his lips
over the fingertips, keeping his eyes on her to gauge
her reaction. The flaring in her eyes told him she was
weakening. Weakening to him. Only to him, if he had

127

anything to say about it. "Even then we were special."

Her lips quivered. "Are you sure you're not Irish with that case of blarney you carry around with you?" she asked weakly, feeling the heat of his stare beginning to melt her resistance.

Travis never looked so serious as he did then. "I want one thing clear: I'll never lie to you and I'll never knowingly hurt you, because hurting you is hurting me. I'll do anything in my power to make sure you never suffer any kind of pain again, and I'll stop anyone who would try to hurt you."

Kali's body trembled. Travis's words were not idle. Deep down she knew that, but he wouldn't be around much longer, and who would protect her then? She would be on her own again, and her time with him would merely be a collage of hours to be pressed away in her scrapbook of memories. She withdrew her hand from Travis's and picked up her fork. She may not have been hungry, but she was going to force herself to eat every bite on her plate.

Travis worried about Kali over the next few hours. Something had changed drastically during dinner. She ate her supper, smiled at the appropriate times, and even initiated conversation, but her heart wasn't in it. Was she still regretting their lovemaking? And what could he do to prove to her that he wasn't like her ex-husband and never would treat her as he had?

Kali excused herself early, saying she wanted to relax in a hot bath. After the hours they'd spent together in bed, Travis wasn't surprised. After all, it had been a long time since she had made love, and she needed to be soothed, body and soul. He remained in the living room listening to the roar of water pouring into the tub. When he heard the soft splash of a body immersing itself in the water, he imagined the bubbles caressing her breasts, floating over her abdomen and covering her arms. He groaned, wishing he were in there with her but knew he wouldn't be invited. At least not tonight. He went back to the book he was reading, but science fiction wasn't holding his attention. He didn't want to read about lovers in another world; he wanted to think about lovers in this world, this country, this state, hell, this cabin! He shifted in his chair. His aroused body felt as if it hadn't been sated in the past eight hours. Maybe it had all been a dream—that was it, he hadn't made love to Kali at all. He had taken a nap and dreamed the whole thing. No, if he had dreamed it, he wouldn't remember the deep pink of Kali's nipples as he had tongued them to a pebble hardness, the sounds of her moans when he touched her, and the sounds of her happy cries when he possessed her. No, they weren't part of a dream; they were a reality he was only too happy to repeat if she would allow him to.

The sound of a door closing roused Travis from his thoughts. He set his book down and rose from the chair to head down the hallway. The bathroom door was open, the scent of honey and almond floating in the steamy air. And the bedroom door was closed—Kali's way of telling him she didn't want his company tonight. He wondered if she was unnerved over what had happened so quickly between them; she might need time to herself. Travis was certain that was the last thing she should have, because that also gave her time for second thoughts.

Kali lay in bed listening to Travis's footsteps. She

closed her eyes, prepared to pretend to be asleep if he opened the bedroom door. Instead, she eventually heard him walking back to the living room. She exhaled. Whether it was a sigh of relief or regret, she didn't know.

She was falling in love with Travis, as sure as the sun would come up in the morning. She was falling in love with a man determined to bring her back to the rat race that had hurt her so badly. But she couldn't afford that kind of love, for it would destroy her in the end. She rolled over onto her side, staring at the stuffed animals on her dresser. She had to remember Cheryl, remember how important it was to find her daughter and bring her home where she would be safe. That was all that mattered right now.

Kali froze when she heard the door opening. A sliver of light flashed over her curled-up body, then disappeared when the door closed softly.

Travis was in the room. She couldn't hear or see him, but she sensed him, swore she could smell him. There was no fear or anger in her body. She should have realized he wouldn't allow her to escape him that easily. He certainly hadn't given up before.

The whispery sounds of clothes dropping to the floor were all that she heard before a heavy weight pressed down the bed on the opposite side and covers were moved aside. Travis eased himself into bed and settled the blankets and quilt over him before turning on his side and gathering Kali into his arms, pressing her head against his shoulder.

"You can pretend you're sleeping all you want, but I know different," he said quietly, kissing her brow.

Kali didn't say a word. She needn't have worried, because Travis was asleep in moments. The relaxed posture of his body and his regular breathing told her that. In time she also slept, slept better than she had in years.

Kali didn't want to wake up the next morning. She knew the floors would be cold, the air icy. The calendar might have said it was spring, but in the mountains the weather was at least a month behind. Here, under the covers, it was warm and cozy. Travis turned out to be better than an electric blanket. She moved her cold toes closer to his warm legs.

"I suggest you move those icicles you call feet or lose them," Travis mumbled, keeping his eyes closed.

Kali stifled a giggle. She should be angry that he was in her bed, that he obstinately took up more than half the covers the night before, but how could she be angry with a man who climbed into bed and held her all night without expecting more?

"My feet are cold," she complained, snuggling closer.

"Wear a pair of your crazy socks to bed."

"But they're cold *now.*"

"So get a pair out *now.*"

"But it's cold outside."

"Honey, you're not telling me something I don't already know." Travis burrowed his head deeper into his pillow as one hand burrowed under Kali's pajama top, finding her breast. He smiled when he found the nipple already peaked. "At least it isn't cold where I am."

"Weren't you afraid of being thrown out last night?" Kali sighed, arching her back under his touch.

"You were asleep, remember?"

She wrinkled her nose. "You're too smart for your own good, do you know that?"

"So I've been told," he replied, looking smug. "Just remember, my mother said I'm the sexy one."

Kali decided to do a little searching of her own. It didn't take long for her to learn that Travis slept nude. "How come you aren't freezing?" Her hand wandered over his bare hip and around to his buttocks.

"The Yates are hot-blooded." He also checked out what her pajama bottoms covered, liking what he found.

Kali gasped when Travis's hand swept over the soft brown curls and below. "Travis, I'm afraid." *Afraid of what's happening to us, afraid of the future, afraid of you.* It was all unspoken but sounded loud and clear in his mind.

He turned her over onto her back and stared down into her wide eyes. His own were black as night and unfathomable, yet warm and comforting as well.

"Three years ago we almost went to bed together, and if we had, it would have been a mistake," he stated quietly, keeping hold of her shoulders so she couldn't move away from him. "It would have been a mistake because it would have been done for all the wrong reasons. You wanted to hurt your husband, and you were just a little bit drunk. I wanted you, wanted you badly, but I don't think the feeling was as strong as it is now."

"Then I would have been a pushover, wouldn't I? So why didn't you take advantage of me?" she demanded, looking miserable.

Travis took a deep breath. "Because while I wanted you, I didn't want you as a one-night stand. I wanted you without any ties, such as that present husband of yours. If you had stuck around L.A. long enough after the divorce, you would have found me camping on your doorstep, complete with candy and flowers and maybe even a poem or two. And then, when the time was right, I would have seduced you into my bed."

"Just as the time was right yesterday?" She wanted to lash out. Why, she wasn't sure.

Travis never looked less like a lover. "I was talking about three years ago, not what happened yesterday. Yesterday was due to the tension building up between us for the past ten days, and a physical attraction we haven't been able to deny. You'd admit it if you weren't so damn stubborn." He looked as if he wanted to shake some sense into her.

"It's all happened so fast!" she protested, wondering how they could have any kind of serious conversation when they were lying in bed, Travis naked and she nearly so.

"Has it? Or did we finally give in to something that has been building for a long time?"

Kali closed her eyes, but the picture of Travis's dark face was clearly imprinted in her mind. He was frustrated with her. It showed in his voice, but there was nothing in his expression to back it up. His eyes showed concern for her.

"My hormones are all out of whack." She sighed, slowly opening her eyes.

Travis's lips creased in a slow smile. "You wanna talk about hormones, we'll talk about hormones," he drawled, rubbing his torso against hers, allowing her to feel his arousal.

Kali's eyes answered his smile with one of her own.

133

How could she remain upset with this crazy man residing in her bed, showing her how much he wanted her? "That's a pretty big hormone," she commented nonchalantly.

"I wouldn't worry. You're more than woman enough to handle it." He eased her pajama bottoms down and kicked them the rest of the way off. The top took a bit of her assistance, which she was only too willing to give.

Kali looped her arms around his neck. "How do you do it? Here I was feeling sorry for myself and mad at you, yet you easily tease me out of my mood?"

Travis bent down and nipped her neck. "It's all those hormones," he said, his voice rumbling, running his hands over her body, finding every sensitive spot with unerring accuracy. "And the fact that I'm learning I can't sleep with you without wanting to make love to you. I may have behaved last night because I felt you needed the rest, but it's morning now. You've had your eight hours' sleep, and my behavior is ready to take a turn for the worse."

Kali was turning to liquid under Travis's touch. "If this is your behavior at its worst, I wonder what it would be like at its best," she murmured, curling a leg around one of his muscular calves. She buried her face against the curve of his neck, inhaling the musky scent of his skin. She decided he smelled just as dark and dangerous as he tasted, and she wouldn't have him any other way.

His mouth covered hers, his tongue plunging in to find the sweetness he knew he would find there. He invited Kali to participate in the love dance as their tongues curled around each other sensually. When Kali's tongue darted into his mouth, he felt fiery stabs

of desire overtake his body. He hadn't been a monk
—there had been more women than he cared to
think about in his life—but none had ever affected
him the way Kali did. All she had to do was smile at
him and he wanted her.

"For a beat-up old model, you've got a very sexy
body, lady," he muttered, his mouth trailing across
her cheek and up to her eyes. The eyelids fluttered
shut as he scattered butterfly kisses across her skin.
One hand covered her breast.

"Models aren't known for having much in that department," she managed to say despite the lack of air
in her lungs.

"More than a handful is a waste." He proved his
theory by cupping the rounded globe and bringing it
up to his lips. He covered every inch lovingly.

If Kali thought she had been cold when she first
woke up, she wasn't now. In fact, she was burning up.
And it was all due to Travis. His mouth turned her
blood to burning lava, and his hands brought her to
the boiling point.

Her own hands were shy in their exploration.
Blayne had never wanted her to participate in their
lovemaking—if it could have been called that, now
that she knew what the real thing was like. Travis
encouraged her to touch him as openly as he touched
her.

"Do you realize what you do to me when you touch
me?" he asked in a husky voice, covering her hand
with his as she tentatively stroked the silky shaft,
showing her what he liked best.

Her eyes lowered. "I hope you feel the way I do."

Travis rolled over onto his back and pulled Kali
with him. She lay sprawled over him, her hair a silky

curtain around her face. His finger traced her moist lower lip, swollen from his kisses, and pressed down lightly until her lips parted.

"With you I feel like the most potent, virile man in the world," he said softly. "I feel as if I can take on the whole world and win. Kali, you're so beautiful and sexy that I want to carry you off and keep you all to myself. I'm afraid someone else will find out just how wonderful you are and take you away from me."

Kali shook her head. "That's why this is all so scary," she confessed. "The feelings are so strong, we don't know where they will lead us—except to bed, of course," she added wryly.

"Do you hear me complaining?" he asked, flashing her a wicked grin. His hands braced her waist and lifted her up to straddle his hips.

It's not enough, Kali thought, but it was a beginning. She knew a lot about starting over and wasn't afraid of the hard work that would be ahead. Travis kept his hands on her hips, helping her move in a rhythm most pleasing for both of them. She looked at his face, dark and taut with desire, the eyes glowing like coals. It was the expression of a man caught up in a maelstrom of passion.

"Flow with it, Kali," Travis encouraged in his voice, watching her face flush and her eyelids lower. "Give in to what you're doing."

"I'm afraid," she whispered, feeling almost overwhelmed by the incredible sensations she was experiencing.

"I'm here with you. There's nothing to be afraid of," he told her as his hand reached down between their two bodies and touched her intimately.

Kali moaned several times as her body quickened

with each stroke. She was no longer frightened, because Travis was with her every step of the way. At the last moment her eyes flew open and she stared down into the dark face that held more than passion; if she had been fully aware of it, she would have seen the love shining in the black depths. Then, suddenly, she cried out and let herself fall against Travis. He held on to her tightly, absorbing the aftershocks that came for a short while.

"You never let me go halfway, do you?" she asked lazily, running her tongue across his jawline.

"Hell, no, this was for me too," he murmured, pulling the covers up around them so they wouldn't catch a chill in the cool room.

The previous fears fluttered through Kali's mind but disappeared just as quickly. How could she hold on to the darkness when the man beneath her banished it so easily?

"I wish I could entice you into getting up to fix a wonderful breakfast." She sighed, enjoying the warmth of the covers, and especially Travis's body warmth.

"You could, but it would be inedible." He grinned.

Kali grimaced. "I guess I can be persuaded to cook, after all."

"That sounds like a wonderful idea. I'd like ham and eggs, hash browns, blueberry muffins or corn bread, and plenty of coffee."

Before Kali scrambled out of bed, she pinched Travis. He immediately retaliated with a swat on her bottom. She shrieked and spun around, prepared to fight back, but the sight of the naked male standing before her changed her mind.

"Just for that you can forget about any muffins or

corn bread," she declared with an injured sniff,
reaching for her robe and wrapping herself up in the
warm depths before leaving the room.

"All I ask is that you make enough for two," Travis
called after her as he got out of bed and hunted up his
jeans.

Travis was happy to see warm blueberry muffins
served with his bacon and eggs; Kali was determined
that he wouldn't have everything his way. The muffins had come from the freezer, but they still tasted
wonderful, as he was only too happy to inform her
along with a thank-you kiss.

"I'd suggest you take me on some further exploration of the countryside, but what with having breakfast at lunchtime, I don't think our going out so late in
the day would be a good idea," Travis said when they
were through with their meal.

"I could take you up to Alf's tomorrow. He lives
over near Common Creek," she replied.

"What's so special about Alf?"

"That you have to see for yourself." With that cryp-
tic statement, she refused to say any more, no matter
how hard Travis tried to find out.

After taking care of the horses, Kali took Travis on
a walking tour of the property, pointing out the small
creek near the back of the house and the many trails
leading up to the mountain.

"There are still a great many people living up
there with no idea of the newfangled inventions that
have come to this world," she said softly as they
walked along a narrow trail. "Then there's others
where you see the television satellite dish right next
to the outhouse. This part of the country has a great

many contradictions, but I couldn't imagine living anywhere else."

"Why didn't you ever talk about your past before? Why was it kept such a big secret?"

She shrugged her shoulders. "I guess I wanted to keep a piece of myself private. It wasn't that I was ashamed of my background; after all, many famous people have less than exemplary pasts. I wasn't trying to hide anything, I just wanted to have something all to myself. I was lucky that I had an agent who agreed with me."

Travis wondered if Kali realized just how lucky she truly had been. When she'd walked away from L.A., she'd also walked away from several lucrative contracts and pending lawsuits. Her agent had sweet-talked the angry employers about breakdowns and mental anguish, and the suits were eventually dropped. Travis had heard about it through the grapevine that traveled endlessly in their business. So why hadn't he known all the problems behind Kali's and Blayne's marriage, except the few rumors regarding Blayne's infidelities? Kali must have worked very hard to keep the truth about her marriage under wraps. No wonder she had been so worn out emotionally when she'd left L.A. She had nothing more to give anyone. Until now. In his arrogance he felt he had arrived in Virginia at just the right time to pull Kali out of her self-imposed exile and bring her back to life.

"And you used 'Human Frailties' to release the rest of the poison of your marriage from your system," he remarked, tightening his hold around her shoulders so she couldn't move away as he anticipated she would when she realized exactly what he was saying.

139

But that didn't stop her body from stiffening in his embrace. Travis turned, wrapping her in both arms and keeping her close to him.

"Why do you persist in talking about my marriage?" Her voice was strained. "You've already heard the worst parts of it. Isn't that more than enough for you? It's a dead issue as far as I'm concerned, so why can't we leave it that way?"

"It isn't a dead issue as long as it keeps you hiding away from the rest of the world," he argued gently, brushing the tangled hair away from her face.

"I am not hiding away. I'm resting."

"For almost three years? That's a hell of a rest in my book."

Kali tried to pull away from Travis, but he wasn't about to allow her to escape. He grasped her chin between his thumbs and pulled her head up for his kiss. There was no restraint this time as his mouth moved over hers relentlessly, his lips and teeth nibbling at every corner, and his tongue possessing every inch of her mouth. He gave her no chance to back away because he wanted her to give in to him. At first she fought him. She knew he wanted her surrender, but in her present frame of mind she wasn't about to give in to him. He kept demanding more from her no matter how much she fought him. In the end she had no choice but to wind her arms around his neck and arch her body against his.

Long moments later Travis lifted his head. "Not here," he insisted hoarsely. He grabbed her hand and practically dragged her back to the cabin. In a matter of moments Kali was efficiently stripped of her clothing and in bed with Travis. The time for talk was over —for the present.

140

Chapter
9

While Travis slept that night, Kali arose and spent several hours in the living room thinking over a few of the things Travis had said. Perhaps he was right; perhaps it was time to leave the safety of the cabin and venture out in the real world again. She was certainly a great deal stronger emotionally now. The trouble was, he just didn't realize how difficult returning to L.A. would be for her. She curled up on the couch with a quilt wrapped around her and a glass of brandy in her hand, but no ready answers came to mind. She decided she would just have to remain tough and make the changes in her life in her own time. If Travis just wasn't so damn sexy, she might have a better chance of standing her ground!

Finally, feeling woozy and sleepy from the brandy she had drunk, she headed back to bed. She slipped under the covers and curled up next to Travis, unaware that he had awakened when she had first slipped out of bed, and he knew exactly how long she had been gone and even had a pretty good idea what she had been doing. He pretended to be asleep and merely shifted his warm body closer to her, and she snuggled against him.

When they had gotten up, Travis didn't mention his knowledge of Kali's nocturnal flight and couldn't help but notice she didn't say anything, either. She acted more lighthearted than usual, fixing waffles and bacon for breakfast, then suggesting they just leave the dishes to soak while they were gone.

"My jeep will take the road better than your motorcycle will," she told him as they walked outside an hour later. Kali carried a large-sized canvas bag which she threw into the back of the Jeep. "And no matter how much you hate how I drive, we'll be better off if I do, since I know the roads better."

"As long as we can stop in town so I can make out my will and notify my next of kin," Travis muttered, earning a glare from Kali.

"Don't worry, I'll make sure Jenny gets your James Dean poster collection," she assured him in a sweet coo as she switched on the ignition and put the jeep in gear.

Travis was about to add another remark when Kali took off down the hill like a bat out of hell. He would have prayed if he had enough breath to do so.

"How far are we going?" he shouted into her ear.

Kali smiled. "You'll see."

Ten minutes later Kali turned off the main road

onto a very rocky dirt road that had more curves than the letter *S*, and steadily climbed upward into the mountains.

"What happens if a car comes from the opposite direction?" Travis asked her.

"We either hug one edge or the other," was her breezy reply.

Travis looked down the side of the mountain, then over to the mountain hugging the other side of the road. Neither looked very safe. He figured the road was a little over six feet wide, and while two foreign sport cars could make it easily, if they were foolish enough to try, two larger cars wouldn't have a chance.

Who was this Alf that Kali would drive up a road that was nothing more than a rough trail to see him? It would have to be someone very special for her to go to so much trouble.

The winding drive up the mountain took more than a half hour, although they had gone barely ten miles. By then Travis's insides had been bounced around so much, he was positive his liver was where his heart should be, and his heart somewhere around his kidneys. He noticed Kali's sideways glances and the tiny smile curving her lips. The witch was testing him! She'd probably figured he would cry uncle a long time ago, but she had to learn he was tougher than that.

The log cabin Kali pulled up in front of was straight out of a movie, down to the three hunting dogs lying lazily on the porch. The dogs lifted their heads at the sound of a strange engine and immediately dropped when they saw that the visitors were friendly.

"Great guard dogs," Travis commented sardonically, raising his arms over his head and stretching the kinks out of his body.

"Alf? Reba?" Kali called out, reaching into the back of the Jeep and pulling out the large canvas bag.

A thin woman pushed open the screen door and peered out.

"Calliope, is that you?" A voice with a musical drawl greeted their ears.

"The one and only," she replied gaily, running up the porch to hug the woman tightly.

Reba looked over Kali's shoulder at Travis, who remained by the Jeep. "That ain't Harold." The distaste in her voice indicated her low opinion of Kali's ex-husband.

"No, this is Travis Yates," Kali told her, gesturing to Travis. "He's a friend of mine from California."

"Oh, landsakes, ain't he a big one," Reba said with a faint laugh, wiping her hands on her calico apron before holding one out. "I'm mighty pleased to meet you, Mr. Yates."

"Travis, please." He flashed her the slow smile that did such delicious things to Kali's equilibrium and equally flustered Reba. "Mr. Yates is my dad." He looked at the woman in her faded housedress, gray hair pinned back in a neat bun, and warm smile, and liked her immediately.

"You are welcome." Reba stepped back and ushered them inside. "Alfred is out by the barn, I'll call him." She turned to Kali. "He'll be so pleased to see you, honey. It's been a long time since you've been able to come up to see us." She left them, practically running toward the rear of the house. "Alfred! You come on in here, we have company."

Travis looked around the small living room that

doubled as a parlor. The furniture was from another era, the kind antique collectors would sell their souls for. The horsehide sofa looked as uncomfortable as he knew they were from his experience with the one that resided at his grandmother's house, but the dark wood was polished to a high shine, as were the various tables, with their knickknacks kept neatly on top.

"I can't remember the last time I saw a tasseled lamp shade," he muttered to Kali, nodding his head toward the floor lamp in one corner.

She grinned. "It's something, isn't it? Reba is in here just about every day making sure there isn't a speck of dust on the furniture. I'm surprised she hasn't rubbed the finish off." She led the way to the back of the house, to a kitchen warmed by a large wood stove. "Would you like some coffee?" At his nod she grabbed two mugs hanging from hooks over the stove and used a pot holder to pick up the metal coffeepot sitting on top of the stove. She looked up when the back door swung open. A tall man, as lanky as Reba, walked inside and hurried over to enfold Kali in a bear hug.

"And here I thought Reba was funnin' me. Let me look at you." He stepped back. "You look good, honey —yes, you do." He also gave Travis an inquiring look.

"Travis Yates." He held out his hand.

"Alfred Warren." He wiped his hand on the back of his worn overalls before taking Travis's hand. "I don't recall Calliope ever talkin' 'bout you."

Kali wrinkled her nose. "Alf tends to forget I'm over twenty-one." She looked up at the older man. "Travis is a photographer in Los Angeles, Alf."

Alf looked over Travis and his blue-and-green flannel plaid shirt and worn jeans with dark gray eyes not dimmed by age. "Hell, son, you don't look like any photographer. I thought they all wore sissy-lookin' clothes and talked funny."

Travis chuckled. "My pa would take a stick to me if I ever showed up wearing anything looking sissy."

"Where ya from?"

"Originally, Texarkana," he explained.

Alf nodded. "A down-home boy." He glanced down at Kali. "He sure seems a sight better than Harold, Calliope, girl. You're finally getting smart."

She reddened and opened her mouth to explain that Travis wasn't prospective husband material, but Travis stepped in smoothly to rescue her—or did he?

"I guess we all have to make our mistakes before we learn what we really need in life. Thank God Kali's finally coming around."

Kali almost choked. She was already beginning to regret bringing Travis with her, and that regret festered over the next few hours.

It didn't take Travis long to charm the older couple. Reba confided in Kali that she thought he was a wonderful young man and just what Kali needed. Alf was a bit more direct, asking Travis if he was going to do right by the girl.

Kali would have hidden somewhere if she could have. Always in the past, Alf and Reba had treated her like their own daughter, telling her she was so much better off without Blayne in her life but never suggesting that she find another man. Of course, she had never brought a man up here to meet them, either, and they would naturally assume he was special to her. She had to admit he was special to her; the trouble was, she wasn't sure how special she wanted him to be.

146

Only Love

"Yep, when Laurie, our youngest, went off to college, we decided to move back up here to my parents' place," Alf told Travis over a dinner of smoked ham, mashed potatoes, biscuits, and vegetables. "She's working as a secretary in Saltville now. Cal, our oldest son, is in the Army and stationed in Germany for two years. Our other two daughters are married with kids of their own, ad our other four sons are scattered among just as many states."

Travis didn't need his fingers to realize Alf was saying they had eight children. No wonder they decided to return to the peace and quiet of the mountains!

" 'Course, it ain't as quiet as I'd like," Alf went on. "Seems like one of the kids is always up here, and Calliope comes up once or twice a month when the weather is good." He grinned. "She brings us up a piece of civilization."

Travis already knew the bag Kali had brought into the house held recent magazines, books, and anything else she thought the older couple might like.

After dinner Travis was taken on a tour of the small plot of land by a proud Alf.

"Calliope's a good girl," Alf told him as they wandered through the spacious barn with its two cows, a horse, several goats, and a pen adjacent to the barn for the pigs. "She went to school with our daughter, Susan. Considerin' how her pa used to treat her, I'm happy she didn't turn out to be a bad girl. Oh, she made her mistake with Harold, but I could see why. That boy had more charm than the serpent in Eden. But she never did anything wrong."

"Then why was her father so rough on her?" Travis

147

asked, glad to be able to talk to someone else about Kali's past.

Alf shook his head, his eyes dim with sorrow. "Rance was a hard man to know. He had his ideas of right and wrong, and he stuck by them no matter who it hurt. You shoulda seen Calliope's ma; she was the prettiest little thing you ever saw. Most people couldn't understand why she married someone as hard-hearted as Rance. Word was because she was pregnant with his child. The other story was that he loved her so much, he was willing to marry her even though the child wasn't his. No one dared to find out which story was true, or even if there was another one, since Rance tended to use his fists for little reason. Leastways, Calliope was born six months after they got married, and Rance was bound and determined to make sure that child stayed a good girl. In the end all he did was drive her away. He died a harsh and bitter man, never bothering to realize just what a jewel he had in Calliope. When she began getting famous in those magazines, he told everyone he had no daughter, because he wouldn't acknowledge a whore of Babylon as his seed." He sighed.

The more Travis heard about Rance Howard, the more he disliked the man and was glad he was dead. No wonder J. C. said Kali hadn't known love from the two men in her life who should have shown it to her.

"When you have a gift, you cherish it, not destroy it," he murmured, remembering the times he had seen the stark pain on Kali's face when she recalled her past losses.

Alf's grizzled face lit up. "Son, that's it exactly," he agreed. "Too bad Rance or Harold didn't see it that way. I'll tell you one thing, that boy wouldn't be able to drive through town without ending up with some buckshot in his ass for what he did to Kali by taking her little girl away from her. A daughter needs to be with her ma, not gallivanting all over the world with a no-good pa."

"I guess he figures she's his daughter too."

Alf made a rude noise. "It's who loves and raises a child who can claim being a parent. It didn't sound like Harold knew how to do either. And Kali is left hurtin', thanks to that bastard. Now, I don't want you to think I'm talkin' out of school, but Reba and me could tell right off that you think a lot of Calliope, and I don't think you're the kind of man to hurt her, either. 'Course, if you were, you'd find out there were a lot of people around here who would go after your hide."

Travis smiled. "The more I'm around this countryside, the more I can understand why Kali loves it—and the people—so much. It appears she needed someone to care about her after what had happened, and she had that here."

"And now it's time for her to go back," the older man announced.

"She doesn't think so."

"That's up to you, isn't it?" Alf rummaged around in one of the stalls until he found what he was looking for. He held up a large jug with a triumphant grin. "Reba would skin me alive if she knew I was offering some of this to you." He offered the jug to Travis.

He took a hearty swig and promptly choked. "Damn, no wonder they call it firewater," Travis gasped, touching his throat to make sure it didn't have a hole burned through it.

Alf drank the liquor without any visible side effects. "Now"—he rubbed his hands with apparent relish—"I'd sure enjoy hearin' about those models you work with."

Kali sat in the kitchen with Reba, drinking coffee and watching the older woman repair a delicate lace tablecloth. She couldn't help wondering what Travis and Alf were talking about and had a sinking feeling it might have something to do with her.

"Your Travis is a nice-looking man," Reba commented in an all too innocent voice.

"He isn't *my* Travis," Kali said, correcting her.

"Oh, I'm pretty sure he thinks he is." The older woman held the tablecloth up to the light to inspect her work. There were no visible signs of repair. "I've always prided myself as a good judge of character, and that man is exactly what you need. He's not at all like Harold."

Kali thought about the time she'd spent with Travis and silently agreed with that point. "Then why didn't you ever warn me about Harold?" She could finally think about her ex-husband without pain shooting through her body for what he had done.

"Girl, you wouldn't have listened to any of us. Harold was a charmer, that was obvious. And that was probably why he thought he could get into television and make a fortune. Trouble was, he forgot charm couldn't get him everything."

"It sure got him me," Kali said wryly.

"That was 'cause you were too young to know better, and you were dead set to go against your pa."

"Too bad I didn't grow up sooner."

Reba leaned across the table and covered the

younger woman's hand with her gnarled one. "It was all meant to be," she said, trying to console her. "You have a daughter who the Lord will restore to you. Don't you worry about that. Just as you were meant to meet Travis. He's a lot of man, honey. I suggest you do everything possible to keep him."

Kali shook her head sadly. "It would mean returning to L.A., and I can't do that, Reba. I just can't go back there."

"Calliope Howard, I don't want to hear talk like that," she said, scolding. "You have never been a quitter, and I won't let you talk like one now. You're not the same frightened woman you were when you first came here. You just remember that."

Kali smiled. "You sound like Travis. He thinks it's time to get rid of my ghosts."

Reba nodded. "I told you he was a smart man. I have faith in you. When the time comes, you'll do what's right."

Kali wondered if she knew what was right anymore. If she'd had a lick of sense, she wouldn't have gone to bed with Travis. But if she hadn't, she wouldn't have experienced something so beautiful, and just thinking about his making love to her was enough to make her cry with happiness.

Less than an hour later they left so they wouldn't have to traverse the narrow mountain road in the dark. Kali promised to see the older couple soon, and Travis was given the invitation to come by anytime.

Kali was pleasantly tired when they returned to the cabin early that evening but knew she would have to check on the horses before she did anything else. Travis offered to help her, and they walked over to the barn together. The large interior was warm with the rich scent of hay and horses.

"One of my favorite places." Travis grinned, cornering Kali near one of the stalls. He placed one hand on either side of her shoulders, preventing any kind of escape. "So, how about a little nooky in the hay? It's just as good as a feather bed."

She laughed. "You are crazy."

He moved in even closer. "Tell me more." His breath fanned out over her face as he lowered his head to capture her lips with sensual abandon.

Kali sighed as her mouth opened for his invasion. But suddenly everything changed. The dark side of her past intruded, a side she would have preferred to keep hidden. She wasn't in her thirties any longer; instead, she was sixteen, at the threshold of her womanhood, and feeling her power over the boy she was convinced she would love forever. This wasn't Travis kissing and stroking her, it was Harold. And the dark shadow standing over her was her father. He may have been drunk, but he could certainly preach fire and brimstone as well as any minister when it came to the morals of his daughter, throwing fear into her without lifting his hand.

"You're turnin' into a slut just like your ma, Calliope. I ain't gonna let that happen as long as I have any say over you. I'll make sure you don't try those shenanigans again."

"No, Pa! We weren't doing anything! I swear to you!"

"Don't lie to me, girl! I saw the two of you kissin' and touchin' each other back there in that rear stall. Boys don't do those kinda things unless you let them. I don't like to do this, but I'm gonna have to punish you, Calliope. I want you to know it's for your own good. No girl of mine is gonna end up a slut like her momma."

"No! No! Please, Pa, don't hurt me. Nothing happened! I'm not lying to you! I'm a good girl! I wouldn't do anything wrong!"

"No," she whimpered, shaking her head from side to side, still lost in the past. "Please don't."

Lost in his desire for her, Travis didn't realize she wasn't acting coy until she lashed out at him.

"No, don't touch me!" she practically screamed, pushing him away and darting out of the barn.

Travis stood still for a moment, unable to assimilate what had happened. He ran after her and caught up with her just before she reached the back door.

"What the hell is going on?" he demanded, shaking her. "You acted as if I were going to rape you in there."

"Just leave me alone," she ordered tautly.

Travis took the time to notice Kali's eyes; they were wild with fear, and her face was paper-white. "What happened in the barn to make you so afraid of a man touching and kissing you?"

She shook her head. "Nothing. I just didn't want you to kiss me, that's all. It's a free country. I have the right to say no."

"Kali, I can spot a lie a mile away, and yours is practically glowing in the dark. Tell me what happened." This was not a request but an order.

She remained mute, still struggling to free herself from his tight grasp but to no avail.

Travis's face betrayed the frustration growing rapidly inside. "Kali, you're allowing your fears to consume you, and that's a mistake. Tell me what happened—let me help you."

She swallowed. She knew that if she didn't tell him, she would be standing there until she did. Travis was just as stubborn as she was, if not more. "My—uh—my father found Harold and me in the barn. We were only kissing, nothing else!" She cried out, wanting him to believe her, even if her father hadn't.

"I believe you." He kept his voice calm and even.

"My father didn't. He was convinced we were doing even more, or were ready to. He said it was all my fault, that I was probably leading Harold on, and if I wasn't careful, I'd turn into a slut like my mother." Her eyes were blank, looking back into the past. "He said he would make sure I'd stay a good girl no matter what it took."

"What did he do to you?" Travis asked warily.

Her voice broke. "He whipped me. He said he was going to cleanse me of my sinful ways one way or another." She took several deep breaths to calm herself. "It certainly cured me of going into the barn with Harold again—or with any other boy."

Travis's hands slid down her arms to her wrists. He took hold of one in a tight grasp and led her away from the cabin in the direction of the barn. It took Kali a moment to realize his intention, and she began fighting him immediately.

"No!" she yelled, kicking at him without success.

"In order to battle your fears, you have to confront them and discover they can't hurt you anymore," he told her, ignoring her protests. "And I'm going to be with you every step of the way. No one and nothing can hurt you now but yourself. Your father is dead

Kali. He can't come after you anymore. Your ex-husband is no longer here and he can't hurt you, either."

Kali continued kicking and screaming, calling Travis every name in the book, determined not to give in easily.

"Lady, words like that will only get your mouth washed out with soap," Travis warned grimly, not giving her an inch as he continued their walk back to the barn.

By then Kali's chest was heaving from her exertions. She resisted every step of the way, but Travis eventually got her back inside the barn. He led her over to a nearby wall and held her against it with the weight of his body. He didn't try to touch her any other way. For the next few minutes he absorbed the sobs and screams of anger she directed toward him with a mighty vengeance. By the time she stopped, she was drained of all feeling and sagged against him.

"A barn holds hay, horses, cows, and whatever else the owner cares to put in it," Travis said quietly, picking a weary Kali up and carrying her back to the cabin. She was too tired to do more than curl her arms around his neck and lay her head against his chest. "There's nothing to fear from it, and the day will come when we'll tumble into the loft and make love, and you won't be scared at all."

"I want to hate you for what you did." Each word came out in a jerky gasp as she was placed on the bed and the quilt pulled up over her.

"Then hate me all you want. I told you before, I'm going to force you to face your fears, and when they're all gone, you'll be a whole person again. That's the woman I want." Travis sat on the edge of

155

the bed and picked up her chilled hands, rubbing them between his own.

"You have a very strange way of talking a woman into posing for you." Her eyes closed.

"You told me that if I mentioned my book again, you'd boot me out, and here you're the one to go and talk about it." He chuckled.

"I may still boot you out," she murmured.

"I doubt it. Then you'd have to fix your own coffee again."

"You're right, I couldn't stand it." Kali's words were slurred, her body relaxed. Travis remained with her until she fell into a deep sleep. When he did leave her, he left the door ajar and the hall light burning so she wouldn't have to wake up in the dark. He knew that the moment she stirred, he would hear her and be by her side.

It was several hours before Kali awoke. She was slow returning to the land of the living. When waking brought on a headache, she was tempted to go back to sleep. She rolled over onto her side and stared at the open door and the light burning from the hallway. A moment later Travis stood in the doorway.

"I see you're awake. Would you like something to eat?" he asked softly.

"You can't cook," she mumbled.

"I can warm up soup in the microwave without any harm coming to it," he assured her with an easy grin.

"Unless the microwave blows up," Kali muttered, sitting up, pushing her hair away from her face. She felt hot and gritty.

Travis disappeared and returned carrying a damp

washcloth. Brushing aside her protests, he wiped her face and hands. "Why don't you put on a robe and come out when you're ready," he suggested.

She nodded. There was a great deal she wanted to say to him, but she wasn't sure how or where to begin. Before she could form one word, he was gone.

Kali washed up and discarded her clothing in favor of a bright coral velour robe. When she walked into the kitchen, she found Travis setting a bowl on the table, along with a plate of warm rolls.

"Don't worry, I didn't set food near the stove or oven," he told her, pouring a glass of wine and putting it near the bowl.

Kali tried the soup and realized it was the homemade chicken noodle soup she'd stored in the freezer along with the rolls. She didn't feel hungry but knew that if she ate something, her headache would probably go away.

"Aren't you eating?" she asked, watching him take the seat across from her.

"I ate a few hours ago."

It wasn't until then that Kali looked at a clock and was stunned to find it was almost midnight.

"I may as well have slept through the night," she said wryly, applying herself to her late supper.

"If you had, you wouldn't have been able to enjoy the gourmet meal I whipped up for you."

Kali looked at the food storage containers stacked on the counter, at the microwave, then at Travis. "Yes, I can see you put a great deal of thought into the meal," she said, teasing.

He relaxed. She was in a better frame of mind than he expected she would be. Perhaps that meant she didn't hate him as much as she had intimated before.

Kali ate most of the soup, one roll, and drank all her wine before sitting back in her chair.

"What you did was the most horrible thing I can imagine," she said without preamble. "I understand why you did it, but I still don't appreciate it."

"I didn't expect you to."

"You can be a bastard, can't you?"

"Yes, but I'm also the man who is in love with you."

Whatever Kali had expected for an answer, it wasn't that. She could only sit there and gape at him, wondering if she had heard right, and so afraid she might not have.

Chapter
10

🌙 Kali didn't ask Travis to repeat his statement, and he didn't bother to elaborate. When morning finally came, she was still reeling from his confession. The last thing she had expected was for him to tell her he loved her. Desired her, yes; wanted her, yes; loved her, no.

"Oh, no, lady, today I drive," Travis informed her after she announced that she needed to go into town to check her mail. "I intend to live to see my next birthday. Besides, I'm tired of riding around with my stomach in my throat."

"Fine." She dropped the keys into his outstretched palm and headed for the passenger side.

Travis knew exactly why Kali was so quiet during

the leisurely drive into town. His telling her he loved her was probably more than she could handle just now. Except he had to tell her; he wanted her to know that his feelings were more for her than just a few nights in bed and then a "Good-bye, see you later." He'd seen too much of that happening in his world, and wouldn't have been surprised if Kali wasn't afraid of just that. No matter what, he had to make sure she knew they weren't just idle words for him.

Following Kali's directions, Travis parked in the dirt lot behind J. C.'s general store.

"I want to stop in Millie's and see if she has any cinnamon rolls," Kali said, jumping out of the jeep and walking around to the street. "No one can make them like her, and I like to buy up as many as possible and freeze them." She headed for a small shop that doubled as a clothing store and bakery.

"I would think most women do their own baking around here." Travis followed her.

"They do, but Millie fixes up some specialty items most people don't care to make themselves, and cinnamon rolls is one of them." Kali hesitated when an elderly couple approached them. She managed a weak smile that didn't reach her eyes. "Hello, Tom, Sarah."

If looks could kill, Kali would have dropped dead right then and there. Their gazes were glacial, their expressions pure fury directed at the younger woman.

"Because of you and your high-and-mighty ways, Calliope, we lost our son," the woman bit out. "I hope you can live with yourself." She stalked on.

Kali's face was paper-white, and she bit her lip to

keep it from quivering. She grasped Travis's hand, holding on to it tightly.

"I—uh—I don't think I really need any cinnamon rolls," she whispered, turning around.

Travis noticed several ladies watching Kali, then grouping together to chatter in low tones. It wasn't difficult to guess who they were talking about.

"Let's go into J. C.'s."

She shook her head. "No, I just want to go home."

Travis draped his arm around her shoulders. "We will go into J. C.'s and you will act as if nothing happened," he advised in a low voice.

"I can't."

"You can and you will." He steered her toward the general store and inside.

Kali held her breath as she searched the interior, until she discovered it was empty except for its proprietor.

"Hello, J. C." She forced herself to smile and failed miserably. "How are you?"

"I'd be better if my arthritis wouldn't act up so damn much," he grumbled, coming around the counter to kiss her on the cheek. He looked at her with sharp eyes. "What happened to get you upset?"

She shrugged. "I'm not upset."

"Someone named Tom and Sarah." Travis supplied the names, even though he had a good idea who they were.

J. C. sighed heavily. "They're so bitter that they only want to believe in one side of the story." He turned to Travis. "They're Harold's parents, and they've always blamed Kali for taking him away from here. They don't understand that he wanted to leave here just as badly as she did. He was the one who felt he was better than anyone here, not her." He hugged her tightly. "They also blame her for issuing that warrant for his arrest if he returns to this country. They think she forced him to leave, and see nothing wrong that he took Cheryl with him."

"They blame me for losing their son but forget that I've lost my daughter," she whispered.

The trio was silent for several moments before J. C. roused himself. "Let me have the list of what you need. I've also got some mail for the two of you." He took her list and disappeared behind the counter.

Kali couldn't keep still and wandered through the tiny store as J. C. filled several boxes with her needs and dropped the mail in one box. She was so immersed in her perusal of a selection of paperbacks on one counter, she didn't see J. C. gesture to Travis and lead him into the back room.

"I'm hoping this isn't what I think," he said in a low voice, handing him an airmail envelope. "But if it is, I don't want her to be alone when she opens this. I also don't want her to see it until you feel the time is right."

Travis looked down at the dark blue scrawl across the pale blue tissue paper. There was no return address, but the burning feeling in his gut told him the name of the sender.

"You're right," he said slowly, still staring down at the envelope. "After what just happened, the last thing she needs is to be upset again."

J. C. nodded in understanding. "She'll yell and scream and cuss a blue streak," he said, warning the younger man.

"She can do anything she pleases, so long as she doesn't shut me out," Travis muttered, pocketing the envelope. He schooled his face into an unconcerned expression as he followed J. C. out into the store.

"What were you two doing back there?" Kali demanded, turning around. "Looking at the pictures in *Playboy*?"

"Now, honey, you know very well I only read it for the articles." J. C. was all innocence.

Kali rolled her eyes in disbelief. She picked up one of the boxes, only to be ordered by Travis to leave them alone; he'd carry them outside to the Jeep. She watched him load the Jeep, noticed the frown in his eyes, and wondered what had put it there. She had a sudden sinking feeling that his worry had something to do with her.

During the drive back to the cabin Travis caught hold of Kali's hand and squeezed it tightly. Apprehension filled her body, but she feared asking the obvious question.

Travis unloaded the boxes quickly, helping Kali put everything away in its proper place. He suggested she look through her mail while he made some coffee.

Sensing whatever he had to tell her would be kept quiet until he was ready, she glanced through her mail, read letters from Jenny and another friend, and opened a box of videotapes and books from Malcolm. She put them aside, knowing they would come in handy when she was left alone again. Alone. That word sounded sad. She had grown so used to Travis's company that she'd forgotten the time would come when he would have to leave. Thinking about it tempted her into going back to Los Angeles, but she still didn't feel brave enough to reenter the fast lane.

Kali walked back into the kitchen, took the coffee

cup Travis extended to her, opened a cabinet, and added a healthy splash of Kahlua to the dark brew.

"Isn't it a little early in the day for that?" he asked mildly.

She spun around and faced him. "That depends on what you have to tell me."

He nodded. It was as good a time as any to get it over with. He slowly pulled the envelope out of his shirt pocket and handed it to her.

Kali's fingers felt stiff as she grasped the envelope. She stared down at the familiar writing and immediately feared the worst. She took a swallow of the coffee before inserting her fingernail under the flap and carefully opening it. A small photograph fell out. The paper fluttered as her trembling fingers unfolded the single sheet of paper. Travis reached down to pick up the photograph and looked at it. The girl in the color picture was probably six or seven years old, with long brown hair and Kali's eyes. Her delicate features and smile was a perfect younger version of Kali's. The sour feeling in his gut intensified. He wished he'd read the letter before giving it to her, no matter how much she might have screamed at him about invasion of privacy.

Kali's face revealed a stark pain Travis had never seen before.

"How he must hate me," she whispered, taking the picture from his hand. Tears glistened on her cheeks as her fingertips lovingly traced the features. "What have I done to deserve this terrible thing?"

Travis took the sheet of paper out of her hands and read the six lines. There was no signature, but the identity of the author was all too obvious.

Only Love

Little Bo Peep has lost her lamb
And doesn't know where to find her
Leave us alone and she'll come home
When little boy blue is ready.

Sorry about the lack of rhyming, love. I never was very good with poetry.

Travis quietly palmed the envelope and slipped it into his jeans pocket. He would take a better look at it later. It was a small clue and better than nothing.

"How did he know I was still here?" Kali wondered out loud, still holding on to the photograph.

"Wasn't this sent in care of your attorney?"

She shook her head. "No, it was sent to me in care of J. C." A look of determination crossed her face. "And I intend to find out how he knew I was here." She picked up her key ring. "I'll be back later."

"Oh, no." He grabbed her arm, stopping her flight. "You're not going anywhere without me."

"Whatever, but I'm going back to town now, and hopefully J. C. will have some answers for me."

Travis only allowed Kali to drive because he sensed she needed an outlet for her frustration. They reached the general store in record time, and Kali walked into the store with fury written on her face.

"First of all, I do not appreciate you giving the letter to Travis instead of me," she said, berating J. C. "Second, it was sent to me here, and I want to know everything you know. And don't try to pull any innocent act with me, you old faker, because this place, along with Millie's, is a hotbed of gossip."

The older man sighed. "Word has it that Harold calls his parents every so often and usually asks for money, saying it's for Cheryl and then promising to bring her for a visit as long as they don't tell anyone he's here."

Kali stiffened. Whatever she had expected to hear, this wasn't it. "They know where he is?" Her quiet voice was deadly.

"No one knows that for sure." J. C. was quick to placate her. He was used to that glint in her eye and knew it meant trouble. He glanced at Travis, silently warning him to beware.

Kali spun around and stalked out of the store.

"She's goin' over to the Gresham place," J. C. told Travis. "You better hurry, or she'll leave you behind."

He nodded and rushed out after her. He barely hopped into the passenger seat when the Jeep was slammed into gear and took off like a rocket. Travis took one look at Kali's grim features and decided it was better not to comment on her driving.

She drove out of town in the opposite direction from her cabin and headed up a narrow dirt road for a short distance. The clapboard house was small and painted a pale gray, with darker gray trim.

Kali jumped out and walked up to the house. She knocked on the door and stepped back to wait. When Sarah came to the door, her face stiffened with cold resentment.

"What do you want here?"

"You know where he is," Kali stated icily.

"If I did, I wouldn't tell you. This was all your fault, Calliope Howard. You with your high-and-mighty ways. You seduced my Harold into taking you to California," she said accusingly. "And because of you, he can't even come back to his own home and family. You're an evil woman, Calliope, and someday you will pay for your sins," she intoned. "I only hope I'm here to see it."

Her smile was cold and deadly. "He didn't take me anywhere. I paid for everything, and I certainly didn't seduce your precious son, who probably had just about every girl in the high school." She deliberately kept her tone even, a calmness just as deadly as a cobra ready to strike. "You can stand here from now until doomsday declaring you don't know where your son is, but I won't believe you. I want you to know that you are covering up for a criminal, the man who stole my daughter."

"We're not covering up for anyone. We're only helping our son because you were cruel enough not to let him see Cheryl after the divorce!" Sarah voice was shrill, her eyes wild. "Why shouldn't he be allowed to see his little girl?"

Kali's eyes narrowed. She thought of the many indignities she had put up with, thanks to Blayne, and how many of them had been hidden from the public. No more. She was past caring.

"Your precious son was an unfaithful husband from day one, because he needed variety," she stated calmly.

"If you had been a better wife to him, he wouldn't have strayed."

"He never wanted a wife, and he never wanted Cheryl. He demanded I get an abortion the day he learned I was pregnant, and he fought with me for the next seven months. If he spent more than five minutes in Cheryl's company, it was for the press, not for himself. He didn't give a damn about her, and I doubt he does now. All he wants to do is punish me for smartening up and getting rid of him. He was

167

lucky I didn't drag all the dirt into court, and believe me, if it hadn't been for Cheryl, I would have." She stared long and hard into the older woman's face. "I have a message I want you to give to your son. You tell him that I haven't forgotten what he did to me, and for that he will be hurt—badly." Without waiting for any reply, she turned around and walked back to the jeep.

She drove blindly down the path, braking to a stop when she reached the main road.

"I would greatly appreciate it if you would drive the rest of the way," she whispered hoarsely, looking straight ahead.

When they returned to the cabin, Kali headed straight for her bedroom. She didn't say a word, but Travis knew she needed to be alone. Deciding some kind of physical outlet was needed, he went over to the woodpile and picked up the ax.

Kali sat in the middle of the bed, hugging her knees against her chest. She couldn't remember the last time she had felt so cold. Why was this happening to her? She hadn't been a bad girl; she'd certainly done everything her father had ordered her to do. She hadn't turned to drugs, alcohol, or indiscriminate sex while in L.A. So why was she being punished? Tears welled up, and raw pain clawed at her chest. She gave in to the tears in hopes it would diminish the pain. A half hour later the pain wasn't gone, and she ended up with a headache and red eyes. She went into the bathroom, grimaced at her reflection in the mirror, and splashed cold water over her ravaged face.

The house was so quiet. Kali was grateful Travis had left her alone, but now she needed him to warm the icy cold invading her body. She wandered through the rooms but found no sign of him anywhere. When she reached the kitchen, she could hear the sounds of an ax splitting wood. Looking out the window over the sink, she could see Travis, an ax swung over his bare shoulder. In deference to the arduous work he had discarded his shirt, and sweat poured down his shoulder and back. She stood for several moments watching the graceful movements of the ax swinging upward over his shoulder then down to slice the logs in half. Kali's mouth grew dry as she studied the bunched muscles rippling. Her fingers twitched in memory of tracing those same muscles when he lay over her, his body possessing hers. She noticed his face grimacing with the effort and remembered his face when he climaxed. Suddenly Kali wanted him. She wanted him not only to warm the ice in her veins but also to make her feel like a woman again. She needed him so badly, she knew she couldn't wait. Moving slowly like a sleepwalker, she left the kitchen and walked outside to the woodpile.

Travis had just lifted the ax when he noticed Kali moving toward him. He lowered the ax and watched her, thinking he couldn't imagine anyone moving so gracefully. Then he noticed the look in her eye.

Kali walked up to Travis and took the ax out of his hands, dropping it on the nearby wood stump before looping her arms around his neck and pulling his head down for her kiss. Her tongue darted into his mouth, sweeping through to savor his dark flavor.

Travis moaned. He put his arms around her waist and pulled her against him, rubbing his arousal against her. Their hips writhed in imitation of the act they both craved.

"I want you," she whispered in his ear, tracing the whirled outline with the tip of her tongue. She smiled when she heard his groans of desire, but it wasn't enough. She wanted him tied up in knots, and proceeded to do just that. She swept her hand down the front of his jeans, finding the swollen bulge of his arousal and caressing it lightly.

"You're playing with fire, Kali." Travis groaned, grabbing her hand and pressing it harder against him.

"I believe that can be said of you also," she replied throatily, rubbing her breasts against his chest. She wished she wasn't wearing anything so she could feel his heated skin against hers. In fact, she didn't want either one of them to have any clothes on at that moment. "I want you."

He grinned. "That can be arranged."

Kali's eyes darkened. "I want you now."

There was no mistaking her meaning. While Travis was not one to turn down the opportunity to make love to the woman he adored, he did hesitate at the idea of making love outdoors in forty-degree weather. At the same time he hated the idea of parting with her, even momentarily, to make their way back to the bedroom. Wrapping his arms around her waist, he picked her up.

"Put your legs around my waist," he ordered thickly.

She smiled and complied. "Do you know what it feels like to have you inside me?" She nibbled on his throat.

Travis thought more about making love outdoors

in cold weather as he walked them back to the cabin. With each step Kali told him what she liked him to do to her. He knew he'd better hurry. When he passed the living room, Kali murmured for him to stop.

"Here, in front of the fireplace," she suggested with a sultry wink.

Travis lowered her to the braided rug in front of the crackling fire. They knelt, facing each other.

"Do you realize how sexy you looked out there chopping wood?" Kali whispered, nuzzling the hollow between his shoulder and collarbone. The warm, musky scent of his skin filled her nostrils, making her feel as heady as if she had drunk champagne. She ran her hands over his shoulders and his back. "As I watched you, all I could think of was our making love. I couldn't wait until you finished. I had to go out and tell you that I wanted you right away."

Travis dispensed with her shirt and sweater and carefully unhooked her bra, allowing her breasts to spill freely into his hands. Staring into her eyes, already dazed with passion, he rubbed the nipples with his thumbs until they were hard, silently demanding all his attention. His lips followed the same path, enveloping one nipple and tugging on it. Kali closed her eyes, preferring to experience the fiery sensations coursing through her blood with lightning speed by feel instead of by sight. In her mind's eye she could picture Travis's mouth covering her nipple, tonguing and teething it to moist perfection, the brush of his mustache against her sensitized skin. She wanted to savor it all slowly.

"You are so beautiful in the firelight," Travis murmured, moving his attention to her other nipple.

171

Kali laughed, a sensual sound that sent shivers down his spine. "It hasn't even grown dark yet."

"It doesn't have to, because I know what you look like in all kinds of light." One hand ventured down to the waistband of her jeans and unzipped them. "And I want to see all of you now." With Kali's help, her jeans were pushed to one side before they went to work on discarding Travis's jeans and briefs. He had deliberately left her tiny bikini panties alone, enjoying the mystery of her half-clothed body. "You drive me crazy," he muttered against her mouth," toying with the ribbons on her hips. "I want you so much but I don't want it over too quickly."

Kali touched his face with butterfly-light kisses. "It will never be over." She gasped when his hand slid under the panties, finding the moist warmth that signified her desire for him.

Travis smiled. She may have said it in the heat of passion, but he knew she meant it whether she realized it or not. Feeling the time for games was over, he ripped away her panties and pressed her down to the rug. They stretched out on their sides, running their hands over each other lovingly.

When Travis at last entered her, Kali sighed in ecstasy. Their lovemaking was slow and leisurely, both of them holding back, wanting to savor each other.

"If I died right now, I'd be a very happy man," Travis whispered, grasping her hips.

Kali smiled. The cold was rapidly receding from her body, thanks to Travis's loving. She felt complete, for the first time in ages.

"Just let me keep making you happy, and I promise you'll have a lot to stick around for," she murmured, leaning down to kiss him. Even as she bent over him, she could sense his warm eyes upon her, revealing the depth of his feelings. Holding on to him tightly, she gave in to the passion he evoked. Soon they were both lost in the heat of their lovemaking.

Chapter
11

The logs in the fireplace were nothing but warm ashes when the couple finally roused themselves and returned to the real world.

"Lady, I sure like the way you seduce a guy," Travis told her as he pulled on his jeans before going over to build up the fire.

She smiled ruefully, shaking her head and looking surprised at herself. "Actually I never thought I had it in me."

Travis wrapped a hand around the nape of her neck and pulled her toward him for a quick kiss. "You weren't around the right man, that's all."

She tipped her head back. "And you think you're the right man?" she asked coyly.

Dark fires flared up in his eyes. "Damn straight I'm the right man for you. The sooner you realize it, the better off we'll be."

Unnerved, Kali frowned and began to step back, but Travis's tight grip on her arms prevented any escape.

"As far as I'm concerned, we were destined to be together three years ago, Kali, but fate kept us apart for reasons of its own," he said quietly, holding her chin steady so her gaze couldn't evade his. "The time has finally come for us to face it."

"I promised myself never to return to L.A. or to get involved with anyone from there, and I intend to keep that vow. I thought that was the only way I could keep my sanity," she murmured, watching the hurt dim his eyes. She wished she wasn't the one to put it there, but it had to be said. She had to let him know how she felt. She loved him—God, how much she loved him!—but she still wasn't strong enough to fight what had happened to her.

"Then you're in for a shock, because we're definitely past the point of involvement, Kali. This isn't some casual affair that we can shrug off and go our separate ways," he said harshly, his fingers digging painfully into her shoulders. "I don't ever want to hear you belittle what we have."

Why did she feel as if she had just been threatened? Kali was afraid to admit what they had because that would make it real. She wanted to tell him how much she loved him and that she was his forever, but dammit, he was going back to California soon. Did he think she would stay behind and pine for him so badly that she'd rush right out there? Is that what he wanted? She jerked away.

Only Love

There was no mistaking the pain in Travis's eyes because of her rejection, but she chose to ignore it.

"I think I'll take a shower," he said quietly, turning away.

Kali crossed her arms in front of her waist, rubbing her elbows with her hands. She wondered if Travis was hungry but decided not to ask him. She doubted she could eat a thing, but she needed to do something, anything, to get her mind off their confrontation. Wandering over to the refrigerator, she took out the makings for a salad and some stew. As she prepared the meal, she wondered at the sad turn of events. Why did she have to hurt Travis? From the beginning, he had been more understanding than Blayne ever was, and he certainly had been patient with her no matter what she put him through. Still, she couldn't bring herself to take that final step and admit how much she really needed him. Not after all this time of telling herself she was on her own and that she couldn't afford to trust anyone, especially another man.

Travis stood under the hot spray, his neck bowed so that the shooting water could ease the tension. He knew why he was upset over what had just happened. His time here was growing short. Within the next three days he would have to leave for L.A., and he still hadn't gotten Kali to agree to come back. Right now he could care less if she posed for his book. He still felt it was a good idea because there wouldn't be the pressure that fashion modeling caused, and she could ease back into the business or ease right back out when his book was finished if she so chose, but he wasn't going to push it with her because he knew that would only increase her hostility, and it had taken him long enough to push back that particular barrier. What a shame the others weren't as easy.

Why was it that the first woman he fell in love with proved to be so troublesome? He thought about some of the women he had been with in the past. They certainly wouldn't have made him as crazy as Kali did, but they wouldn't have given him the joy, either. He exhaled a shuddering breath as he turned off the water and stepped out of the shower.

Their meal was consumed in silence, neither of them eating much at all. Travis offered to wash the dishes while Kali took a shower. When he walked into the living room with two glasses of brandy, he found her sitting in front of the fireplace brushing her hair dry. The firelight flickering across her pensive features and hair added even more beauty to the scene. Without thinking twice, Travis set the glasses down and headed for the bedroom to dig something out of his duffel bag.

Kali looked up when he returned, and she froze when she saw the leather-covered item in his hands.

"What is that?" Her voice was tense.

He smiled wryly. "After all these years you still can't recognize one?" He took the camera out of the case and checked the shutter speed and experimented with the flash attachment to make sure it worked properly.

Kali looked down at the brush in her hand, not surprised to find her hand shaking.

"It's just that I can't imagine you're going to take pictures of the scenery at this time of night." There was a return of her old sarcasm.

"There's your idea of scenery and my idea of scenery." He took off the lens cap and set it to one side. "Mine doesn't necessarily have to be outside."

Her eyes narrowed. Her mouth felt cottony and her eyes burned, but she wasn't going to allow him to frighten her. "If you want to take my picture, it's going to cost you five thousand dollars."

As if he had anticipated her rash dare, Travis dug into his jeans pocket and pulled out a checkbook. He filled it out and handed it to her. Kali looked at the amount and the boldly scrawled signature across the bottom, folded it in half, and put it in her robe pocket. Smiling with only her lips, she stood up.

"What kind of pose do you wish?" She moved from side to side, looking provocative with each graceful movement. "Demure? Sensual? Downright sexy?" She lowered the shoulders of her robe until the curves of her breasts were revealed almost blatantly. "Do you want to see some leg?" She lifted the hem and extended her bare leg, her toes pointed daintily. "Perhaps you'd like me to use some makeup? My skin tone tends to wash out under the bright lights if I don't wear the proper base. Do you want me to wear heavy eye makeup? Light? Surely you have your preference." Each word carried a cutting edge. "Just tell me and I'll give you whatever you want. After all, you're paying for it."

Travis remained impassive, aware that she was trying to bait him to anger.

"Give me what you feel most comfortable with." He lifted the camera to his face.

Kali was determined to do that and more. She adopted her most haughty look and whirled around, the full hem of the robe swirling around her ankles. She raised her arms and lifted her hair up, her head tipped back and eyes closed. Travis didn't hesitate and shot frame after frame, using the firelight as a backdrop and adjusting his f-stops to accommodate the lesser light.

Working to a nameless tune in her head, Kali moved from one pose to another, her lips moist and parted, her eyes half closed, her thick lashes looking like dark crescents against her pale skin. To Travis she had never looked more beautiful. Pretty soon her movements flowed into a sensual dance. She may have started out angry, but she couldn't remain that way for long. Unconsciously she wanted to show Travis just what she could do in front of the camera. She was unaware that Travis had hurriedly reloaded the camera two more times so he would miss as little as possible. When she eventually halted, her skin was damp from her exertion, her shoulders bowed with weariness. Travis lowered the camera and remained quietly in his crouched position, watching as she lifted her arms over her head to ease cramped muscles.

"You seem to make me do things I don't want to," she said finally, pulling her robe up and bending to pick up her brush. "You talk about what's between us, and I've been wondering about that. All I can see is the physical attraction. The stuff affairs are made from."

"All you *want* to see."

"It's a free country. You see what you want to. After all, I see what I want to. You'll be leaving for Los Angeles soon."

"Yes, in about three days." He saw no sense in lying to her. "I told you I could only stay a couple of weeks, and I've been gone longer than that now."

Her lips curved in a bitter smile. "Three days. No wonder you thought you should bring out your camera as a softening-up technique. You knew you didn't have very much time left. What a shame it didn't work."

Travis thought differently. His actions were far from some kind of "softening-up technique." He had brought his camera along because he never went anywhere without one. This trip had enabled him to take pictures of the scenery during his ride, and also of some very interesting people he had met along the way. He even had taken several pictures of a very proud J. C. the day he had gone into town alone.

As for the pictures he had taken of Kali, he knew they were good without having to look at the finished product, and vowed to develop them as soon as he got back to his studio. Kali may have thought she needed a special base makeup and proper lighting to look beautiful, but he knew otherwise. All she needed was the right setting.

"I probably shouldn't have done this tonight after all you've gone through today, but usually emotion helps a model give more to the camera instead of hindering her."

Kali collapsed on the rug, the very same rug she and Travis had made such beautiful love on hours before. She took several hairpins out of her pocket and twisted her hair on top of her head, securing the knot with the pins. She had three days. Would she allow Travis to walk out of her life, or would she agree to go to California and pose for his book? She thought all her major decision making had been done years ago. She should have known better.

"I should have shot you that very first day."

181

He grinned. "To be honest, I'm surprised you didn't. You looked more than prepared to do so."

"I was thinking very seriously about shooting first and asking questions afterward. You just caught me at a weak moment, that's all." Her earlier fire had returned with a vengeance.

Travis dropped the rolls of film in airtight containers and cleaned the lenses before putting the camera back in its case.

"Believe me, I'm glad you gave me the chance to talk first." He walked over to her and began kneading her neck and shoulders with strong fingertips. Kali rolled her head forward, groaning in appreciation as the tense muscles began to relax under his ministrations.

"Why anyone thinks posing is easy is beyond me," she murmured.

"Maybe you should try a hot shower to get the kinks out."

"If I wanted the kinks out, I would definitely have shot you weeks ago." Laughter laced her tone now that her earlier anger toward him was gone.

"Am I to assume you aren't mad at me any longer?" he asked softly.

"You make it pretty hard to be," she admitted with a sigh. "You're right, a hot shower would do me a lot of good." That she wanted to be alone was implied, understood, and honored.

They didn't make love when they retired for the night but instead curled up in each other's arms, not falling asleep for a long time. Both were thinking of what would happen in three days' time when Travis left Virginia and Kali was left alone again.

The subject was left unspoken the next day by

mutual consent. Instead, they spent the day riding up to the meadow they had gone to long ago and talked about any other subject but the one that preyed most on their minds. Kali withdrew more and more as the day progressed. She didn't want Travis to leave, and she couldn't bring herself to return to L.A. to pose for him. Was she being selfish? Probably, but she didn't know any other way.

She thought about many troubling things that evening as they cleaned up the kitchen after dinner.

"How about a few hands of poker?" Travis suggested, folding the dish towel and putting it to one side.

Kali shrugged. She knew how to play, not very well, but well enough to hold her own. She had come to a few decisions and knew she should voice them before her courage ran out.

"I've decided that I will pose for you," she said quickly.

Travis watched her closely. He sensed there was a condition behind her agreement, and he didn't have long to wait to hear it.

"But I have to pose for you here," Kali told him, her tone telling him she wouldn't consider otherwise. "I made a vow I wouldn't go back to my old way of life in California, and I intend to keep it. If you want to photograph me so badly, you'll have to do it here—and my whereabouts must be kept secret. I want that written in the contract." She faced him with her chin held high.

Travis took his time taking the deck of cards out of the desk drawer and popped them out of their package. "Then I'm afraid it's no deal. I have other commitments that I must keep, and I have no more time to roam around the countryside according to the whims of one subject." He finished shuffling the cards and slipped them back into the package.

Kali flinched at his blunt choice of words. "Then you must not want me very badly." She kept her chin in her usual gesture of defiance.

Travis's dark eyes were hot in their intensity as he watched her. "Oh, I want you, all right. I want you badly enough that I wouldn't think twice about carrying you into that bedroom and making love to you so long and hard, you wouldn't know what had happened to you. But as a model, no, I can't afford to want you that badly. I've dealt with temperamental models enough in the past, and I won't give in to one now. Not even you."

Kali smiled to herself. So he saw her as a temperamental model, did he? Well, perhaps she was acting like one, but her true reasons for her harsh demands were much more complicated than that. Didn't he understand how impossible this was for her?

Travis walked up behind her and placed his hands on her shoulders. "Maybe it's best that I'm leaving soon," he said quietly, resting his chin on top of her head. "All of this has happened so fast that maybe some time on our own is what we need to sort it out."

The tears she had denied all day filled her eyes. "I don't want to say good-bye."

"But you don't want to come to L.A., either."

She opened her mouth, closed it, moistened her lips. "I can't." Her voice cracked. How could she explain her fear of going back to that fast-paced town? Too much had happened there for her to feel comfortable. Here she was safe; there were no medi-

people, no pressures, no worries, except for her dream of getting Cheryl back.

"I could always try a bit of emotional blackmail," Travis said, breaking into her thoughts. "Such as, 'If you love me . . .'"

She stiffened and spun around. "That isn't fair, Travis." Her voice trembled with sorrow.

"Is it fair to want to keep me here in this hideout with you for as long as you can?" he asked harshly, his fingers digging into her arms. "That's what you really want, isn't it? For me to stay here keeping you satisfied in bed while you run away from all your troubles?"

"My, you really think you know me well, don't you? You know every inch of my body, exactly what buttons to push—" She would have gone on, but Travis's mouth had covered hers in a hard, wild kiss. She was helpless in his embrace. Then suddenly his touch changed. With soul-searching tenderness his tongue slid across her lips, caressing them with unhurried thoroughness before wandering back inside her mouth to tempt her into a straining union that lasted until they were both breathless.

"Maybe we're better off keeping our discussions personal," Travis muttered roughly, covering her face with biting kisses. "This seems to be a better way to communicate."

Kali's hands clenched his shoulders tightly. Her head was thrown back, exposing the slim column of her neck to his marauding mouth. Long moments later, Travis lifted his head and looked down at the soft mouth he'd just tasted, the slightly parted lips glistening with moisture from his own mouth.

"You taste so delicious, I could keep this up for days," he murmured.

Her slumbering eyes were answer enough. *Take your time*, they invited silently.

Travis's mouth descended again. He was determined to take his time, to discover and claim every inch of her as if he had never tasted her before.

Feeling the fire race through her veins, Kali let her hips arch up against the taut cradle of his thighs. Keening moans left her lips in a plea for possession, but he ignored her. He was determined to give her a night she would never forget, and one he would carry in his heart for all time, because until they reached a compromise, they could never have a life together. Her insistence on staying in Virginia couldn't be part of that compromise.

He picked her up and carried her into the bedroom with all the expertise of Rhett carrying Scarlett up that long stairway. He could easily identify with the man. Both dealt with extremely strong-willed women.

No lights were on. Travis set Kali on her feet long enough to strip her of her robe before guiding her to the bed. His own clothing was discarded quickly. He stood before her, his darkly tanned skin glistening with perspiration, his body hard and aroused. Kali gasped at the sight of him. Even if this were to be the last time they made love, she never would be able to forget him. She lay back against the pillows and watched Travis slowly approach the bed.

For the longest time he stood there, one knee bent on the bed. He watched her, imprinting her in his mind. He didn't need artificial light for this; he knew the exact color of her eyes and hair, the delicate peach blush of her skin, the enticing mole just above her right buttock. The more he looked at her, the more he began to hate her for doing this to them. They could have so much if only she was willing to trust him. By now she should know he would never hurt her. If anything, she was the one doing the hurting, and he had the pain in his gut to prove it. That was when he made his decision: This would be a night never to be forgotten by either of them.

Travis stretched out on the bed next to Kali. He noted her watching him with unspoken questions in her eyes. Without a word, he rolled onto his side, facing her. One hand coasted along the delicate curve of her shoulder, the gentle slope of her breast, the narrow indentation of her waist, and down to her rounded hip. With each touch he left fiery imprints on her skin. After his fingers trailed over the sensitive skin on the back of her knee, they moved back up to her throat. This time the path veered, beginning with her throat, down to the valley between her breasts, keeping that straight line down to her navel. Kali quivered under his touch. She wanted more than this light, maddening touch but knew her pleas wouldn't be heard. He intended to drive her crazy, and he was doing an excellent job of it. Travis's fingertips danced downward, barely brushing against her, but it was enough to send shock waves traveling through her body.

A dark, sensual cloud blanketed the lovers as Travis began trailing his fingertips over her side again. All the time his eyes snared hers, watching the way her pupils dilated. Her skin was flushed and moist, her breathing erratic. When Travis's hand brushed over the damp nest of curls, he found her more than ready for him.

"You are making me crazy," she whispered.

"I'm making both of us crazy," he countered, bending his head to press a light kiss against the curve of her shoulder. Now his lips duplicated each caress his fingers had begun. Kali closed her eyes, allowing each sensation to seep through her by touch only. Besides, she didn't need to have her eyes open to see the lambent fires burning in his eyes, and the deliberate way he aroused her. It was all so calculated, her heart told her. Oh, he might be making love to her, but it wasn't the same as the other times. This time it was all deliberate, as if he meant to prove something to her. She was afraid he was doing just that, and she knew the reason why. He was showing her that this was much more than physical attraction. Lust could never bring about this dark intensity between two people.

Unable to lie still any longer, Kali began exploring Travis's taut body. When his velvety mustache touched her navel, her hands traced the muscles along his shoulders and down to his buttocks. The skin was slick, the muscles fluid under her fingertips.

"You are so beautiful," she whispered, pressing her lips against his hair.

Instead of answering, Travis parted her thighs gently with his tongue. Kali gasped and arched up as the lightning seared her veins. Travis held nothing back. His tongue probed, his breath teased, and his voice murmured dark, loving words against her sensitive skin. Kali's head thrashed from side to side on the pillow. She couldn't get enough air into her tortured lungs as she flew out into the stars. Just when she began to return to earth, Travis moved up and thrust into her with one deep stroke. Kali's eyes opened wide.

"You fit me so perfectly that I doubt you'll ever find another man to replace me," he told her in a voice of midnight. "That's why I intend to leave you with a lot of memories to tide you over those long, cold nights, my love."

Oh, what beautiful memories he made! Kali felt filled and possessed by Travis. She wrapped herself around him, inhaling the musky scent of his skin and relishing the feel of him. She chose not to listen to his words because a naïve part of her still felt he never would leave her.

Travis made love to Kali all night, giving them scant time to rest. She fell asleep sprawled across Travis, her body limp and satiated. He remained awake, stroking her hair and the lines of her body until his own body hardened with desire. He began touching her intimately until she moaned and woke up. She didn't protest when he lifted her on top of him because she wanted him just as badly. Afterward Travis fell into an uneasy sleep.

Chapter
12

When Kali awoke, she was alone in bed and couldn't hear anything to indicate that Travis was in the cabin. She immediately panicked. Grabbing her robe off the floor, she put it on and ran into the living room, then the kitchen, only to find those rooms empty also. The roar of the motorcycle outside alerted her to Travis's whereabouts. Not caring that she was barefoot, she ran outside to find him straddling his bike, revving the engine. Judging by the bags loaded on the back, he was in the midst of leaving—and without a word to her.

"Travis!" she cried out, running toward him. "You were going to leave without saying good-bye, weren't you? Why?"

He took his time removing his helmet. The lover of all those beautiful nights was gone. His harsh countenance and cold eyes left her feeling as if she were looking at a stranger. She didn't know this man.

"I figured it would be better if I took off so we wouldn't have to worry about unnecessary good-byes."

Kali blanched at his very cold and very blunt words. "I thought that after everything . . ." She gestured helplessly.

"Everything?" Travis refused to look at it the same way. "You were the one who decided we would just have a fling until I went back to California."

"You're asking the impossible from me!"

"Am I? Believe me, if I could work from here, I would, but we both know that's just as impossible as your idea that you can't come to California. Instead, you prefer to hide away here in your own little self-erected castle of safety. For a while I thought I had breached your defenses enough that you would brave anything. I should have known better. You're still afraid to come back to the real world. Fine. I don't like what you're doing with your life, Kali. I know I have no choice, and I won't put up with it." He slipped his helmet back on and turned back to the handlebars. "Good-bye, Kali, it's been an education."

She stepped back as he slipped the bike into gear and rolled down the hill. When he reached the highway, he roared off without a wave or a backward glance.

Kali remained standing there for more than ten minutes, disregarding the chilly morning air. She couldn't believe Travis would leave her so callously. No, it had to be some kind of sick joke he was playing on her, and soon she would see him driving up the hill. But twenty minutes later he still hadn't returned. He was gone for good. She moved slowly into the house and poured herself a much-needed cup of coffee to warm her chilled body. Too bad it wouldn't have any effect on her chilled heart.

Kali didn't do very much that day. She felt as numb as she had after Cheryl's kidnapping. She was barely able to function. She built a fire in the fireplace and curled up in a corner of the couch, watching the flames dance. How many times had they made love in front of a roaring fire? Travis had even carried her up to the loft one night, insisting they make love in the bed in which he had slept alone so many nights and in which he'd dreamed about making love to her. The entire cabin was filled with memories; new ones that she wouldn't be allowed to forget easily.

Kali left the cabin early the next morning and arrived at J. C.'s store before it opened. That didn't deter her from pounding on his back door.

"All right, all right, dammit, can't a man eat his breakfast in peace?" he grumbled, opening the door. His frown disappeared when he saw his visitor, swollen red eyes and all. "Come on in," he said in a rumbling voice, stepping back.

"He stopped by here before he left, didn't he?" Kali demanded, walking into the small kitchen.

"Yeah, he did. You don't mind if I get back to my breakfast, do you?" He sat down at the square Formica table in the middle of the kitchen. "There's some coffee left, and juice in the refrigerator."

She shook her head. Placing her hands on the table, Kali leaned toward him. "Well?"

J. C. sighed. It didn't look like he would be able to

finish his breakfast after all. He set his fork and knife down on the edge of his plate and looked up. "He stopped by, made a few phone calls, and bought some beef jerky and some cans of soda." He stared at her with those sharp eyes of his. "He also told me to look after you."

"Anything else?"

J. C.'s silence was answer enough. Her shoulders drooped.

"You've really done it this time, my girl," he told her in his usual blunt manner. "You had the perfect man for you in the palm of your hand, and you let him get away. Never knew you could act so stupid."

"He wanted me to pose for his new book," she threw back.

J. C. didn't say anything, but the expression on his face told her what he thought about that. "So he bedded you and stuck around for so long just so you'd pose for him. Seems he would have lit out sooner if you weren't going to do what he wanted. I'm sure there's plenty of women in L.A. who'd pose for his book and wouldn't give him no back talk, neither."

Kali's eyes blazed at the idea of Travis making love to another woman.

"You're not being fair."

J. C. stood up and carried his plates over to the sink. "No, Kali, *you're* the one who isn't fair. That man loved you, pure and simple. It was pretty obvious yesterday when he asked me to look after you. You've been hidin' yourself out here for too long. In the beginning it was all right, because you were hurtin' and needed to heal. The time for that healin' is over. It's time for you to go back and deal with what happened there."

194

Only Love

"Back to what?" she demanded shrilly, slicing the air with her hand. "There's nothing there for me. All I had out there was pain. Why should I go back to a place that only hurt me?"

"Because there's a good man out there who will take away the pain and give you more love than you know what to do with if you'll only let him," J. C. said gently.

Tears welled up in her eyes. "I do love him, J. C. I love him so much, but I'm also afraid I'll end up hurt again."

He looked exasperated. "What else is it going to take for you to wake up and see you don't belong here anymore?"

"Don't belong," she murmured, shaking her head. "This has always been my home."

"No, lovey, your real home is where your man is, and right now your man is on his way back to California. I suggest you go back to the cabin and think long and hard about it."

Kali nodded and slowly walked outside to her jeep. How could she not belong here? She'd grown up here. All during the drive back to the cabin she thought over what J. C. had said. Had all she done here was hide from real life? Yes, she had come here to heal her wounds and get her life back together, and since there was no pressure and she'd had enough money for personal expenses, she saw no need even to think about returning to L.A.—or going anywhere else, for that matter. Her agent already knew she had no desire to continue her modeling career. It didn't fulfill her anymore. She didn't like to think about the days ahead without Travis, but was she truly brave enough to go back? No matter what, she couldn't make the decision just because of Travis; it had to be for her too.

Travis had been back to work for almost a week, and his employees were beginning to wish he had stayed away longer. While he wasn't known for having a bad temper, his moods had been erratic since his return, and only Jenny was brave enough to go up against him.

"Travis, you're well on your way to being voted the most unpopular man in this galaxy." She cornered him one morning before he had a chance to escape into the studio.

He grimaced. "I guess I haven't been Mr. Congeniality, have I?"

"You got it."

Travis ran his fingers through his already tousled hair. "Okay, I'll work on being nicer, I promise."

Jenny watched him move restlessly around his office.

"You love her, don't you?"

He dropped wearily into his desk chair. "I love that woman so much, it hurts," he admitted. "Trouble is, she doesn't love me enough."

Jenny perched herself on the edge of the desk. "I figured something like that had happened. What I can't understand is why she didn't come back with you."

"That's where 'she doesn't love me enough' comes in." He sighed. "Kali doesn't want to come back to L.A.—ever."

Jenny's lips pursed in a silent *oh*. "She still hurts that much?"

He shrugged. "She thinks so. I could be wrong, but

I think she's afraid that if she comes back, all the pain from her divorce and her daughter's kidnapping will surface again. She has private detectives working to find the girl, but nothing has surfaced so far."

"And that's why you hired some people of your own?" Jenny asked, then went on, clarifying. "The statement came a few days before you got back. It wasn't difficult to figure out why you did it."

He pounded the desktop with his fist. "Dammit, why can't she allow herself to feel something real? Why does she have to be so afraid of getting hurt again?" He groaned with the defeat he had felt from the moment he had left Kali's mountain cabin, and cursed himself roundly for not just hoisting her on the back of his bike and kidnapping her.

Jenny looked at the raw emotion scoring Travis's face and knew just how deeply he cared for Kali. She only wished there was something she could do other than offer advice, and prayed Kali felt as deeply for Travis as he did for her. Yet if she did, why wouldn't she come out here to be with him? Surely she couldn't be hurting as badly as she had in the beginning.

"She may come to realize it when you aren't around," she offered quietly. "As long as you were there, she could believe you'd never leave her. Now that you aren't there, she might come to see how important you are to her."

The stark hope in his eyes was enough to make her cry. "I'd like to think that, Jenny. I really would."

She smiled. "Now, I know you've got it bad. You haven't called me hoss once since you've been back." She held up a hand in warning. "Of course, I'm not complaining, mind you."

197

Travis sighed. "Okay, I've been a first-class bastard. I do promise to shape up, hoss," he added with a trace of his old wicked grin.

Jenny rolled her eyes. "I will probably come to regret our little chat." She strolled out of the office, throwing over her shoulder, "Besides, Deke expects you to shoot those pictures of him this weekend, and you're going to need to eat your Wheaties to keep up with him."

Travis's reply to that was short and to the point. He stared down at the paperwork littering his desk, determined to push Kali out of his mind, however temporarily, and get some work accomplished.

Late that evening he worked in his darkroom, processing the photographs he had taken during his ride eastward and the ones he'd taken of Kali that fateful night.

As each print sat in the developing tray he watched the paper darken and each delicate feature take shape. He had been right, and Kali wrong. The lighting wasn't what he would have used, her lack of makeup discernible, and the first pictures showed her display of temper, but soon the play of emotions on her face revealed sorrow, desire, and love, all rolled up in one beautiful package.

When he was finished, he studied each glossy photo carefully. Memories flooded back in a painful rush as he recalled each time they argued and each time they made love. Just remembering sent his blood rushing to his head. In a fit of temper he had even called an ex-lover of his, determined to put Kali Hughes behind him once and for all. He had wined and dined the woman and escorted her back to her apartment with every intention of spending the night. Instead, he drank a glass of brandy, kissed her, and said good night. He couldn't dredge up the slightest desire for the lovely woman with her perfectly coiffed hair, French perfume, and designer dress when all he wanted was a woman wearing inexpensive clothing and only the hint of a lemony soap added to her own natural fragrance. He was determined never to go through that hell again.

Travis left the darkroom with the collection of photographs of Kali in his hand. The negatives were locked away in a cabinet so no one could inadvertently find them and perhaps find a use for them. While he trusted his employees, there was still the cleaning crew and temporary help that came and went in the studio, and he wasn't about to allow anything to hurt Kali.

It had already been a hellish two weeks, and he wasn't looking forward to the rest of his life. Maybe he should just give her some time and then find a way to take another one or two weeks off and go back there to try to persuade her again to come back with him. Meanwhile, if he had any of the smarts he was supposed to have been born with, he'd get to work on his next book and allow that to fill his otherwise empty hours.

Kali was unhappy. Anyone who saw her shadowed eyes and pale face knew that, especially J. C. He talked to her until he was blue in the face, but he still didn't get anywhere. She still refused to relinquish her fear of going back to L.A.

"Then be prepared to live out your life a lonely, embittered woman," he told her bluntly during his latest lecture. "Because there's no guarantee you'll ever get Cheryl back; not if Harold has anything to say about it. You had a man who loved you and would have done anything for you, and you threw him away. I wonder how you're going to feel when you read about his marriage and later the birth of his kids; kids that should have been yours. You just remember that and I hope you can live with it."

Kali was horrified that he would talk to her in such a cruel manner and ran out of the store without saying anything. But she couldn't run away from his words as easily.

During the drive back up the hill his lecture echoed over and over inside her head. The idea of Travis marrying, having children with someone else, made her feel wretched. No, it couldn't happen! No one could give him what she could.

Give him what? her conscience demanded. *You did throw him away, just as J. C. said. He wanted to give you the world, and you refused without giving him a chance.*

When she reached the cabin, she rushed inside and flew through the house, doing twenty things at once. Within two hours she led the horses into the trailer she had already hooked up to the jeep.

J. C. didn't look surprised when Kali marched back into his store carrying two large cartons.

"Would you keep an eye on the cabin and the horses for me?" she asked without preamble, setting two cartons of food on the counter. "And I'd like to use your phone too." She headed for the basic black telephone in a corner without waiting for an answer.

J. C. grinned. "Hot damn!" He chortled, slapping his knee. "She's finally gettin' some sense in that thick head of hers."

* * *

Travis had been out of the studio for two long and frustrating days due to working with Deke, who had decided to go on a binge. Travis had taken it upon himself to dry his old friend out. When he returned to the studio late one morning, Jenny attacked him with a vengeance.

"Why haven't you returned my calls?" she demanded, stalking him back to his office.

"I've been busy." He looked at her quizzically, surprised that his usually unflappable assistant acted so upset. "I can't believe something came up around here that you couldn't handle, so you might as well tell me why I'm in trouble."

She stood in front of him, her hands braced on her hips. "True, any emergency I can handle, but this isn't something I should have to worry about unless you want *me* to pick Kali up at the airport."

Travis froze. "When?" he asked sharply, afraid to believe his ears.

"The telegram came two days ago. It wasn't marked 'personal' so I opened it. It was just as well I did; otherwise, you might not have been at the airport and she would have thought the worst, wouldn't she?"

His lips thinned. "When, dammit!"

"Ten o'clock tonight."

Travis looked down at his desk, cluttered as usual. He was positive there was work there that required his immediate attention, but he couldn't think about anything but the fact that Kali was coming to him.

"I called your cleaning lady to come in today and get your house ready. I also made a hotel reservation in case Kali prefers privacy," his assistant went on.

"And, yes, there's work here you should be doing, but I doubt you'd be of any use to us. Go on home, do whatever you do there to remain calm, and be sure to arrive at the airport with time to spare."

Travis ran over to Jenny and picked her up, spinning her around in a circle.

"Do you realize how happy you've made me?" He grinned, feeling more lighthearted than he had in a long time.

"I have a pretty good idea." She laughed. "Don't you think you ought to get going?"

Travis stopped long enough to drop off the film he had taken of Deke before running out of the studio. His motorcycle kicked up a great deal of dust as he roared off, and how he managed to arrive home without a speeding ticket was a miracle. Of course, the way he felt now, he firmly believed in miracles.

Not knowing what to do with himself, Travis wandered through the house until his cleaning lady ordered him out by suggesting he take a ride, go to the beach, *anything* but bother her.

He rode for several hours, ate the dinner his cleaning lady had left for him, and watched the clock hands move slowly until it was time to leave for the airport.

As it was, the flight was late, since the evening flights were stacked up overhead. Travis strode into the bar for a drink, changed his mind because he didn't want liquor on his breath, then changed his mind again. His insides were knotted up with anticipation of seeing Kali, and he decided he needed something to calm him down. A whiskey was just the ticket.

Only Love

* * *

Kali sat in her first-class seat wishing they were on the ground. She wasn't a good flyer to begin with, and a bumpy four-hour flight hadn't helped. She drank several Kahluas with milk to soothe her jumpy nerves, but all she ended up with was a woozy head. She looked out the window but could see only tiny lights below.

Had Travis gotten her telegram? Would he be there to pick her up or would she find herself on her own? That was silly. If he hadn't wanted her in L.A., wouldn't he have let her know? He wouldn't have let her come all this way to be humiliated, would he? Why not? She had done a number on him; why shouldn't he be allowed some revenge? She looked down at her hands, lying tensely in her lap. She had tried reading a book, then several magazines, and even attempted to watch the movie but couldn't concentrate on any one thing but the thought of seeing Travis again. She was so frightened. She had planned never to come back, but she hadn't known Travis would be a part of her life then. After meeting him, she knew her future would never be the same. Her flight to L.A. was proof of it.

She made another trip to the small lavatory in the front of the jet but saw the same person in the mirror she had seen before. Pale face, large eyes, makeup long worn off; she had only put if on for moral support, anyway, her hair pulled back in a French braid, a raspberry wool sweater with a matching striped shirt beneath and jeans. She certainly didn't look like anything to write home about. But Travis knew what she looked like. He had seen her looking even worse. She just wished the damn plane would land so her period of turmoil would be over. If she'd been smart, she would have drunk her way cross-country. Then she wouldn't have cared whether Travis was there or not!

Travis spent the time wandering through the terminal, watching people, idly noting if a person looked like a good subject or not. It was a habit of his, and he always made sure never to stare at someone for too long that they became uncomfortable. He glanced at his watch again. They kept announcing that the flights were stacked up. When would they announce Kali's flight? He wasn't always the most patient of men, and right now he felt ready to chew his nails. He wanted to see her walk off the plane and into his arms. He needed to feel her, to taste her, to hear her voice. Then he would know everything was all right. Okay, maybe *everything* wouldn't be all right, but if she was with him, that would be close enough for him after he took her to his home and made love to her. He needed to have her wrapped all around him, to feel himself buried deep inside her, to wake up next to her. Hell, he just plain needed her. His head lifted when he heard the dispassionate voice announcing the arrival of Kali's flight and the gate number. He hurried over to the appropriate gate so he would be sure not to miss her when she stepped off the plane.

Finally! Kali gathered up her heavy jacket, nylon tote bag, and purse. She stood up, fully prepared to leave the plane as soon as possible. She passed a trembling hand over her hair, found a few loose strands, but nothing to worry about. She was glad she had spritzed on some cologne a little while ago, so she wouldn't feel completely grubby.

She walked slowly behind the other passengers as they disembarked. The tunnel from the plane to the terminal never seemed so long. Was he there? She took several deep breaths to calm her ravaged nerves and wished she hadn't turned down that last drink on the plane. Oh, well, she'd never been one for false courage.

Travis stood back a short distance and to the side. From that position he was able to see Kali before she saw him. She looked tired and very tense. He wanted nothing more than to run to her and enfold her in his arms, but he would wait for her to see him, to walk that final distance.

As if sensing his presence, Kali's head swung around to face the dark, enigmatic gaze. She halted and stared long and hard at him before her feet moved slowly in his direction.

"My plane was late," she explained unnecessarily, standing before him.

There was the faintest touch of a smile lurking in the corners of his lips. She looked so forlorn, she was irresistible.

"I'm glad you came," he said finally, leaning down to press the lightest, but no less potent, of kisses on her lips.

The breath Kali had been holding for so long left her body in a silent rush. "I was afraid you wouldn't be here," she said honestly.

"I almost wasn't."

Her faint smile disappeared.

Travis relented. "I was out in the desert shooting

some publicity photos for a friend of mine and just got back into town. Jenny cornered me the minute I got into the studio and gave me your telegram." He draped an arm around her shoulders as they walked toward the escalator. "You needn't have worried, Kali, I would have been here, come hell or high water."

She ducked her head. "I don't know why I came." Her voice was muffled and sounded suspiciously tearful.

He hugged her more tightly against his side. "I don't know why, either, but I'm glad you did."

They walked slowly, since they knew it would take some time for the baggage to be unloaded.

"How was your flight?" Travis hated small talk, but everything else he wanted to say couldn't be said in a public place.

Kali wrinkled her nose. "I've had better. I'm not a good flier to begin with."

They entered the baggage area and located the carousel that would carry Kali's flight. A few pieces had already been unloaded, but nothing that matched her nylon tote.

"There it is." She pointed out the small bag coming their way.

Travis lifted an eyebrow and glanced at her sideways. "That's it?"

"I don't have much in the way of clothing for out here, so I figured if I need anything, I can do some shopping."

Travis picked up the bag and led the way outside to the parking garage, Kali following.

She looked around the exterior of the new terminal, feeling very much like a hick coming to the big city for the first time. Much had changed and much had stayed the same. The terminal was new, and Travis mentioned that there was also a new international terminal, and the parking garages had been expanded. Kali was sensitive to the noise, the gas fumes, the cars honking, and loud voices speaking loudly in several languages. She could feel a headache coming on, and the knot in her chest tightening.

I shouldn't have come back here! she cried out to herself, hurrying to cross the street with Travis. *Why didn't I stay where I felt safe?* That was when she realized that she was more apprehensive about the noise and the people than the fears she thought she would have: the idea of her divorce and Cheryl's kidnapping being brought up again, and other fears that only lurked in her mind. After all, why should she be afraid when Travis was there to protect her? If she could keep a tight hold on that thought, she'd be all right.

Travis noted Kali's unease and correctly interpreted it. He glanced around the empty garage and stopped a few paces from his parking space near the elevator. He grabbed Kali's hand, pulled her into a dark corner, and backed her up against the wall.

"And now for the appropriate welcome back," he murmured, lowering his head and capturing her mouth with hungry ease, a hunger Kali was feeling as well. Soft moans welled up in her throat as she dropped her bag and slid her arms around his neck, arching her body up against his warmth.

Travis's tongue thrust roughly into her receptive mouth and foraged every sweet corner. He hadn't forgotten the taste of her; he just wanted to reinforce it. His hands fumbled with her heavy jacket, lowering the zipper so his hands could reinforce the feel of her breasts, already swollen with their need. As swollen as his own need.

"You little witch, I should strangle you for making me wait so long for you," he muttered, rubbing his torso against hers. Her nipples puckered under his slightest touch, which only served to drive him crazier. He knew if he didn't draw back now, he would be taking her against this wall, and he wanted all the privacy he could get for their reunion. He pulled back reluctantly. "I think we'd better get going before we give any unexpected visitors a show." He led her toward his Corvette.

"Not what I expected." Kali couldn't help but admire the classic fire-engine-red racing machine.

"Not expected of me?"

She nodded. "I guess I thought you would have something rougher." She felt apologetic.

Travis grinned. "Don't worry, I have a truck with four wheel drive if that will make you feel better." He placed her inside the low-slung car and walked around to the driver's side. Within seconds they were racing down the ramp to the exit.

Kali looked around as they drove down Century Boulevard. The heavy traffic, even that late at night, was a shock to her system.

"I feel so out of it," she confessed, turning back around in the bucket seat to face him. "A traffic jam in Newton's Gap usually consists of two cars wanting to make the same turn. I've been gone so long, this is a shock to me."

"You'll get used to it."

Would she? She wasn't so sure.

Only Love

"Where are we going?" She noticed Travis took the south on ramp to the freeway.

"My house." He shot a quick glance in her direction. "Any problem with that?"

Was there? At least he wasn't taking her to a hotel. Kali knew she didn't want to be alone tonight, and she also knew she needed Travis more than she had ever needed him before.

"No, none at all."

Chapter
13

Even for the late hour, the freeway was busy. Kali looked around at the cars racing past them, even though Travis was driving at a little over sixty-five miles per hour.

"Whatever happened to the fifty-five-miles-per-hour speed limit?" she murmured, forgetting she hadn't kept to the speed limit since the first day she'd started driving.

He flashed her a wide grin. "That's only for when the California Highway Patrol is sneaking around." He changed lanes and took the next off ramp.

"Where exactly do you live?" She stared straight ahead. *I shouldn't have come. In time I would have gotten over him.* She noticed that even the side roads seemed crowded.

"Rolling Hills." *Why is she so stiff? Is she that afraid of something happening? What will it take for her to realize I'm not going to let anything happen to her, that I'd protect her with my life?*

Kali repressed a shiver. The party where she had first met Travis had been in Rolling Hills, an exclusive community that was zoned for horses and not far from Palos Verdes, another exclusive residential area that overlooked the sea.

"I usually don't attend parties given by neighbors, but I'm glad I made that exception," he told her, aware of her unease. "They got a divorce a year ago and sold the house. A very strange lady who collects cats lives there now." He reached over to grasp her hand and squeezed it tightly. "Why don't you close your eyes. I can imagine you're dead on your feet, and a little bit of rest wouldn't hurt. We'll be there soon."

Closing her eyes sounded like a good idea, but Kali was afraid of falling asleep. She wanted to see the place where Travis lived, to see if it matched his rough-edged personality.

She wasn't disappointed. The house was set high up in the hills, amid enough acreage that it appeared to be entirely secluded. She caught a glimpse of the barn, lit up by the headlights when Travis drove around to the rear of the sprawling ranch-style house.

"We don't stand on ceremony here." Travis helped her out of the car before pulling her bags out of the trunk. "Through there." He used her tote bag to point the way under a covered walkway to a door with a floodlight overhead that lit up the area leading to the detached garage.

They entered a kitchen that was sparkling clean with modern appliances and absolutely no personality. Kali looked over the room, noticed the absence of any usual clutter and gauged it was used for little other than making coffee and keeping the beer cold in the refrigerator.

"Actually I'm surprised there isn't six inches of dust on the counters," she said dryly, shrugging off her heavy jacket in deference to the heat flowing through the vents.

Travis grimaced. "Jenny sent the cleaning lady in so the place wouldn't scare you off."

Kali spun around, revealing a wariness in her eyes. "Jenny knows about us?"

"She did a lot of guessing. I didn't tell her if she was right or wrong." Travis watched her closely, thinking she probably should have kept her coat on. Then he wouldn't be so interested in the rise and fall of her breasts, remembering how they looked when they were pink and moist from his kisses. "If the idea of you staying here bothers you so much, I can still take you to a hotel. Jenny made a reservation for you."

She shook her head almost violently, her eyes wide and dark. "Please, Travis, I don't want to stay somewhere impersonal. I won't be any trouble, I promise."

He stifled a groan. Trouble, her? He steered her into the den and, before turning on any lights, dropped her bags and pulled her into his arms with one easy motion. His mouth covered hers just as hungrily as it had in the airport parking garage, if not more. Here there was no fear of interruption. Kali's arms looped around his neck to provide easier access as her sweater was jerked upward and her shirt ripped open. His hands were cool on her bare breasts at first, but warmed rapidly.

"You sure took your time getting here." Travis's voice was a deep rumble in his chest as he pressed hungry kisses all over her face.

"I missed you so much, it almost seemed sinful." She sighed, arching up under his caresses.

"I can't remember the last time I've been able to eat a decent meal what with thinking about you."

"You probably haven't eaten a decent meal unless someone has cooked one for you." She shivered with delight when his tongue teased the curved whorls of her ear.

"If you're asking in a roundabout way if there's been any other woman cooking for me, you can be rest assured the only women who've cooked a meal for me worked in a fast-food restaurant." His breathing grew raspy with desire.

Buttons were undone by swift fingers, zippers nimbly released, sensual explorations made by curious hands. Sighs echoed in the empty room as they fell slowly to the carpet, first kneeling as they continued running their hands over each other's bodies to reacquaint themselves with the hard planes and soft curves, and then lying on their sides, their bodies lightly touching as if afraid to part for the shortest time.

"The bed seemed so large after you left."

"Mine was cold without you in it."

"J. C. called me a coward for not coming after you sooner."

"No, not a coward, just stubborn. Good thing I love

stubborn women." His mustache brushed erotically over the nipple, already puckered from the cool air and the long wait for the warm possession of his mouth.

"I am a coward."

"Cowards don't make love the way you do."

"Your skin feels so warm."

"If you think my chest is warm, you should try a tad south. There's a regular heat wave down there."

"Mmm, you're right about the temperature of the southern hemisphere. I wonder if there's a foolproof method for cooling it off."

"Not the way you're doing the job." He gasped as her hand encircled the part of him pulsing with life and desire for her.

"I need you so badly."

"I second the motion."

"Um, *this* motion?"

"That will do for a start."

"And then?"

"And then this." Travis showed her by thrusting deeply into her waiting sheath. Their caresses had been hurried in an attempt to make up for lost time, and their lovemaking was now frenzied, hot, and hard. He had made only a few deep thrusts before Kali arched upward with a cry, her body convulsing around his. She wrapped herself around him as her skin flamed with fires hotter than a volcano, fires that Travis felt just as strongly. This was no leisurely coupling; they needed each other's possession to feel whole again. Before long, Travis's body also convulsed, and he cried her name in the heat of desire. They remained locked together, their breathing erratic as they slowly returned to the present.

After a while the air in the room began to feel cold. Travis stood up, swept her up into his arms, and carried her to the rear of the house to his bedroom, where he made sure the covers were piled around her before he climbed into bed next to her. It wasn't long before they were reaching for each other again. A long night of loving lay in store.

Kali was too comfortable to wake up fully. The covers around her were warm, as was the body lying next to her. Her eyes were still closed against the morning sun, her lips curved in a smile. All in all, she hadn't felt so good in a long time, not since the last time she and Travis had shared a bed. She half turned when a hand stole across her abdomen and began rubbing a warm caress across her soft skin.

"Do you always look so happy when you wake up?" Travis's whiskey-rough voice was music to her ears.

"It depends on who I wake up with," she couldn't resist saying.

Travis took the bait very nicely. He rolled her over the rest of the way until she had no choice but to look up at his scowling features.

"I suggest you amend that statement to 'when you wake up with *me*,'" he advised darkly, lowering his body over her so she could feel his potent desire burning her skin. He framed her head between his hands and looked deep into her eyes, seeing the smile echoed on her lips.

Her eyes sparkled, her smile tinged with feminine provocation. "Make me," her voice almost purred with invitation.

"Darlin', I thought you'd never ask." He lowered his head, his lips brushing across hers before slanting more fully over them and taking her breath away with incredible ease.

After their hurried lovemaking the night before, they should have wanted to take all the time in the world, but it wasn't possible. They still needed each other too much to wait. Kali's fingers encircled Travis with love, urging him to join with her, an invitation he was loath to refuse.

"Why did you have to wait so damn long before coming to me?" he said raspily, sliding easily into her.

She smiled through a mist of happy tears. "Because I'm stubborn, just as you said." She wrapped her arms around his back and held him tightly against her.

As before, they loved furiously. Kali was positive she had died and gone to heaven, with Travis's arms around her and his tongue thrusting into her mouth in loving imitation of their bodies.

As Kali felt herself climaxing, her body arched upward to receive even more of the man she loved so deeply. Her nails raked his bare back as she shattered into fiery pieces.

"Oh, Kali!" Travis cried out as pleasure burst over him.

Kali looked up to see the fierce love shining in Travis's dark eyes, and she felt safe at last, and secure.

When she next awoke, the sun was shining high in the sky, and only shadows lingered in the bedroom due to drapes drawn halfway across the large sliding glass door. She half sat up to study her surroundings when the door opened and Travis walked in carrying a tray.

"Good, you're awake," he said, greeting her with a

warm kiss. "I brought you some breakfast." He set the tray in front of her.

Kali looked startled at the array of food before her. Scrambled eggs without a burned edge to them, sausage, two slices of French toast topped with syrup, juice, and coffee.

"I'm impressed," she told him after taking her first experimental bite. "And you said you couldn't cook," she accused lightly, offering him a nibble of her French toast.

"I can't. But I can open packages and throw them in the microwave with the best of them. It's amazing what you can find in the frozen-food section nowadays."

Kali looked down at her food again and back up at Travis to see if he was teasing. There was no doubt he was telling the truth.

"So you slaved over a hot microwave just for me. Now I *am* impressed." And she proved it with another, much more satisfying, kiss.

Travis exhaled a deep breath when they finally parted. "As much as I hate to say this, I've got to go into the studio today. I've got something going that needs to be finished by this afternoon, and I'm going to have to bust my butt to finish it by then, due to a very sexy lady who decided to seduce me this morning."

"I don't recall hearing any complaining on your part."

"I was lucky I could breathe, much less say anything."

For one brief moment Kali felt the irrational fear of his leaving her. She wanted to throw her arms around him and beg him not to leave her alone, but she knew she couldn't do that. After all, he had probably held up a great deal of his work for her sake, and quite possibly lost clients, due to his staying with her so long in Virginia. The least she could do was understand and send him off with a smile.

"Then you won't mind if I relax in a long hot bath and spend the day exploring your house?" she asked lightly.

Travis noted the tension darkening her eyes and knew why it was there but said nothing. He was relieved that she was trying so hard to sound matter-of-fact.

"It's all yours." They both knew he wasn't speaking idle words. "There're a few things in the refrigerator. My cleaning lady stocked up, although I have no idea what's in there. The studio number is coded into the phone, so all you have to do is dial two. With luck I should be back by six-thirty, seven at the latest." He looked down at the tempting sight of bare shoulders, tousled hair, and swollen lips and thought of saying the hell with his work and staying home, but knew he couldn't do that. Kali was going to have to learn to cope with California living all over again, and perhaps in the beginning she should do it at her own pace.

She managed to flash him a bright smile. "Have a good day. I'll fix you dinner."

"We can go out."

Tension rippled across her face for a bare second. "No, that's all right. I enjoy cooking," she managed to say brightly. "I'll rummage through the refrigerator and see what I can find. You go on. The sooner you're gone, the sooner you'll be home again."

Travis silently rejoiced at her referring to his house

as home. "Fine, see you later, then. Don't worry about any unwanted company. My cleaning lady only comes about once a week usually." He couldn't resist one last kiss and groaned as he pulled back with a great show of reluctance. "You're right. If I don't get out of here soon, I won't leave at all." He stood up and strode briskly out of the room.

A few moments later Kali heard his motorcycle roar past the house and gradually fade away. She finished her breakfast, put the tray to one side, and got out of bed to take her bath. While the water ran into the tub she carried the dirty dishes into the kitchen and washed them up quickly. She smiled at the memory of finding her suitcases and discarded clothing from the night before sitting sedately in the bedroom that morning. Instead of pulling on her robe, she wore Travis's shirt while doing the dishes. With his musky scent surrounding her she felt comforted as she performed the domestic chores. A glance into the refrigerator proved Travis's cleaning lady had stocked up with the basics and gave her a few ideas on what to fix for dinner that evening. A search of the freezer showed her what Travis normally ate. She hadn't realized there were so many frozen dinners available that were microwaveable. As she explored the kitchen she noticed a separate hand-held dialer attached to the wall phone. Every space was taken up with a name and number. Curious as to why he needed so many numbers, Kali looked down at it closer, then burst out laughing. The numbers appeared to be lumped together in categories: Mexican, Chinese, Italian, Korean, Thai, and a few others that had to be good old-fashioned American. A quick look in the phone book told her the rest of the story. Travis had a phone system that connected him to just about every restaurant in the county that delivered or had take-out facilities!

A long, relaxing soak in the tub eased a few aching muscles and allowed Kali to think about what she would do while here. That was certainly something she hadn't thought through as well as she should have. Travis still wanted her to pose for him, she was sure of it, but could she really go through with it? Even with Travis there would be pressure. It couldn't be helped, because that was part of the game. She stirred restively in the hot, bubbly water. Deciding it was time to do something useful, she climbed out of the tub and dried off quickly, dressing in jeans and a warm sweatshirt that carried brightly colored letters on the front saying "I Don't Want to Grow Up," a birthday gift from Jenny.

An exploration of Travis's property revealed the small horse barn with two Arabians housed inside. She took the time to greet them before moving on to peek into the garage and wander around the grassy property. He was right, with the large acreage a person did feel as if there were no one else around for miles. It was a feeling of privacy she enjoyed and thought she could have only in Virginia.

Kali spent the rest of the day cutting up vegetables and browning meat for stew and looking through Travis's meager supply of magazines. Admittedly, most weren't to her taste, being motorcycle and photography periodicals, but there were a few recent fashion and women's magazines that she thought he might have purchased with her in mind. She also found herself listening to the answering machine click on each time the phone rang. Nine out of ten calls were from women.

"At the tone, please leave your name, number, and a brief message." Travis's voice sounded just as sexy on tape.

"Travis, honey, it's Donna. I haven't heard from you in ages, and your assistant said she won't accept any more calls at your studio. Give me a call." The syrupy voice was more than any one person could handle.

"Travis, this is Andrea. Lyle Sloane is giving a party next weekend, and I hope you can go with me. Would you call me as soon as possible?"

"Travis, you SOB, we're getting together next Saturday afternoon at Deke's place for a beer bash. You'd better show up, or we'll invade that fancy house of yours for a *real* party, and you know the kind I mean." This had to be one of his motorcycle buddies.

With a brief grin Kali wondered how Travis managed his busy social schedule. She also couldn't ignore the twinges of jealousy at the idea of his going out with other women. She believed him when he said there had been no one else in his bed since his return to California, but that hadn't meant he had lived a monk's life before that.

During her inspection of the large den, which held a large-screen television and a complex stereo system, she also found a wall covered with photographs. Several of them were obviously of his family, a tall woman with his smile and eyes, several men of varied ages with the unmistakable family resemblance, and one of a tall gray-haired man that would be the perfect picture of Travis when he grew older. She also found many photographs of herself, the ones that had been taken that night in her cabin. With her unerring eye she saw the same magic Travis had. As clear as day, her love for Travis showed in the way she posed, in the glow in her eyes and the smile on her lips. The woman in the photograph held a beauty only one in love could possess. She stood there for the longest time looking at the pictures, seeing a woman she hadn't known existed. And there had been no pressure when those pictures were taken, except the kind under which she had put herself.

"All right, you've been running around all morning ignoring me, but now you're cornered and I want to know that Kali is here and all right." Jenny fixed Travis with a no-nonsense glare as he dropped into his desk chair.

He grimaced. "You're the worst nag I have ever known. Okay, okay, Kali is doing fine. She's at my house." He glowered at Jenny's knowing expression. "And she's staying there." He made it sound more like a threat than a statement.

"I guess that means you won't be staying late tonight."

"You got it." The idea of Kali in his home, waiting for him, left him feeling warm. He wished he were back there now instead of waiting around here for a temperamental model. He sincerely wished he hadn't taken this assignment, even if it was for a friend. Working with bad-tempered models wasn't worth the money, and the next time such a request came through he was going to turn it down flat, friend or no friend.

Travis unwrapped a couple of sticks of gum and

popped them into his mouth. He glanced down at the outline he had made regarding his new book. On paper it looked great. In two days he was due to see a woman who had lived in Paris under the German occupation during World War II. He knew of someone who had written an article about the woman, and he wanted to photograph her for his book. This woman had undergone trials few people could understand, and he wanted that strength to be revealed on film. He thought about asking Kali if she wanted to tag along. Perhaps if she saw how he worked, she might relent long enough to allow him to photograph her.

"Jenny!" he bellowed. "If she isn't here in the next ten minutes, I'm not using her. I don't get paid for sitting around on my ass waiting for God knows what. I've got other work that can be done."

"Okay," she called back. "And, Travis, next time use the phone and save your voice. That's why we have an intercom system."

"Maybe, but it isn't as satisfying."

Kali had checked the stew, glanced at the clock, and knew Travis should be home at any time. It all felt so domestic to her, nothing like what she had felt with Blayne. Possibly because he never cared to eat at home or have her cook. That was better left to the servants, he had enjoyed informing her.

Not wanting Travis to catch her looking her worst, she brushed her hair until it shone, added a spritz of cologne, and was in the midst of debating what to change into since she didn't have any sexy lounging outfits when she heard the sound of a key in the lock and the kitchen door opening and closing.

"Kali?" Travis's shout was music to her ears.

She ran from one end of the house to the other to reach his open arms.

"Um, the best part of the day," he murmured, capturing her mouth with his. "I missed you."

She smiled under his kiss. "I believe you said something very similar last night."

"That was missing you because you lived in another state," he explained, taking a great interest in the delicate arch of her throat. "Today I missed you because I knew you were in my house and I couldn't be here. Something smells good."

"I made stew." She found it difficult to catch her breath when his hand slipped under her sweatshirt and found her unbound breast. He mumbled a few incoherent words has he palmed the warm flesh.

"Enough for two?"

Kali chuckled, remembering a few of the meals she had delighted in making. "More than enough. In fact, a few extra minutes on the stove wouldn't hurt it a bit." She rubbed herself invitingly against him, taking delight in his instant arousal.

"Make it an hour and you've got a deal." He grasped her hips and brought her fully against him.

"I'll turn down the heat, you turn down the bed." She slipped away to head for the kitchen.

"Honey, if you're serious about turning down the heat, you'd better come with me," he called after her, a wicked laugh underlying his words.

When Kali returned to the bedroom, she not only found the bed covers turned down but also Travis lying there in all his glory. A glory she was determined to savor to its fullest. She was glad she had turned down the heat, because they didn't return to

225

the kitchen for an hour and a half to eat their dinner of stew and buttermilk biscuits.

"I like your house," Kali told him as they relaxed after dinner with glasses of wine in the den.

"I'm glad. I admit it's a bit large for one person but I like the space, and the idea of horse property was appealing." He settled back against the couch more fully with Kali nestled securely on one side of him, his arm around her shoulders. Damn, it all felt so right to him! Why couldn't she see it and stay out here with him where she belonged? Travis was tempted to say just that to Kali but knew he would only meet with resistance and he didn't want that, not after her covering her fear long enough to make a visit. What she didn't know was that he didn't intend to allow her to return to her hideaway.

"I saw the pictures you took of me," she said quietly, leaning forward to place the wineglass on the coffee table.

He waited until she was back in his arms before speaking. "And?"

"And you're brilliant, which I'm sure you already know." She sounded peeved at her admission.

Travis chuckled. "Talk about someone hating to admit the truth."

"Talk about someone so arrogant that he's breaking his arm patting himself on the back."

He brushed aside the hair covering her ear and nuzzled it with his lips. "I only wish I could act arrogant where you're involved," he murmured, half turning so that his body covered hers.

"You do."

"Do I? So why don't I feel as if you're all mine?"

"I've been yours since that New Year's Eve so long

226

ago," she said breathlessly, feeling his hand sweep up her leg from knee to thigh.

"Have you?" His lips traced the sensitive skin from her ear to the curve of her collarbone, his mustache leaving tactile sensations along the way.

"Yes, I—I couldn't let—" She gasped for air as the heat flowed from his body into hers. "I didn't want him touching me . . . making love to me after you kissed me."

Travis exhaled a deep breath. "You mean, after you saw him with that woman." He wanted complete clarification from her. He wanted to hear the words from her and not have to figure it out for himself.

She shook her head. "No, by then it was too late for us." She shifted her legs when his hand found the juncture at the base of her jeans zipper. "You—you made me see that. You made me feel things I hadn't known existed, and now . . ." She breathed deeply, wondering when he would stop this erotic teasing. "I know no one else could give me what you have."

He smiled against the upper curve of her breast where he had pulled the soft material down. "I do believe the neckline is stretched beyond repair. I guess I owe you a new sweatshirt."

Kali pressed her fingertips against the base of his neck and pulled him back up to meet her loving gaze. "You could rip all my clothes to shreds and I wouldn't put up a word of protest. Of course, you'd have to buy me a new wardrobe, and I can prove to be expensive."

He grinned. "I do believe the prospect would be more than worth it. But for now let's just help each

227

other ease these clothes off," he began, showing her exactly what he meant, "and we'll get into the ripping at a later date."

"Sounds good to me."

Chapter
14

"Why is it so important that I go along with you?" Kali demanded, a touch of her old antagonism resurfacing.

He sighed. How did one simple request turn into such a big deal? "I didn't say it was important, I merely suggested that you might like to go with me. You could see how I work."

"I don't think so. I'm still so tired from my trip, I'd really prefer staying here and getting in some relaxation time." She refused to look at him.

Travis braced his hands on his hips, looking down at the floor as if all the answers would magically appear. "You're tired," he stated flatly. "You've been here for almost a week, and all you've done is relax.

At least *your* idea of relaxing, since you usually cook, clean, or go horseback riding along the back trails. Yet, you don't want to go out to breakfast, lunch, or dinner. Not to mention going to a damn movie where no one would see you because it's dark inside!" His voice remained quiet but deadly all the same. "I thought you had gotten rid of some of those fears when you came out here, but you haven't, have you? The only difference is instead of hiding away in your cabin, you're hiding away in this house."

Kali stiffened. "If you don't like having me here, just say so. I can just as easily go to a hotel."

His jaw tightened with the temper he was working hard to contain. "That isn't what I mean, and you know it. Besides, did you ever stop to think that if you were in a hotel, you'd be *forced* to go out among the masses for meals and such? Here you only have to go as far as the kitchen."

Kali knew she was acting unreasonable, that her fears were irrational. She also knew she was hurting Travis after all the love and kindness he'd showered upon her the past week. Didn't he surprise her with flowers the day before, and a box of her favorite candy the day before that? He had never asked anything of her except for her to accompany him on this assignment, but she was afraid to go. It wasn't a fear of crowds or meeting new people that plagued her but a fear that once she got back into the mainstream, she wouldn't be able to return to the peace and quiet of the mountains. J. C. may have said she was better off leaving Virginia, but she wasn't so sure.

"You'll be busy doing your work, and I'll just feel like a fifth wheel among your crew," she argued.

He smiled and shook his head. "There will be no

crew save you carrying my case if it would make you feel better to help out. These will not be studio shots that are carefully posed and backlit. I prefer natural light and natural poses. I'm talking about people here, not models in a fancy magazine."

But Kali still felt uneasy. If she hadn't left L.A. years ago, perhaps she wouldn't be undergoing these self-made fears now. And as Travis had told her, he would have been on her doorstep as soon as it was humanly possible. Would she have allowed him inside her home and, ultimately, her heart? Probably, but not without the same kind of fight she was putting up now.

"Is it that important to you that I come?" Her question was scarcely audible.

"I want you to see how I work, Kali, and I want you to be with me. Haven't I made that plain enough before?"

She nodded. "Give me a few minutes." She turned away and walked back to the bedroom.

It was twenty minutes before Kali appeared in a pair of jeans and a cornflower-blue silk shirt.

"I don't have any citified clothes left," she explained, gesturing to herself.

Travis looked down at his own well-worn jeans, scuffed boots, and plaid shirt. "I don't think you have anything to worry about, but if you'd feel better, we can always go shopping later today or tomorrow," he suggested.

Kali managed a weak smile. "Can we take it one day at a time?" she requested.

"Anything."

Travis had told Kali little about the woman he was going to photograph other than that she had been in

231

Paris during the German Occupation and had been part of the French Underground. The woman had lost her husband and three sons during that time but still managed to do a great deal to fight for her country. She had moved to the United States when her daughter married an American serviceman, and it was only recently that her story had been told in a women's magazine. Travis wanted her in his book and had contacted her immediately. He also wanted Kali to see how he worked in hopes that she might feel more receptive about posing for him.

The house they arrived at looked more like a tiny country cottage in San Pedro, with its neatly clipped front lawn and colorful flower beds framing the walkway and around the house.

Helene Dumont was another surprise. Kali assumed she had to be in her late sixties or early seventies, but she looked much younger, with silver-streaked hair and a virtually unlined face considering the hard, and many times dangerous, life she had led. Over the years her outward beauty had diminished, but she had a inner beauty that would never fade.

"I am pleased to meet you both." The older woman greeted them with a warm smile, her accent still heavy, even after all the years of residing in the United States. She studied Travis with a sharp eye. "So you are the man who wants to put my picture in a book. You shouldn't be taking pictures of me when you have someone so lovely to focus your camera on." She gestured toward Kali.

He smiled back. "Perhaps I look for more than a pretty face."

Helene offered them coffee and light-as-air pastries before seating herself in an old-fashioned armchair. "We have discussed your book on the phone, but I would like to talk about it now where I can see your face while you speak of it."

Travis inclined his head in agreement. "All right." From there he went into a thorough outline of what he wanted to show in his book. "People suffer for many reasons and reveal that suffering in many ways," he finished. "I want to show that it doesn't mean the end of one's life, but perhaps the beginning."

Kali sat through the exchange with a sense of wonder. Was this truly what he meant when he had first talked about his photo book with her? All she had thought about were the many books published about various countries, exotic tropical fish, and other subjects, but nothing like this. Had she underestimated him that much?

For the rest of the day Kali learned even more about Travis and his work. He was unfailingly patient with Helene as he urged her to remain seated in the overstuffed chair and merely rearranged the curtains by way of controlling the lighting. As he shot roll after roll of film he urged her to talk about her days in occupied Paris, and that was how he caught the facial expressions he was looking for. Kali remained in the background, watching him work with an incredible amount of patience that she never would have credited to a photographer.

"I enjoyed listening to your stories, Madame," Travis told Helene several hours later after he had packed up his equipment. "I only wish I had the gift of words to write them down. They should be told, and not just in a magazine article."

"Perhaps one day I will find someone I can work

with," she replied before turning to Kali. "I still believe, my dear, that you should be the one before the camera."

"I used to be," Kali admitted a bit shyly. "I was a model until a few years ago."

Helene studied Kali carefully, then the truth dawned on her. "Ah, yes, now I remember." She grasped Kali's hand with her two warm palms and held it tightly. "I'm sure everything will turn out all right for you. It is not a good way for someone to gain inner strength, but it will make you better able to fight when the time comes. You are always welcome in my home." She scanned both to indicate that the invitation was for each of them.

"Well?" Travis glanced at Kali after they had left the house.

She shrugged self-consciously. "All right, it wasn't what I expected. Does that make you happy?"

"Not as happy as I'd feel if I could take you out to dinner tonight."

"All right." The two words came out in a rush before she could lose her courage.

Travis showed no signs of victory from her capitulation, although inside he was shouting for joy. He turned at the next corner.

"In the mood for seafood?" he asked casually.

"That sounds good."

"Fine, let's go over to Ports O'Call. Afterward you can drag me into all the shops."

When they first arrived at the seaport doubling as a shopping arcade with several restaurants, Kali felt apprehensive. Without feeling egotistical, she convinced herself someone would recognize her and her time of anonymity would be over. By now she had realized that running away had only intensified the problem when she should have stayed and worked out her problems. She could have quit modeling without resorting to fleeing the state. She could have gone back to Virginia for a few months, then returned here. But she hadn't, and her emotions were paying the price.

In time she was able to relax, with Travis's help. Who couldn't relax and have fun with such a personable escort? He was the perfect dinner companion, alert to her every need, and every wish was granted before it was even aired. She couldn't have asked for more. After dinner they wandered through most of the shops, Kali enchanted with many of the gift and clothing items she found. Smiling self-consciously, she bought a knit dress of a deep sea blue, then declared that they'd better leave before she succumbed to more than just one dress.

"Saying 'Charge it' was much easier than you thought, wasn't it?" he said teasingly, hugging her against his side.

"Much too easy," she agreed ruefully, circling his waist with her arm. "I haven't done any frivolous shopping in so long, I forgot how fun it can be."

"Does that mean we'll be hitting the shopping mall tomorrow?" He unlocked the passenger door to the Corvette and helped her inside.

"I think so." Kali's expression was pure mischief. "I have a lot of time to make up for."

Once Travis had seated himself, he leaned over and caught Kali in his arms. "We both have a lot of time to make up for," he whispered, possessing her mouth in a bone-melting kiss and pulling back only with extreme reluctance.

Kali guessed the direction of his thoughts and wholeheartedly agreed. "Then I suggest we go someplace where we can discuss this at great length," she murmured, placing her hand on his thigh and feeling the muscles jump under her touch.

"Great idea." He winced when he put the car in gear without engaging the clutch. "Next time around, I buy a car with an automatic gearshift. Saves time." After making sure there weren't any police cars lurking about, he took off with the speed of light. It was another night where their clothes were scattered on the floor from the kitchen into the bedroom. How they got that far was a miracle.

The next day Travis kept his promise and took Kali shopping after they consumed a late breakfast. She knew this shopping trip would be a true test of her newfound, and still very delicate, courage.

"What I am doing to myself is so egotistical," she told Travis as they drove to a nearby mall. "After all, I haven't been in the business for several years, and Blayne and I are old news by now. What makes me think I'd be recognized? I have been acting very foolish, haven't I?"

"Do you mind if I don't answer that question?"

"Oh!" She punched him in the shoulder. "You know very well what I mean."

"Sure I do, and I've thought the very same thing."

"That I'm egotistical?"

"No, that you're old news, but I figured you wouldn't want to hear that, either."

Kali grimaced. "You're right."

When they reached the mall, Kali made sure her

charge cards were in her wallet. She couldn't wait to purchase a wardrobe of new clothes—she'd fallen so behind in the fashions lately. She also planned to find herself some very sexy lingerie to entice Travis with. She just hoped she could escape from him long enough to do some of her very special shopping.

"You don't have to tag along, you know," she told him as they entered the first store. "It may be hard for you to believe, but I've been shopping for years and know what to do."

He looked down at her, that sexy half grin of his sending very erotic thoughts through her suddenly overcharged brain.

"You mean, I don't get to watch?"

"No."

"I'd be happy to accompany you into the dressing room to zip up zippers and button buttons, you know."

"I think I can do that on my own."

"Yeah, but I'll bet I can do a better job."

She couldn't resist saying, "Only if you're unzipping or unbuttoning."

Now Travis had erotic thoughts. He considered picking Kali up and carrying her back to the truck and driving back to the house at top speed, but he wasn't going to cause her to miss out on this day.

Kali felt like a kid let loose in a candy store. She wandered from department to department, fingering fabrics, picking up various items of clothing and standing in front of a mirror holding them up in front of her. Travis refused to leave her side, preferring to nod yes or shake his head no on each item.

"It's terrible that you have such good taste," she

237

grumbled, putting one blouse back on the rack after Travis gave it a thumbs-down.

"Do you want me to leave you alone?" he asked, finally taking pity on her.

"Yes," she replied without hesitation.

Travis's fingers traced the delicate lines of her jaw. "All right, I'll give you two hours. We can meet in that little French café downstairs. Fair?"

"Fair." Her mind was already concentrated on the racks of clothing around her.

While Kali had fun going through clothes, she didn't linger. A few times she had the uneasy sense that someone was watching her, and even looked around but saw nothing amiss. After a while she knew exactly what she wanted and wandered through several stores picking up dresses, casual clothing, and lots of beautiful silk and lace lingerie. When she finished, she had to check most of her packages before meeting Travis at the café.

She found him sitting at a small table in the rear of the café, drinking a cup of coffee.

"Are you trying to tell me you only bought two items in all this time?" He looked suspiciously at the packages she held.

"You have to be joking." She dropped into the chair across from him. "Right now my feet are killing me."

"They should be. You're only an hour late."

Kali's eyes flew to her watch. Where had the time gone? "I'm sorry," she apologized, feeling guilty he had waited for her all this time. "I guess I lost track of time."

"I figured you would. That's why I got here forty-five minutes late."

"I'm glad you didn't let me grovel very long," she grumbled, setting the bags at her feet. "Wait until you see all the packages I had to check! What a wonderful idea that is! It saves walking out to the car all the time. And this way I'll have an extra pair of hands to help me." She picked up the menu and scanned the offerings. "Um, everything looks so good."

Travis made a disparaging sound. "More like a nibble for most of us. I never was one for quiche or a fancy salad."

Kali hid her smile. She was all too used to Travis's large appetite, for food and other things.

"I'll have a bowl of the onion soup and the roast beef sandwich," he told the waitress after Kali had requested the spinach quiche and a salad. "And coffee."

Needing to talk about something that had been bothering her lately, Kali leaned forward, resting her elbows on the table, her fingers laced together. "Travis, I appreciate your doing all this for me, but I have a pretty good idea I've kept you from pursuing some of your regular activities."

"Like what?"

She shrugged her shoulders. "Well, hobbies."

"Don't have any other than working on my truck or riding my horses, which I've done even with you here."

"Answering your telephone calls." She didn't look pleased at the number of women who called Travis, although as far as she knew, he hadn't returned one call.

His dark eyes revealed nothing of his thoughts as he looked at her. "I only return the important phone calls. As for anything else, they'll soon get the idea that I'm not interested and go on to someone else."

Kali looked down at her food as it was set in front of her and couldn't help smiling. How wonderful it felt to hear those words!

Travis found out soon afterward that Kali wasn't exaggerating when they picked up her many packages.

"Are you sure you left anything for the other shoppers?" he grumbled as they loaded up the back of the truck. "Good thing I brought this instead of the 'Vette. On second thought, maybe I should go out and rent a moving van to get all of this back to the house."

"It isn't that bad," she protested, handing him the last of the bags and boxes.

"No? Then why is the truck suddenly sitting lower to the ground?" He couldn't resist teasing her.

"I won't even dignify that with an answer." With her nose held high, Kali climbed into the truck, but her haughty manner lost its bearing when she tripped and almost fell onto the seat. Travis thought it safer not to comment on her klutzy retreat.

"I spent too much money," Kali said with a moan as they carried the bags into the bedroom and tossed them on the bed and a nearby chair. "I can't believe I went this crazy. When I said I was making up for lost time, I wasn't kidding."

"*Now* you think of it." He dropped the bags on the floor and circled her waist from behind, placing a kiss on her neck. "You mean, we're going to have to go back and return most of this stuff?"

Kali sighed, thinking of the many items and why she'd bought them. "No, I want you to see me in more than a pair of grubby jeans and a beat-up sweater."

"Actually"—one hand snaked under that same beat-up sweater and traced the edge of her bra—"I like you best in nothing at all, so if you want to get technical about it, you wasted your time and money buying all those clothes."

She closed her eyes, losing herself in the magic of his touch. She leaned back, resting her hands on his arm, feeling the muscles contract under her fingertips. "It isn't fair," she whimpered when the abrasive pad of his thumb rubbed over her responsive nipple. "All you have to do is touch me and I melt."

"You don't even have to touch me to get me rarin' to go." He pulled her back against him to indicate the hard arousal straining the front of his jeans.

Kali tried to turn around, but Travis refused to loosen his embrace. "Look at us," he ordered. "Look in the mirror."

Her head lifted slowly, as if in slow motion, watching their reflection in the mirror along one wall. It wasn't difficult to guess how strongly they both were aroused. Kali's face was flushed a deep rose color, her eyes soft and dreamy while Travis's features had sharpened, his black eyes bright with the knowledge of what he was doing to her. He kept his hand under her sweater, rubbing his thumb back and forth over her nipple, then transferring it to the other breast for the same careful attention.

"I once wanted to photograph you like this." His voice was harsh with desire. "But then I was afraid someone else might see the pictures, and I didn't want anyone to see you this way. I'm selfish because I

241

don't want anyone else to know how beautiful you are when you're aroused."

Kali's breath caught in her throat. She couldn't stop staring at their reflection in the mirror. There was something erotic about the way they were both dressed while Travis caressed her breasts and traced the shadows of her neck with his mouth and tongue. She wanted to turn around and return the favor, but she couldn't move. She stood there and savored his expression as he murmured all the loving things he wanted to do to her. A hazy light surrounded her while she swayed in his arms.

"Please," she whimpered, wanting more.

"Please what?" He cupped both breasts in his hands, watching in the mirror as her eyes fluttered closed in ecstasy.

"I want you to make love to me," Kali pleaded, placing her hands over his, urging him to squeeze tighter.

"How much?" he growled, driving her wild with his caresses.

"So much that if you don't do something very soon, I . . ." Her voice drifted off helplessly, leaving no doubt in his mind how much she wanted him.

"I wanted to hear you say that," he whispered. One of his hands inched its way down the front of her jeans to the zipper, lowering it by a fraction of an inch with each deep breath she took.

In retaliation, Kali decided to do a little exploration of her own. Letting her fingers roam recklessly, she smiled when she found the male bulge, knowing it wouldn't be long before Travis would have to surrender to his own body's needs. She caressed him with teasing fingertips, bringing a throaty groan from his lips.

"It appears, cowboy, you're not as safe as you thought you were," she whispered.

Travis turned her around in his arms, never letting his hands cease their erotic possession. "Right now you're the one who can't be considered safe," he said roughly, pulling her sweater over her head. When he had stripped her of her clothing, he gently pushed her onto the bed. Dropping down beside her, taking full pleasure with her mouth, he continued his sensuous exploration of her breasts.

Kali could still see their reflection in the mirror and found the sight of her naked body and Travis's still fully clothed unbearably titillating. Her hands roamed freely over his muscular form, needing the comfort of the feel of his body just as much as she needed his touch and his loving.

"Do you realize how much I love you?" he asked with a groan, rolling over until she lay beneath him. "Kali, I would do anything to make you happy."

She smiled, reaching up to caress his face with her hand. "Then make love to me. Please . . ."

"Whatever you command, I'll do." He quickly rid himself of his clothing, and before Kali could draw another breath, he was back beside her. Travis didn't wait long. Taking hold of Kali's hips, he thrust himself into her, smiling to see her tremble when he entered her. She closed her eyes, feeling herself rapidly reaching a climax. What made it beautiful was that she knew she wasn't alone. Just as she felt the shudders of her orgasm, Travis cried out her name. When they finally returned to earth, their breathing was erratic. They lay in each other's arms, savoring the closeness.

"I talked to Malcolm this morning. He called while you were in the shower." Kali decided to bring up something she needed to share with him.

Travis was instantly alert. "And?"

"Still no word about Cheryl." She snuggled closer to him for comfort. "One of the detectives is positive she isn't in France any longer, but he isn't sure what country they moved to. He's advised giving up the search, since he feels he's doing nothing more than wasting my money." One lone tear streaked her cheek.

Travis cursed under his breath. He wished he could do more than stroke her and say meaningless words. He wanted to tell her he had taken up the search for her but he didn't want to infuse her with false hope. He made a mental note to contact his people in the morning to see what news they had. One thing he hadn't brought up was the idea that Cheryl might not want to see her mother anymore. After all, it had been over two years. How much did a little girl remember? Since her father was such a bastard, he could have told her any number of lies about her mother, and Cheryl might not want to come back. How could Kali handle it if her daughter rejected her after all this time and pain? One thing was certain, though: He intended to be present if and when Kali was reunited with her daughter, because he wasn't going to see her hurt again.

"You don't want to give up," he stated quietly, continuing to rub her back.

She shook her head. "If I give up, it's the same as saying there's no hope in finding her. Malcolm did suggest we cut down the number of detectives and only follow good strong leads." She buried her face against the curve of his neck, her loose hair falling across his chest. "What he meant was that he didn't think we'd get her back, either." Her voice was muffled with unshed tears. "And now you've turned my life upside down."

"I have?" He betrayed mild surprise at her charge.

"Yes, you know very well after I came back out here that I would have trouble returning to Virginia. You knew I wouldn't be able to go back into seclusion again because I'd see so much out here to keep me busy. Who knows, maybe I should talk to someone about 'Human Frailties,' if it's as good as you and Jenny say it is. I just hope I can convince everyone else it's fiction, even if there is a strong parallel between the fictional characters and my own life. I can imagine you're proud of getting through to me about that too. You're a horrible man, Travis Yates, because you always seem to get your way." She braced herself up on one elbow looking down at him with accusation in her eyes.

He grinned unrepentantly, yet he was serious when he told her, "I meant it when I said I wouldn't let you go once I truly had you."

Kali chewed on her lower lip. "Then I guess there's only one thing for me to do."

"And what's that?" He thought he knew the answer, but he wanted to hear her say it out loud.

"Pose for your damn book!" she shouted, jumping on him to show him she meant every word.

Travis wasn't about to complain.

Chapter

15

Three days had passed, and Kali was surprised Travis hadn't brought up her agreement to pose for him. Instead, he had taken her to the beach one day and to the Norton Simon Museum another, so she could have her fill of the beautiful artwork the building housed. Today he had gone into the studio, explaining there was work to do. A few hours after he left, she was surprised to hear a knock at the door. Since the house was set so far back from the main road, she knew it couldn't be a salesperson. She laughed with joy when she looked through the peephole and found Jenny standing outside.

"I can't believe it!" Kali squealed as she jerked open the door and hugged her friend. "You look so wonderful! You let your hair grow!" She stepped back to get a better look at her.

"You don't look so shabby yourself," Jenny replied, teasingly, eyeing Kali's lilac shorts and pullover shirt. She sobered. "I'm sorry I wasn't here sooner, but well, Travis and I thought you should have some time to yourself before anyone else descended on you."

"You mean Travis decided," Kali countered. "Believe me, I've had firsthand experience on how that man works. But why would he keep you away? Come in. You have time for coffee, don't you?" She stepped back so the other woman could enter.

Jenny looked amused. "Don't give him all the blame. This was part of my decision too. I knew how traumatic coming back here would be for you and that Travis would take excellent care of you, so I didn't worry. If there had been a problem, then I would have been out here like a shot. And, yes, I have time for coffee. In fact, the slave driver gave me the day off."

Kali looked at her with skepticism. "Give me a break. If you're anything with him like you were with me, I know exactly who gave who the day off. In simple terms, you went in and told him you were taking it off—no ifs, ands, or buts!"

Jenny followed her into the kitchen. "Yeah, that sounds about right. I was only helping out the poor man by taking the decision out of his hands." Once they were seated with steaming cups of coffee, Jenny took a closer look at her former employer. "My God, you look more beautiful than ever, and I have a pretty good idea Travis has something to do with it. You're in love with him, aren't you?"

Kali ducked her head. "I guess you could say something like that," she admitted.

"Something like that? Hey, I had to work with him after he came back here. Attila the Hun would have been a pussycat compared to Travis. He was *unbearable* to be around. He didn't straighten out until I threatened him with dire consequences!"

"Meaning you were going to fire him." Kali giggled, sipping her coffee. She looked at Jenny with amazement. "I forgot how it felt to laugh and feel carefree again. I wasn't alive back there, Jenny, I was just going through the motions. It took Travis to make me realize where I was going wrong."

"So are you going to pose for him?"

"I already told him I would."

Jenny frowned. "When did you tell him?"

"Several days ago."

"He never said a word," she murmured. "No offense, but do you think he might not have believed you?"

"Meaning words said in heat of passion and all that?" Kali shrugged. "Perhaps he didn't. I'll have to set the record straight when I see him tonight—although I will admit I'm not too sure I can go through with it. It's been a long time."

"Travis doesn't work like most photographers."

Kali thought about that afternoon spent with Helene Dumont. "Yes, I know," she responded softly.

"He loves you a lot, Kali. He'd do anything for you."

Kali looked at her quizzically. "You sound like you're trying to reassure me for some reason." She laughed, but her laughter halted when she saw her friend's serious expression. "Something's wrong, and both of you are keeping it from me. What? Is it Cheryl? I want to know!" she demanded.

Jenny sighed, digging into her large leather tote. "I told Travis he wouldn't be able to keep this from you for long, but you know how stubborn he can be." She shoved a newspaper toward her.

Kali looked down at the tabloid. It was a sleazy paper known for its sensationalism, and her blood froze. Pictures of Travis meeting her at the airport, kissing her in the garage, walking with her at Ports O' Call, and even one of her holding up a scanty piece of lingerie in a department store. She swallowed the lump in her throat.

The headline read, MODEL KALI HUGHES CUDDLES UP WITH NEW LOVER, PHOTOGRAPHER TRAVIS YATES. And below, the first lines of the article read: Is she in L.A. to make a comeback, or just for a bit of recreation? There's still the big question: Where is ex-husband Blayne Savage and her daughter?

"Why?" she whispered, remembering her feeling of being watched in the stores.

"Kali, Travis is furious about this." Jenny reached across the table to grasp her hand and found it ice-cold. "He's been on the phone for hours today, threatening everyone from the photographer to the publisher."

She felt close to tears. "It won't do any good, and both of us know it. Now I have to go back to Virginia."

"Come off it, Kali, I know you too well. You're not that much of a coward," she said sharply.

"Why couldn't he tell me about this himself? Why did he send you here to do his dirty work?" She pushed the offending newspaper to one side.

"Because he thought you might prefer having a woman present," Jenny said softly. "Plus he was afraid you'd cry, and he's absolutely helpless when it comes to tears. I slammed a file drawer on my fingers one day, and he almost came apart while begging me to stop crying. He even promised me a raise." She hoped to lighten the atmosphere. "Look, Kali, tomorrow the headline will be about someone else and you'll be old news again. You know how it goes in this town."

Kali forced herself to think rationally. "You're right," she finally had to admit. "I'll be old news soon enough. And Travis is right; I've been doing enough running. I may as well stand and fight, and the best way to begin is to pose for his book."

"Are you planning on going back to modeling?" Jenny asked her.

She shook her head. "No, I'm too old, and it doesn't hold the fascination for me that it used to. I've discovered I enjoy writing. In fact, I've been keeping a journal while I've been here. I'm going to talk to Malcolm about suggesting a literary agent, and I'll submit 'Human Frailties' to see if it's publishable. Maybe that's where my talent lies now."

Jenny lifted her cup in a silent salute. "And to think I was against Travis seeing you. You'll never know how glad I am that I gave in to his bullheaded insistence on finding out where you were."

Kali smiled. "So am I." She knew her next job would be to prove to Travis that she was willing to pose for him.

She would have been stunned if she had known that Travis was on the phone to Europe most of the day, insisting he be contacted immediately if there were any solid leads.

He was just as surprised when he returned home that evening to find her setting the table for a cozy little dinner. He listened to her reasons for posing for him. Yes, he had thought her promise was just spoken in the heat of passion, and he was pleased to learn that she was serious. He didn't waste any time and arranged to photograph her in a few days' time, before she lost her nerve. All through the evening he waited for her to bring up the subject of the tabloid, but she never said a word. He could only feel that having Jenny with her while she read the story had done the trick. At bedtime Kali made love to him as fiercely and passionately as always, and he clasped her to him tightly, as if afraid he'd lose her if he let her go. Travis prayed that the sensationalism would die down and she could finally lead a normal life again. She more than deserved it, and he would make certain it would happen.

Kali was in a nervous state the morning she was due at Travis's studio. After refusing to eat any breakfast, she walked into the bathroom for a shower. She stood in front of the bathroom mirror, a washcloth in one hand and her cleansing lotion in another. The longer she stood there, the more she grew to hate the face staring back at her, the face that was due to be photographed in two hours. She dropped the plastic bottle and cloth in the sink and returned to the bedroom where Travis was finishing dressing.

"I can't go through with this," she told him flatly.

"All right, why can't you go through with this?" He acted much too calm to her way of thinking.

"I'm not doing this for myself but for you, and it's

all wrong!" Her voice began to rise several decibels. "From the beginning you've tried to change my life, and like the fool I am, I allowed you to—just the way I allowed Blayne to change my life around to please him." Travis's face tightened at that statement, the dark expression revealing his displeasure as his gaze swept over her pale features. *"I can't do it!"*

Travis remained in the same position, his arms crossed in front of him. "There's a lot of things in life we feel we can't do, but we somehow find the strength to do them. Just as you will, as soon as you realize you need to do this work to prove to yourself it wasn't modeling that caused your pain but your ex-husband. I'll wait for you in the den."

"I hate you for doing this to me," she shouted after his retreating form.

He halted and turned around. This time there was nothing but sadness in his dark eyes. "If it will make you feel better, you can hate me all you want." He walked away without looking back.

Tears glistened in Kali's eyes, but she refused to give in to them. She knew she didn't hate Travis, but she felt she had to blame someone for her awful state, and he was the only scapegoat around. She went back to the bathroom to finish getting ready.

Travis was seated on the couch reading a magazine when Kali walked in. He looked up and, without saying a word, got to his feet and led the way out to his car. They rode into town in silence, and he dropped her off at the studio while he went on to another appointment. He thought she might relax more if he wasn't around while she was getting ready.

At the studio, Kali was surprised and pleased to

find Larry and Karen, the makeup artist and hair-dresser she had worked with most often in the past. It did a great deal to set her mind at ease, until she saw the large studio with its many cameras and light fix-tures. That was the final straw. She ran into the bath-room, slamming the door behind her.

"Where is she?" Travis demanded, walking in and fearing the worst when he didn't see her.

"In the bathroom throwing up," Jenny said bluntly. "Travis, she is scared to death. Admittedly, having Larry and Karen here has helped, but it wasn't enough."

He cursed softly. "So what are you trying to tell me?"

"Go over there and let her know you're here. I know you were trying to help her by staying away, but the one person she needs now is you." She pushed him none too gently.

Travis walked over to the bathroom door and knocked softly. "Kali, honey, it's me."

A few minutes later the door opened. She looked pale but composed.

"Would you believe me if I said I throw up the first day of any assignment?" she said, making a feeble attempt at a joke.

He pulled her into his arms and kissed the top of her head. "Hey, they did a good job on you. You almost look like a model."

She punched him in the stomach. "Don't make me laugh. I don't feel like laughing." She wrapped her arms around his waist, digging her fingers into the small of his back. "I'm sorry I was such a bitch ear-lier," she mumbled against his shirtfront.

"You're more than forgiven if you'll give me one or

two smiles for a picture," he said coaxingly, reveling in the soft feel of her body against his.

She drew back. "Thank you for bringing in Larry and Karen. That was very nice of you."

"I'm a nice man. I also thought you'd feel better with familiar faces around you. I asked Jenny for a recommendation, and she said they were two of the few who had stood behind you years ago."

"I never really knew," she murmured, shaking her head with wonder. "I guess I was so wrapped up in my troubles that I didn't bother to find out if anyone still cared to be my friend. I was too convinced that I was all alone."

"And what about Jenny?"

She smiled against the front of his shirt. "You know Jenny. She refused to go away all the times I told her to leave me alone, and in the end I was grateful for her presence no matter how many times I cursed her."

"The story sounds a bit familiar," he replied ruefully. "Now, as much as I enjoy having you in my arms, do you think we could get some work done before I lock us in that bathroom and make love to you?"

"All right, but don't expect anything spectacular," she warned.

Travis knew differently, but he preferred to prove it to Kali the same way he had before.

In the beginning Kali moved stiffly under the lights. Travis kept her talking, encouraging her to move at her own pace as he kept shooting. He wanted it simple; therefore she was dressed in a plain dress of wild-rose-colored silk that floated around her ankles. He wanted nothing to detract from her se-

255

rene beauty. He ordered an assistant to turn on the stereo, and the rock music kept the mood on an up beat. He was prepared to halt at the first sign of Kali's tiring, but she didn't appear to tire easily. In fact, she looked as if she were having fun. He also insisted on taking several serious poses, some whimsical ones with her seated in a large wicker chair, and others perched on a stool. More and more, Travis wished he had photographed her years ago.

"Enough," Kali announced finally, collapsing on a stool. "I'm too old for all this!" Larry came forward to blot her perspiring face.

Travis handed his camera to one of his assistants. "Okay, why don't you change. I know I got what I need from these." He walked over to check the rolls of film he took, counted each roll and marked them. He quietly informed his two assistants that if any of the rolls were tampered with or any of the pictures turned up anywhere but in his files, he would fire them both. One look at his dark features told them he meant every word. He didn't bother to tell them he would personally process the photos that night and make sure the negatives and prints were locked away. He wasn't taking any chances. Not after what Jenny had told him about Kali's reaction to the pictures and accompanying article in that supermarket rag. He had been furious when he saw it and read the innuendos about how he and Kali had carried on a torrid affair for years under her husband's nose. If he'd had the writer of the article in his office, he would have throttled the man. He could understand why Kali wanted to stay away from Los Angeles if all she saw was filth like that.

"Travis?" Kali approached him hesitantly when

she noticed the fierce expression on his face and wondered what could have angered him so quickly. "You didn't discover that you left the lens cap on, did you?" She tried a bit of levity in hopes he would lose his dark scowl.

He looked down at her and couldn't help smiling. "No, we're safe there. I've got some work to do here, so if you want to go on home or do some shopping, feel free."

"What I want to do is go to the movies," Kali announced. "It would be nice to see something on a large screen that hasn't been out for six months. I know I've resisted going out so far, but today I feel in the mood."

"If you want company, Jenny can go along with you," he offered, not wanting her to be out alone.

"Don't you think she should have the choice of saying yes or no?"

"Would anyone really want to give up a fun-filled day here to go to the movies?" Jenny broke in, having heard the last part of their conversation. "Let me get my purse. I know a theater with six screens not far from here. We can load up on popcorn and junk food while drooling over some hunks on the wide screen."

Travis looked as if he didn't like the idea.

Jenny grabbed her purse and came back to wait for Kali to change her clothes. "Since this is your idea, boss, I guess I get the day off with pay," she declared mischievously, guiding Kali to the front door. "You are so good to me."

"I'm surrounded by mercenary women," he muttered, walking back to the darkroom after giving instructions that he didn't want to be disturbed.

Kali loved the idea of six movies in one place. She

and Jenny ended up watching four of the films that day.

"I think I'm in love with Jeff Bridges," Kali announced when they finally walked out of the theater in the early evening.

"Don't let Travis hear you say that, or he'll lock you away," Jenny joked as they walked to her car.

"In a way, that's what I've done with myself these past two weeks," Kali mused. "And Travis has fought me on it all the way. Now it's time to prove that I'm made of tougher stuff." She glanced down at her watch. "Could we stop by the studio and see if Travis is still there? That would save you driving me home if he is."

"Sure." But a swing by the studio showed it was closed up, and Travis's car was missing from the parking lot. Jenny insisted it was no problem taking her the rest of the way home and swung out onto the boulevard.

But when they arrived at the house, they found it dark, save for the outside light that came on automatically in the early evening.

"Good thing I have a key," Kali said with a cheerfulness she didn't feel inside.

"He didn't mention any other appointments," Jenny muttered. "But then Deke or Bull could have stopped by and insisted he go out for a beer. With them, anything is possible."

"Deke or Bull, those are friends of his from his motorcycle-riding days, aren't they?"

Jenny nodded. "Deep down they're very nice men, but they have the mentality of teenagers at times. They like nothing better than to chase girls and drink beer. I used to wonder how Travis got hooked up with guys like that until I finally realized he was probably their stabilizing force, because I can't imagine him ever acting like them."

"And now all he has are the memories, a tattoo, and his bike," Kali mused as she got out of the car. "Thanks for spending the rest of the day with me, Jenny. I really appreciate it."

"Hey, I should be thanking you." She laughed. "I know very well I'll be walking into a mess tomorrow, but it was worth it. I'll call you in a few days about getting together for lunch."

Kali entered the house and looked around in vain for some kind of message from Travis. When she found none, she decided to take a quick shower and change her clothes. She would put off dinner until she had an idea when he would be home. She couldn't imagine he would just take off without telling her first. That wasn't his way.

It was just as well that she didn't go to any trouble fixing dinner. Travis didn't come home until late that night, sporting a black eye and smelling of too much beer.

"Wonderful," Kali muttered, evading his amorous embrace. "You're drunk."

He looked down at his feet and saw that they were swaying before his very eyes. "Yeah, I guess I am," he said slowly.

"I want you in the shower posthaste," she ordered, ducking his beery breath before he could kiss her. "Ugh, Travis, you stink! Couldn't you call to say you'd be late?"

"Nah, then they would want to come here to meet you, and I don't think you're ready for those guys yet." He allowed her to take off his clothes. "Hey, honey, I'm not that kind of guy."

Kali rolled her eyes. She was just grateful he was a cheerful drunk and easy to handle—a far cry from what she had endured after her father's binges.

Travis loudly protested the cold shower but stood under it long enough to sober up fractionally.

"I didn't want to go," he told her as she heated up a pot of coffee. "But these guys are hard to refuse sometimes, and this was one of those times."

"Jenny mentioned that Deke and Bull might have called." She placed a steaming mug in front of him.

He swallowed the hot coffee in two gulps. "Yeah, she's not a real big fan of those guys. It takes women a while to get used to 'em."

Kali sat down across from him. "Travis, I'm afraid."

He looked up at her sudden confession. "What are you afraid of?" A cold feeling invaded his bones. "Did you hear from Malcolm about Cheryl? Did someone harass you while you were out?"

She shook her head. "Everything is going too well. Except for that newspaper article, of course. But for the most part, it's all so easy. That's what frightens me."

Travis put down his mug and reached for her hand. "That's ridiculous and you know it," he said harshly. "You've had to shoulder these burdens alone too long, and you're still afraid to relinquish them. Just give me a chance to help you. That's all I ask."

She stared down at their linked hands. What he said made sense, but it was so hard to let go of her fears. . . .

"If you think you're sober enough, I'd appreciate i

if you would take me to bed and make love to me," she said in a small voice.

He heaved a silent sigh of relief. "Thank God you asked for something I could do even if I was dead."

But Kali's fears couldn't be easily resolved by Travis's lovemaking. She tossed and turned in bed that night, dreaming horrible dreams about Blayne and Cheryl. When she awakened in a cold sweat, Blayne's demonic laughter was ringing in her ears. Sensing something was wrong, Travis opened his eyes instantly.

"Honey, what is it?" He saw her rigid figure.

"Hold me," she implored, curling up against him. "Make me warm again."

He obliged by holding her tight and rubbing his hands up and down her cold skin. He didn't ask for details, just comforted her until her shivering stopped.

"Want to talk about it?" he prompted quietly when he felt her body finally relax.

She shook her head. "It was just a bad dream." She cuddled even closer, needing his warmth to feel whole again.

Travis felt it was much more than a bad dream bothering her, but he didn't pressure her into telling him. For a long time they lay together with her back nestled warmly against his chest.

"Kali . . ." Travis hesitated, warring with himself whether this was the right time to tell her or not. "I think there's something you should know." He stopped when there was no response, only the sound of her soft breathing. She had fallen asleep. Perhaps it was better that she didn't know he was also looking for Cheryl. He didn't want to raise any more false hopes for her. She'd had enough of those in the past.

While Travis was gone the next morning Kali spent the time doing laundry and puttering around the kitchen making bread. She was in the midst of putting the second loaf in the oven when the phone rang. She listened to the answering machine clock on, and when she realized the call was for her, she picked up the receiver.

"I'm here, Malcolm," she said in greeting.

"What is going on, Kali?" He spoke in his usual brusque fashion.

"I have no idea unless you give me a clearer picture."

"Namely, why is your boyfriend making inquiries about Cheryl?" Kali stiffened. "My office got a telegram from Blayne stating bluntly that if you don't call them off, he'll tell Cheryl you're dead and you'll never see her again. He seemed to insinuate that he was going to send her back to you soon, but he's taunted you with this before the few times we've heard from him, so it really doesn't mean anything, I hate to say."

Kali dropped into the chair before her legs could give out from under her. "Travis hired detectives?" she asked weakly.

"It appears so—and not the best sort, either. At least not the kind of men I would think about hiring. As much as I have to admit it, though, he's had better luck than my men have in getting close to Blayne."

She shook her head, unable to comprehend. "Forgive me for sounding dense, but what you're saying is that Travis is also looking for Cheryl?"

"And without checking with me first," Malcolm

rumbled, indicating that was what angered him. Knowing how he always insisted on being in charge, Kali could understand his irritation.

Kali pressed her fingertips hard against her forehead to stave off the rapidly approaching headache. Why would Travis do this without saying a word to her? She knew Blayne better than anyone, and his threat was very real. As for the insinuation that he was going to send Cheryl back to her soon, she couldn't believe it. If she'd thought it would have done any good, she would have gone to Europe long ago, but Malcolm always dissuaded her, saying it would only make matters worse. Now she wondered if she shouldn't have gone ahead with her first impression.

"I can't tell Travis what to do or not to do," she said faintly. "He has a mind all his own."

Malcolm's comment to that was pithy. "Tell him to get the hell out of a matter that has nothing to do with him," he ordered.

Kali couldn't help smiling. "Malcolm, you are the epitome of the arrogant male."

"Just tell him to knock if off before he screws it up!" He slammed the phone down.

"And good-bye to you too," she murmured, putting her phone down a bit more gently. She wasn't happy with Travis taking matters into his own hands and intended to tell him so just as soon as he got back.

The more she thought about Malcolm's phone call, the angrier she grew with Travis. She knew it was a kind gesture, but the least he could have done was talk it over with her. She could have told him what the detectives had found and where they had looked, and she also would have told him this was her problem and not his. She was standing under the shower still fuming when the shower door suddenly opened and a grinning Travis stood in front of her.

"Now this is what I like to come home to," he told her, beginning to unbutton his shirt. "A naked woman in my shower. A man's dream come true."

Kali's eyes narrowed. She picked up her soapy washcloth and threw it at him with all her strength. It landed against his shirt with a wet plop and slithered down to the floor.

"Who the hell do you think you are, looking for my daughter without telling me?" she demanded shrilly, still standing under the water, her hands on her hips. "Who died and put you in charge?"

"Does this mean we're going to fight?"

She stepped out of the shower, shouldering him out of the way as she picked up a towel and wrapped it around her body. "A fight? Buddy, prepare yourself for World War III!"

Chapter
16

Travis followed Kali into the bedroom, watching her rub her wet body dry and pull on a pair of jeans and a T-shirt. Her movements were uncoordinated and jerky, indicating that she was still angry with him. He had a pretty good idea this was the kind of anger he couldn't tease her out of.

"I knew how badly you wanted to find Cheryl, and I figured if there was something I could do to help speed the process up, you wouldn't mind." He preferred getting it all out in the open. "I'd sure like to know how you found out."

She spun around to face him. "Malcolm called me today. He isn't at all happy that you've stuck your nose into this business."

Only the tightening of his jaw indicated he was impatient. "Kali, I love you and I want to spend the rest of my life with you. Now, I figure that gives me a few rights in your life, including helping you find your daughter," he said quietly.

For the first time she was speechless. That was the last thing she'd expected to hear from him.

He stepped forward and grasped her shoulders firmly. "How many times have I told you how much I love you?" he demanded. "How many times have I proved it? *That's* what gives me the right to try to help you when you need someone. I love you more than life itself, and I'll protect you and yours with whatever it takes. I love you so much, I can't see life without you. I'm even willing to compromise by living a few months of the year in Virginia if you're willing to live here with me. And just to make it all very clear, I'm talking about marriage, not just a long-term relationship." Travis lowered his head. "It won't be easy for us. We're both too stubborn for our own good," he said softly, "but if I'm willing to give it a chance, why can't you?"

Kali thought back over the many days they had spent together at the cabin. He had given her so much, and what had she given him? Had she given as much to him emotionally as he had to her? That answer was very apparent, and she felt ashamed.

"I do love you," she said finally. "I've been afraid because I didn't want to get hurt, even though I knew you'd be the last person to hurt me. I'd like to try living here, and perhaps we could keep the cabin as a vacation home." She raised her face to look up at him, her eyes glistening, her lips parted. "And I cannot think of anything more fulfilling than to be your wife."

For the first time she saw a faint glimmer of hope in his eyes. "You're not mad that I've been trying to find Cheryl for you?" She shook her head. "Then I suggest we crack open a bottle of wine and plan a wedding to end all weddings. If you're a good girl, I'll give you a month to plan it but no more, because I don't intend to lose you again."

She laughed, unable to take it all in. The last thing she'd expected when she was yelling at him ten minutes ago was a marriage proposal!

"One month," she agreed. "Just be prepared for one very special wedding."

He bent and kissed her swiftly. "Good, because it will be one to last forever and a day."

Where did the month go? Kali wondered as she dressed in the rose-pink suit she had chosen to wear for the ceremony. There had been so many details to take care of, and she often felt she needed more time than thirty days. Most importantly, where had Travis gone? He'd told her four days ago that he needed to take a quick trip but would be back in plenty of time for the wedding. Well, the wedding was now a little under two hours off, and there still hadn't been word from the groom.

"Here's your something borrowed." Jenny entered the room with the handkerchief she had carried in her own wedding.

"Have you heard from Travis?" Kali demanded, spinning around.

"He called from the airport a little while ago.

Don't worry, Kali. He said he'd be here in time, and he will be."

She clenched her hands together. "If he isn't, I swear I'll kill him."

Jenny chuckled. "Don't worry, he'll be here."

Kali was still worrying all the way up to twenty minutes before the ceremony. She had vivid thoughts of being abandoned at the altar. She paced the chapel's anteroom, thinking up dire ways to get even if Travis didn't make it in time.

"Kali!" Jenny shouted from outside. "Come here, quickly!"

"Oh, no, he's hurt," she said with a moan, rushing out of the room. When she reached the steps of the church, she caught sight of a weary Travis standing beside a taxicab. Standing beside him was a small girl who held tightly onto his hand. She was looking around curiously. At last her eyes came to rest upon Kali, who stood frozen at the doorway.

Kali's hands flew to her heart, and she gasped. Standing before her was her mirror image, a child unmistakably her own.

"Oh, my God," she breathed, walking slowly forward. "Cheryl?" Tears filled her eyes. She had grown so much! Where was the little girl she had known? Her heart ached with the knowledge that she had lost so many years. Yet here she was. . . . Kali longed to touch her, make sure that this child would not turn out to be a dream. But would Cheryl remember her?

"Mommy?" Her voice was timid, and she looked anxious. But as she gazed up at the woman before her, recognition flooded over her. This was the woman in the photograph her father had given her to keep by her bedside! How many nights had the little girl hugged that picture, wondering why her mommy was gone, crying for her to comfort her? In the beginning she had asked her father to take her to her mother, but after his cold threats, she'd never asked again. But she'd never forgotten her mother. And when this tall man named Travis had come to talk to her father and later explained to her that he would be bringing her home to her mother, she'd left with him gladly. Now she glanced up at him and he squeezed her hand reassuringly.

"That's your mommy, Cheryl," he murmured. He let his eyes take in the beautiful picture Kali made. "I'm sorry I'm late, but I had to pick up your wedding gift," he murmured, his voice husky. He knew he would carry with him the image of his future wife's joy for the rest of his life.

She looked up, her face filled with overflowing love for the man who had moved heaven and earth to bring back her child. "How did you find her?"

"We can go into that later," he told her. "Right now I think we have a wedding to attend."

Kali hesitantly held out her hands to Cheryl, fearful that the girl might be reluctant to come to her. Her heart sang when Cheryl ran into her outstretched arms.

"You've brought me something so special that I don't know if I'll ever be able to thank you," Kali cried, gazing up at Travis with tears in her eyes.

"The look on your face is enough," he assured her as the trio walked into the chapel amid the many well-wishers present to view the reunion of mother and daughter, and later the wedding that was all the more poignant because of the deep love between the bride and groom.

* * *

It couldn't have been a more perfect day. In less than twelve hours Kali had regained her daughter and gained a husband. Knowing how loath she was to be parted from Cheryl for even a short time, Travis suggested they put off their honeymoon for a while so they could have time together as a family, and Kali loved him for it.

The wedding reception was now long over, and an exhausted Cheryl was put to bed in the guest room while Travis and Kali shared some time alone in the master bedroom. A champagne bottle sat in an ice-filled bucket near the bed while they lay under the covers in each other's arms. Travis moved away long enough to set his glass on the nightstand.

"Now, I think it's time to get this marriage consummated," he growled, pulling her on top of him.

She placed one hand on his chest and pushed away.

"My darling, this marriage was consummated many times before the fact," she informed him with a sultry smile.

"Yeah, but I'm a henpecked husband now. Hey!" He flinched when she socked him in the arm and jumped out of bed.

"You will not put me off, Travis Yates. All these years I have gone crazy trying to get Cheryl back, and you accomplished it in a short period of time. How?"

He shrugged. "I sent some friends of mine a description of her. They found her and called me, and I flew over. Say, Paris is some city. We'll have to go there sometime."

"Travis!" she wailed.

He took pity on her then. "Some old friends of

mine are living over in Europe now, and I contacted them about Cheryl and Blayne. Using what many would call unorthodox methods, they were able to track the two of them down and get word to me before he disappeared again." He made it sound much simpler than it had really been.

"Why didn't you tell me when you first heard?" Kali demanded, dropping down to sit on the end of the bed.

His dark eyes softened with love. "I didn't know if I could get there before they disappeared again, and I didn't want to get your hopes up if nothing came of it. You've been hurt enough, love," he told her, leaning forward to take her hand.

Kali would have dropped into his arms right then if she hadn't wanted to hear the entire story so badly. "I'm surprised Cheryl went with you so readily."

He grinned. "I had a little help. I stopped off in Virginia first and picked up her teddy bear, dragon, and a picture of our wedding announcement. She definitely remembered the stuffed animals, remembered you, and after we talked for a while she was glad to return to the States as long as I threw in a trip to Disneyland as a bonus."

"What happened in Paris?" she wanted to know. "Where did you find her? At least she's been eating well. Blayne could never even boil water, so who took care of her?"

"She was staying at a house belonging to a friend of your ex-husband's."

Kali's eyes narrowed. His casual answer sounded much too pat. Why did she feel as if there were a great deal more to the story? "A girlfriend?" she pressed.

271

Travis stretched his body, his hands braced behind his head as he stared up at the ceiling. "Sort of."

"Sort of? Either she was or she wasn't, Travis." She rolled over onto her side, placing her head in her hand. "Which was it?"

Travis mumbled something.

Kali angled her head forward. She wasn't sure he'd heard correctly, and she sincerely hoped she was wrong.

"Travis, tell me now or consider yourself celibate until the year 2000."

He turned his head and grinned lazily at her. Angling himself up, he leaned over her and rested his hand against a full breast, the nipple immediately peaking against his palm.

"Wanna bet as to who can hold out the longest?"

A tiny groan left her lips before she could call it back. "*What* is his friend who took care of my daughter?"

He took a deep breath, already anticipating her reaction. "A hooker."

"*A hooker?*" she screeched, then quickly lowered her voice. "Are you saying you found my little girl living with a hooker? With God knows what kind of men around?"

Travis sighed. This kind of conversation wasn't what he had planned for his wedding night. In fact, he hadn't planned any at all.

"She's a very nice woman. She told me she didn't entertain her—uh—clients when Cheryl was around." He decided he would be better off not telling Kali how beautiful Marie Bouchet was, or how she had offered the tall dark American a freebie.

Kali thought of a little girl who had grown up too

quickly due to her years in Europe and from probably spending so much time with adults instead of playing with children her own age. She wanted to think of Cheryl playing with her dolls and wearing play clothes, not watching orgies or whatever they did over there. Her imagination ran wild at all sorts of perverted activities her daughter may have observed.

Travis grabbed her hand and pulled her back against him, rubbing his hips suggestively against hers.

"Stop thinking the worst," he chided. "She seems to be a pretty together kid, and with us as parents she'll do even better. First thing tomorrow I'm calling my lawyer to draw up adoption papers if it's all right with you."

She stared into his dark eyes. "Blayne gave up all rights to Cheryl?"

"Let's just say I persuaded him to."

Kali's lips quivered in a smile. "Oh, Travis, did you do what I think you did?"

He nuzzled her throat. "Let's just say he won't be playing any more pretty-boy parts for a while." His voice hardened. "I had to, Kali. I took one look at his smirking face when he found out we were getting married"—he would never tell her the exact words Blayne had used about Kali because they were too obscene—"and I knew I had to do something. He signed readily enough and gave me his promise that he would stay in Europe."

Kali hugged him tightly. "Did I ever tell you how much I love you?" she whispered, blinking to keep her tears back.

He leaned down to kiss away the salty tears. "Many times, but I'll never tire of hearing it."

Kali moved closer to Travis, whispering over and over that she loved him, and promising to show him how much before the night was over.

Epilogue

✥ Travis's photo book portraying a woman's strength was well received when it came out a little over a year later. The cover photograph was of Kali. Inside, there was a different shot of her, a fashion photograph taken five years before. With maturity had come strength and even more beauty, and Travis never tired of telling Kali how lovely she was and how lucky he was to be married to her. He had even dedicated the book to her.

Kali had delivered "Human Frailties" into the hands of a literary agent and several months later rejoiced when it sold. Her first work would be published shortly. To celebrate their mutual success, Travis held a cocktail party at the studio.

Kali was there, irritated with Travis's overly solicitous manner.

"Are you sure you don't want to sit down?" he asked for the hundredth time. "After all, you've been standing for well over an hour, and I don't want you to become tired."

"Travis, you're a real pain in the rear," she told him bluntly, gesturing with her glass of soda water. "I'm pregnant, not dying."

"Is he acting like a first-grade pain again?" Jenny asked as she approached them.

"Yes!"

"No!" was said simultaneously.

Kali ordered Travis to be silent. "Ever since he found out I was pregnant, he hasn't let me be alone for more than two minutes. He even told the doctor something must be wrong, since I haven't had any morning sickness. He's even bribed Cheryl to keep an eye on me when he isn't around to make sure I don't get into any trouble."

Jenny smiled at that. Kali had been very patient with the young girl over the first few months of Cheryl's return. She spent many hours explaining to her that she hadn't been the one to abandon her, that her father had taken her away, and about how long and hard Kali had worked to regain Cheryl. Surprisingly, Blayne hadn't talked against Kali very much and only explained their reason for living in Europe as it being crucial for his career. Kali learned of the many "aunts" Cheryl had stayed with while her father worked and was grateful that Cheryl didn't know exactly what Blayne did for a living. She decided to wait a while before going into all the details behind the divorce and Cheryl's kidnapping until the girl was old enough to understand. No matter what, though, Kali would not show Blayne to be the black-hearted villain, because he had taken good care of Cheryl and she was grateful for that.

She had finally learned from Travis that when he'd first learned of Blayne's whereabouts he had flown immediately to Germany to confront the man. He'd given him one option: Blayne could save his health and pretty face only if he gave up Cheryl. Kali had a sneaky suspicion that money had also changed hands, but Travis never spoke of it and she never asked.

From the beginning he was the father to Cheryl that Blayne had never been, and the two were now inseparable. Kali's recently confirmed pregnancy was the frosting on the cake.

Jenny leaned over and lowered her voice. "Is it really true that Travis fainted when you told him you were pregnant?"

Kali's lips curved upward. "Out cold."

"And yet he plans to take childbirth classes with you and be present in the delivery room?"

"Yep."

"What if he faints in the delivery room?" Jenny's eyes sparkled with amusement at the idea of the tall man's passing out on a linoleum floor.

Kali looked across the large studio at the man she couldn't imagine not loving. At the man who had basically given her a reason to live and love again.

"If he does, I'm sure he'll have the grace to wait until we know if it's a boy or girl and make sure mother and baby are fine."

Two hours later, husband and wife were alone in their bedroom talking over the events of the party.

Kali related her conversation with Jenny and laughed when Travis grimaced.

"Talk about ruining my macho image," he grumbled good-naturedly, tossing his clothes in the hamper and ducking in for a quick shower. When he came out, a towel wrapped around his hips and another being used to dry his hair, Kali couldn't keep her eyes from straying over his masculine form with an undisguised hunger. Travis saw her expression and grinned wickedly. "Hey, lady, for someone who's pregnant, you sure get some funny ideas."

"You've never complained before," she retorted, reaching into the tiny refrigerator they kept in the bedroom and withdrawing a pitcher of juice. She poured some into two goblets and handed one to him. "In fact, if I recall last night correctly . . ."

"Okay, I get the picture," he said hastily, drawing her into his arms for a lengthy kiss. "Mmm, you taste better than any juice." From there it was inevitable that they retreat to their large bed for some leisurely loving. Afterward they curled up beside each other, sipping their juice.

Kali looked up at him wordlessly and raised her glass in a silent salute that spoke so eloquently of her love for him. Likewise, Travis lifted his glass, his dark eyes loving her as thoroughly as the rest of him just had. All of Kali's doubts were gone now.

Ever fantasize about having a mad, impetuous

FLING

Sensuous. Discreet. Astonishingly passionate, but with <u>no strings</u> attached? Kelly Nelson did, as she approached her 32nd birthday, so her two best friends arranged a one-night fling as a surprise present. Only problem was that Kelly, accustomed to juggling the demands of a solid marriage, two children, and a successful career, wasn't prepared for what happened next. Neither were her two best friends...her kids... her husband...or her incredibly sensitive, sensuous lover.

by PAMELA BECK and PATTI MASSMAN

12615-0 $3.95

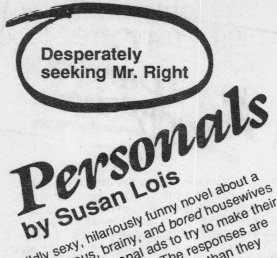